S N

It starts with a KISS

Yesterday she was a suicidal middle-aged housewife.
Today she's 21, with the looks of a goddess.

S N WEDDLE

It starts with a KISS

Yesterday she was a suicidal middle-aged housewife.
Today she's 21, with the looks of a goddess.

MEREO
Cirencester

Mereo Books

1A The Wool Market Dyer Street Cirencester Gloucestershire GL7 2PR
An imprint of Memoirs Publishing www.mereobooks.com

It starts with a kiss: 978-1-86151-166-9

First published in Great Britain in 2014
by Mereo Books, an imprint of Memoirs Publishing

A CIP catalogue record for this book is available from the British Library.

The address for Memoirs Publishing Group Limited can be found at
www.memoirspublishing.com

Cover design - Ray Lipscombe

The Memoirs Publishing Group Ltd Reg. No. 7834348

The Memoirs Publishing Group supports both The Forest Stewardship Council® (FSC®) and the PEFC® leading international forest-certification organisations. Our books carrying both the FSC label and the PEFC® and are printed on FSC®-certified paper. FSC® is the only forest-certification scheme supported by the leading environmental organisations including Greenpeace. Our paper procurement policy can be found at
www.memoirspublishing.com/environment

Typeset in 11.5/17pt Plantin
by Wiltshire Associates Publisher Services Ltd. Printed and bound in Great Britain by
Printondemand-Worldwide, Peterborough PE2 6XD

ACKNOWLEDGEMENTS

A heartfelt thank you to all my long-suffering family and friends who have backed me throughout, especially when I became a pain in the derrière. I am so grateful for your patience, understanding and encouragement. And to the wondrous Melanie Clements and her fabulous mum, Lynne Horton at Mere Green Copy Shop (www.meregreencopyshop.co.uk) for their superb secretarial support, without which I would have been totally lost.

Also, a thousand thanks to the totally gorgeous Charmaine Hampson and the completely lovely Lorraine Rimmer, my inspirational hairdressers at Trilogy (www.trilogyhair.co.uk), who never stopped believing in my dream.

And to glamorous Lesley Feely and Kenidi Star at the Clarence (www.theclarencespa.com) for listening and laughing with me, and the Ten Lit Chicks And A Couple of Cocks Book Club for getting me to read outside my comfort zone.

Also to Cornerstones Literary Consultancy and their Readers for their perceptive analysis and feedback, even when it hurt.

And last but not least, to the awesome Chris Newton and Tony Tingle at Memoirs Publishing for turning my dream into reality. Now that's magic.

THE AUTHOR

S N Weddle has worked for BBC TV as a Producer on both prime time and daytime TV, including numerous make-over shows, and currently lives in Sutton Coldfield in the English Midlands.

In memory of my wonderful
mum and dad, without whom...

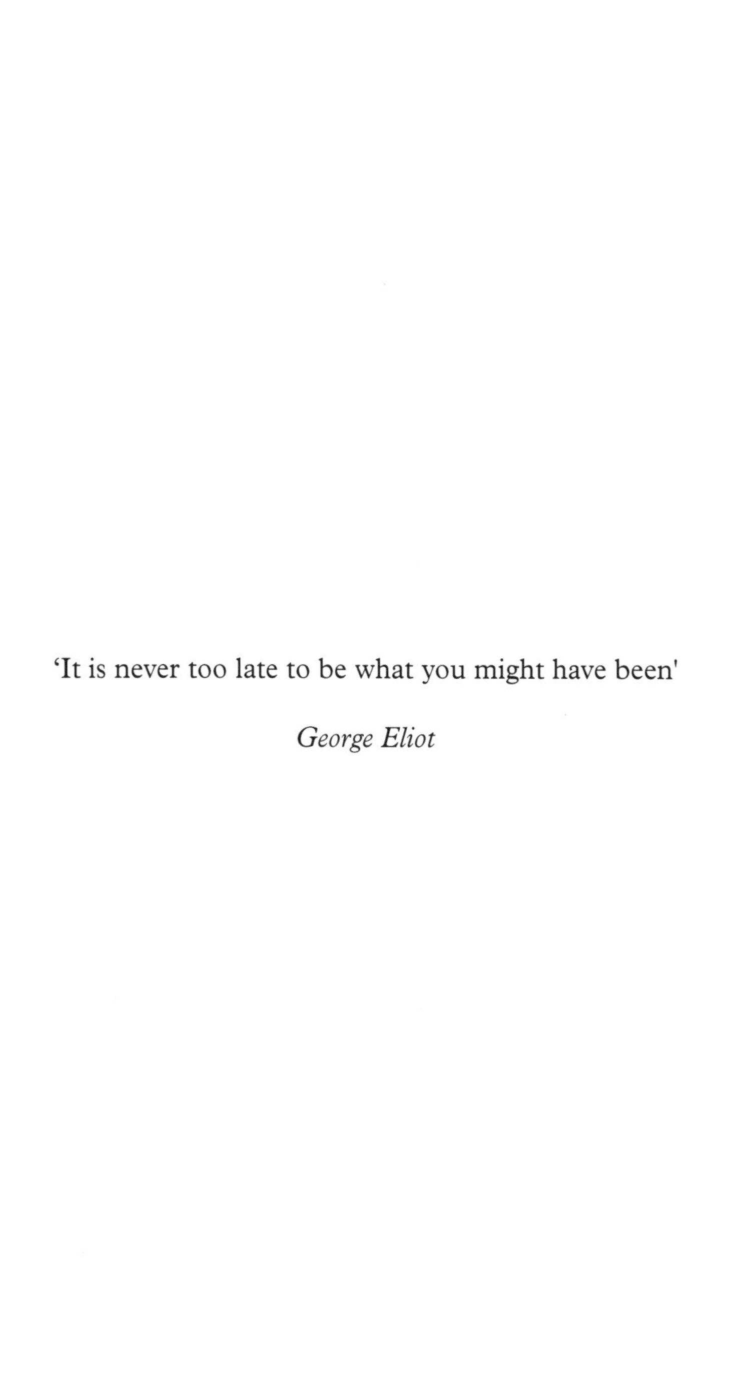

‘It is never too late to be what you might have been'

George Eliot

PROLOGUE

On my wedding day, which should have been the happiest day of my life, I committed myself to a truly wondrous man. If only he'd been my husband.

I hadn't planned it that way, although my Uncle Bill's little bombshell in the car en route to the church didn't exactly help.

"You don't have to go through with it, you know. If you've got any doubts I'll instruct the driver to turn the car around and we'll go for a beer and a steak instead."

Who was he kidding? The invitations had been printed, the congregation had gathered and the honeymoon in Acapulco was booked.

"I'm really not joking," he said. "Nothing is certain but death and taxes. Weddings are a piece of cake."

If only my father had been alive to give me away.

And it wasn't like I'd been harbouring any serious doubts about my husband-to-be either. In fact, I'd been longing for this day ever since I'd first met him. I wouldn't claim it was love at first sight, I just knew ideal husband material when I saw it – Greg Green, so strong, so sensible, and above all a good, kind-hearted man. Looking back, I didn't think I really deserved him then, so I thanked my lucky stars that this handsome all-American boy had chosen me. Besides, I'd had enough of those wild, irresponsible, devil-may-care guys. Not that I'd been exactly overwhelmed with suitors, as 'plain' was how I would have described myself in 1986.

"But you've got a great personality," my mother would constantly try and reassure me. She meant well.

Our limousine continued its relentless glide towards the church. Almost everybody, except my uncle and me, were already there.

"You've never liked Greg, have you?" I challenged him from the back seat of the car.

"I don't have to spend the rest of my life with him, do I? Whereas you are about to make a lifelong commitment."

"Drive around the block," I instructed the chauffeur as I saw the church coming into view.

"What's up, Jen?" I could see Jacqui, my head bridesmaid mouthing as we drove away from the Plymouth Episcopal Church at speed.

The clock was ticking, yet I needed time to think.

***

So what if Greg wasn't exactly my dream guy? I'd already met that man. You see, once upon a time I'd had this dream, so vivid that when I awoke it still felt ridiculously real to me. In sleep, I had encountered this mesmerising figure, as if while unconscious I had truly found the most perfect man imaginable. I could even taste him – like prime beef – such was the power of this supposedly illusory being; Latino dark, WASP tall and worldwide handsome. He talked of important events and magical places he'd visited, but what's more, he actually listened to me like I mattered, as I expressed my hopes for all that I might do and achieve in the life ahead of me. And then he kissed me – devoured would have better described it. If it had all been for real I would never have been the same again.

So I'd been an 18-year-old girl who'd had a dream. Hardly Martin Luther King, was I? Time to get real; this was my wedding day after all, and I wasn't about to forsake my husband for a fantasy. And truly, I wanted to marry Greg anyway.

***

"Shall we go steak or chicken?" my uncle said.

"Wedding cake," I replied. "But not quite yet," I cautioned the driver. "I need time to think. Greg's a good man. If I hadn't heard that commitment for life stuff you were going on about I would be walking up the aisle by now. You could put a girl off marrying Richard Gere."

"Sorry cupcake. I just wanted to test your resolve. You might have thanked me one day. Next stop, church," he then advised the bewildered driver as I nodded my agreement.

If I had any doubts they soon deserted me as I prepared to make my grand entrance into the church. Even so, I'd never enjoyed being on display, and my uncle knew it.

"Happy?"

I nodded.

"Then let your face know it," he whispered into my ear as we awaited our signal to enter. So I unleashed what I considered to be a killer smile, glad to be going where I was meant to be, alongside Greg, who looked at me in a way which can only be described as adoring.

"I don't deserve you," he whispered into my ear. "Stay with me forever."

"I will," I later vowed, not a seed of doubt in my mind as the service progressed.

"Those whom God has joined together let no man put asunder," the Minister proclaimed, and then, duly satisfied that nobody in the congregation objected to our union, he pronounced us man and wife.

Hallelujah! I rejoiced inside.

What's not to rejoice when everything in the kitchen tasted that delicious?

"Smile. Say cheese!" the photographer instructed the assembled guests for the group shot outside.

"I wonder what the French say when they are having a photo taken. Fromage doesn't exactly cut it," I overheard my uncle say when I momentarily took leave of my senses.

"Over here!" Uncle Bill shouted to this apparently random passer-by who just happened to walk past the church. "The stranger at the feast. It's good luck. Come and join us," he commanded this unknown, unprepossessing average Joe, dragging him off the sidewalk to stand between me and Greg.

I couldn't have cared less about him; just another of my uncle's irritating little pranks to be endured.

"You may kiss the bride," my uncle advised him.

How dare Uncle Bill dictate who I could and couldn't kiss? This was 1986, after all. And yet I chose to take the easy option and go along with Uncle Bill's absurd wedding tradition, otherwise he would never have let me forget it. And only as I turned to the stranger did I fully comprehend who it was I'd been invited to kiss.

This ordinary guy had only managed to transform himself into the man in my dream. You know the one; Latino dark, WASP tall, and worldwide handsome. The man of whom I had once said, had he kissed me in real life, I would never be the same again.

I looked at him in disbelief, at this beyond-handsome guy, enchanted by the contrast between his broad, muscular shoulders and his extravagantly long, almost feminine eyelashes, while his deep brown eyes enveloped me, observing me quizzically as he hesitated, awaiting my consent.

You so don't need to ask. Wedding or no wedding, just kiss me, I wanted to tell him, I'm now ashamed to admit.

"Go on. Don't be shy. Kiss her," my Uncle Bill urged him one more time. God bless you Uncle Bill.

So he did.

On the lips.

Inappropriately, yet thrillingly, and as surely as Isolde loves Tristan, Juliet Romeo or Rachel Ross, I knew I had found the one. He tasted sublime as the full force of him pressed down upon me. I stepped back in astonishment, overwhelmed by his maleness.

"Where have you been all my life?" (I can't believe I actually said that.)

"I would have come sooner," he replied, gently brushing back a tendril of my hair which had fallen into my eyes.

"You're too late," said my wise and wonderful mother, intervening to take the stranger by the arm and send him on his way. I yearned to chase after him – how excruciating would that have been? – but my mother held me back.

"Let him go. It will pass. No good will come of it," she urged me, as if she already knew of his power.

He was gone in seconds and nowhere to be seen, as if our kiss had never happened. In my dreams? So what else could I do except turn to Greg and attempt to kiss his confusion away as the crowd cheered, mostly in relief. But please don't imagine I was kissing Greg just for show – I was not going to sacrifice my marriage for one moment of madness with an illusory man, and in time, I even began to doubt whether the stranger ever existed anyway.

From that moment on I gave our relationship my very best shot, truly I did. And yet, however much they say you have to work at a marriage, all work and no play had eventually, 24 years later, made Greg and Jennifer a dull boy and a dull girl.

CHAPTER ONE

In our twenty-fifth year of marriage I had become accustomed to our uneventful journey. The two of us had been like a couple of pilots on a long-haul flight, an extended period of boredom brought to a halt by a moment of blind panic when Greg, my good-hearted, reliable, sensible husband, suddenly announced he'd been having an affair.

Maybe that memory of our wedding day and my inappropriate moment had persuaded me even to consider forgiving him, although please don't imagine that I took Greg's news in my stride. Whereas my infidelity existed only in the realm of fantasy, his remained sickeningly real.

I guess I should have felt anger, hurt or despair, yet once the initial shock had subsided I could only do numbness, as if my emotions had been dulled by novocaine.

"He ended this thing over two years ago," I told Annie, my friend and closest confidante at the homeless centre where I worked as a volunteer. "He said it had been preying on his mind and he couldn't possibly carry on living a lie for another day longer."

"Confession is good for the soul," she replied, "so now he feels a whole lot better about himself."

He had been unfaithful with one of his company's interns, a girl scarcely older than our own daughter. He begged my forgiveness. I struggled to grant it, so we slept separately that night.

Greg made his way upstairs, and I hadn't even bothered telling him about the young Latino man who had brandished a knife at the homeless centre earlier that day. I'm not ashamed to admit that I'd been scared out of my mind when I felt the point of the blade prick the skin on my neck. One sudden move and I would surely have died, all because of the whim of a drug-crazed kid.

"You can go far. I believe in you" I'd told Javier often enough. Perhaps I had been beguiled by his soulful brown eyes, as he became my pet project, even it meant inviting him to live at our home – strictly against Shelter rules, incidentally.

"Please Javier, let me go, and there will be no more questions asked", I had pleaded with him before he had mercifully eased the pressure of the blade upon my skin.

"OK, get me out of here", he'd agreed, handing me his knife, a trace of blood glistening sickeningly on the blade as he took flight down the mall to lose himself in a crowd.

"Are you all right?" said fellow volunteer Jed, rushing to my aid.

"Surprisingly, I'm fine", I replied, confused by how

much I wanted to live when only that morning I had nonchalantly contemplated killing myself.

***

I watched the local late night news alone - my errant husband now safely tucked up in bed - and my blood ran cold when I recognised that same young man on TV. He had been shot dead during a raid on a city liquor store.

I'd truly believed that I could inspire Javier to lead a better life, yet there he lay, as dead as my marriage. And in spite of tasting perfection on my wedding day, I'd genuinely striven to live happily ever after with my husband Greg, only to fail miserably. So there I was, surrounded by the ruins of my existence, as sadness engulfed my soul.

***

When making decisions I like to make lists, drawing a line down the middle of a piece of paper, one side for and one against. To die, or not to die: that was today's topic. It was the most important list of my life.

Nobody who knew me would have guessed that prosperous, respected, even admired, Jennifer Green could be contemplating the end of her days. Yet unknown to them all, I was living a life of quiet despair. Whereas they might have imagined me making lists arguing for and against whether to stay over when I went to visit my grown-up daughter in Manhattan, or which local politician I ought to be lobbying to aid my chosen charity for the homeless, they would never have believed I was considering the end of my days.

I knew of those who considered me to be a fine upstanding pillar of the community, while others could barely conceal their contempt for my devotion of time and energy to what they perceived as hopeless people who would inevitably let me down. And weirdly to me, I aroused envy too, accused by some who would greet me as a friend yet bad-mouth me behind my back of being unduly spoilt, the indulged wife of a rich man. I blame those Desperate Housewives.

Of course, I shouldn't have cared about what people thought. I should have risen above it, recent events having made me unduly sensitive, as my life appeared about as significant as a piece of discarded wrapping paper caught on the wind in a deserted shopping mall. And that's bad.

Against: to prevent the pain of loss to my beloved daughter, I wrote in favour of living.

I recalled the previous twenty-four hours, an earthquake of a day and a tsunami of a night – a life-changing experience, no less, although that's an expression more normally associated with a positive outcome than my double whammy of despair.

For: I have been betrayed by my husband Greg, by Javier, and by those who killed him.

CHAPTER ONE

Unless you are suffering from a dreadful, incurable disease, surely suicide is the most selfish thing a person can ever do. Of course, it was my duty to carry on and besides I had read somewhere that people who help others are the least likely to destroy themselves. So I would call in to my lifelong family practitioner for a good old-fashioned dose of common sense. And if that didn't work, well it's amazing what they can do with pills these days.

It wasn't so much the two great catastrophes of the last twenty-four hours as the little things which had turned my life a deeper shade of blue. To illustrate my point, a dinner party held last week in honour of our daughter Elaine and her increasingly significant other, Brad. I have to admit he was agreeable – Jane Austen's word for hot – as my daughter had earlier warned me. I positively glowed upon sitting next to him – was that appropriate? – but my happy moment was soon sabotaged by Greg complaining about the overcooked beef and the undercooked vegetables. Since when had I claimed to be Martha Stewart? The little things, you see.

"Can't you do anything right?" He reprimanded me.

I might just surprise you, I wanted to reply.

For: at least I could use my death to highlight the plight of the likes of Javier, I wrote in praise of extinction.

Apart from being agreeably hot, Brad was a polite young man who treated me, his girlfriend's mother, with respect. That's what I had become – his girlfriend's mother – always defined by my relationships to other people.

I've mislaid me, and I don't know where to look, I scribbled in the 'For' column.

I don't suppose Brad would ever think of me as a woman in my own right – why should he? I was Elaine's mother – that was my job – and I was unconditionally pleased for Elaine, beyond glad that she had found happiness with a handsome and amiable young man. So what if he gave me, his girlfriend's mother, barely a second thought? That's just the way of things. Get over it.

***

I suspect I had this strange affinity with the homeless because like me, they didn't belong either. I was a volunteer at the shelter, only working part time, although it had become a great passion of mine.

"Why would you want to waste your time with those no-good nicks?" my husband Greg would berate me. Not that he was a bad man, simply blinkered by too much certainty, oblivious to the numerous patterns which constitute the intricate mosaic of life.

Against: I love, even if I'm not in love with my husband.

For: he reduces me.

Putting the list to one side I caught sight of myself in a mirror, confirming, as if I needed it, that my youth had long since flown. The emerging lines on my face and the panda patches under my eyes were completed by a frown, indicative of a hundred thousand compromises there for all the world to see.

CHAPTER ONE

For: the world seems to have passed me by.

48, my age, had a neat mathematical symmetry, which would stand out in the local paper if they should bother to report my death.

Jennifer Green, champion of the Valley Stream Centre for the Homeless, aged 48, was found unconscious at her home after swallowing a lethal cocktail of vodka and barbiturate.

A Tragic Death, screamed the headline in my head – I'd always been a touch dramatic. Nobody knew I was unhappy. That was somebody else's tragedy. With surprising nonchalance I picked up a bottle of vodka and poured a powerful shot into a long tall glass, adding tonic spiced with something grievous, obviously only going through the motions, like a hundred thousand self-obsessed, neurotic, attention-seeking people before me.

Greg had left early for work, on his way to his thriving accountancy practice with a spring in his step, as if liberated by his unexpected disclosure. Boy, was my friend Annie right about confession being good for the soul. You couldn't have blamed me for resenting his tangible sense of relief at the expense of my peace of mind, but strangely I didn't.

"You did the right thing, owning up to your affair like that" I had said, although I also wanted to scream at him, "What took you so long, you bastard?"

He'd claimed it meant nothing, just a simple case of an older man being flattered by the interest of a young woman, and had lasted only as long as it took for him to see sense, which it later emerged was a whole ten months. So just how long does it take for a cheating man to get his head together? Until the novelty wears off, or so I feared.

I'd earlier learned her name was Britney. I'm saying nothing.

"Did you ever tell her that you love her?" I dared to ask him. "No, never in a million years" he said, so I kissed him on the lips as he stood dumbfounded on our front doorstep, his mouth tasting of toast and cornflakes. Instinctively he recoiled, bemused by what he saw as my outlandish show of affection. Typically Greg, yet so unrecognisable from the bronzed, blond young student dressed in a sleeveless T-shirt and ripped jeans, cycling past the Harvard Book Store where I worked during the school vacation in the summer of '84.

Youth had been treating us kindly when along came a marriage set against the backdrop of Greg's burgeoning career as an accountant, in time upgrading to an impressive four-bedroom house surrounded by a white picket fence to protect our beautiful baby girl. Truly we were blessed with so many desirable, wonderful, precious things, yet perversely, most of them dulled our senses further.

How I had once longed to be transformed by love, and to express it through mind-blowing sex. Maybe *Cosmopolitan* had lied to us all along, or perhaps I'd expected too much, as like most women of my generation,

I'd wanted it all. Or had I been cursed – crazy I know – by my obsession with that awesome man first seen by me in my dream, and then on my wedding day when I should have only had eyes for Greg? That man – handsome didn't do it, more beautiful than any man I had ever seen before. Awestruck, I would have pursued him, creating mayhem at the church - a bride in her white wedding dress chasing a strange man down the street on her wedding day! - had not my lovely mother intervened, grabbing me by the arm while counselling me to resist.

"Let him go. It will pass", she had urged me. And just as quickly as he'd materialised, so he had vanished. As the years passed I had slowly begun to take refuge in my memory of him, summoning up this mirage of a man as my ideal lover – Latino dark, WASP tall and worldwide handsome, with deep dark brown eyes and unfeasibly long, almost feminine, eyelashes. In due course he became my comfort, not only in dreams but in waking hours too, so real that in fleeting moments I genuinely believed I had seen him on the sidewalk, in a car or on a plane, always close yet tantalisingly out of reach.

So consider the state I was now in, perched precariously on the edge, toying with suicide, having devoted my life to an illusion. Sure, I know what you're thinking – she needs a check-up from the neck up. If only my wise and wonderful mother were still alive; she could have made me see sense.

CHAPTER ONE

★★★

Distracted and disorientated, I produced a rolling pin from the kitchen drawer and meticulously began crushing lethal pink pills into dust, primed to poison the drink of my choice. Then, absentmindedly, I once more poured a sizeable shot of vodka and a significant splash of tonic into a long tall glass. It was a little early in the day for alcohol and far too early in my life to die.

What a drama queen, only testing myself to see how far I would go before baling out, having already gone through this ritual twice before. So maybe I would carry on living, if only in a half-dead kind of way.

Precisely at the moment I decided not to drink the poison, the phone rang; some guy wanting to sell me plastic windows. His fake friendliness momentarily distracting me from debates about life and death.

"And should you choose to take up this offer you will automatically qualify for a holiday for two in Hawaii", he announced in his automated voice.

"You can count me out, I hate beach holidays, lying there smothered in sand and sun cream, there for all the world to see. It's my kind of hell", I replied. As a suitable response to my frank admission was nowhere to be found on the guy's script, he hung up.

For – I hate my body.

Whenever I flicked through the pages of stick-thin,

perfectly-proportioned models in *American Vogue* or *Cosmopolitan* I would recoil from those alien creatures. They were women, Jim, but not as we know them. Maybe I was just plain envious, although I'd read that most guys prefer something more rounded. Not that it was about attracting men anyway, which would hardly have figured high in my list of priorities given I had a husband, albeit a cheating one, and a fantasy man who would put any other male on the planet to shame.

So I felt queasy about looking at models in glossy magazines. Hardly life threatening, was it? In fact, I hated mirrors almost as much as I despised glossy magazines, two sides of a coin, one a reflection of a woman of a certain age claiming to be me, the other someone I had once aspired to be.

So I was past my prime.

Against: Beauty is in the eye of the beholder.

For: Bullshit.

I went back into the kitchen, staring quizzically at the long tall blue glass and its contents. I assumed it must be the poisonous cocktail, until I noticed a long tall green glass on an adjacent work surface which might equally have contained the toxic drink.

Amid the fog of despair, gradually it dawned upon me that only one of the glasses was a cocktail to die for, the other harmless.

I had once yearned to make a difference, but the stark

recall of Javier going crazy at the Homeless Centre acted as a timely reminder that my mission to make my town a better place had become mission impossible.

So what if I had received more than one glowing tribute from esteemed social scientists for my paper, 'Explaining Homelessness', which they praised for its valuable insights into why some vulnerable people were driven to live on the street? Inside I felt worthless.

Mercifully the phone rang again, and I was glad to hear my daughter's voice, calling from Manhattan.

"Are you OK, Mum?" she enquired in a concerned tone. I must have come over as strangely flat.

"I'm fine," I replied unconvincingly.

"Get a load of this - I've been offered a job!"

"That's brilliant," I observed, feeling ashamed of what I had been threatening to do.

"And not just any old job, it's the kind that comes with a salary. How incredible is that? Working in public relations for a reputable company."

"I couldn't be more delighted" I said, and I truly couldn't have been.

"Except that I'm not going to take it."

Count to ten, then recite the chorus of *I Will Survive* when I really wanted to scream out loud at her for being so wilfully, absurdly, stupidly perverse in rejecting a great career opportunity.

I rationed myself to a one-word enquiry. "Why?"

"Because I don't want to give up on TV."

"And by TV you mean that freak show of a talk show. And they don't even pay you expenses, let alone a salary."

"Oh mother" she said, in that certain world-weary voice she employed to remind me that I had absolutely no idea what I was talking about. "It's only a matter of time before I get a proper paid position. Melissa so rates me. She says I've got a real instinct for what makes great television."

We said our goodbyes – I mean how could I possibly compete with a talk show legend like Melissa Parker? – and while wallowing in self-pity I threw in for good measure the vacuum left by Elaine leaving home and pursuing a career in television among the shiny bright things in Manhattan, a sort of desolation descending upon me at the thought of it. Home had never felt so homeless. And how Greg and I struggled to fill that gap – empty nest syndrome, I think they call it.

I had remembered as a teenager seeing bored middle-aged couples sitting opposite one another at restaurants in ill-at-ease silence, talked out, loved out, lived out. I had vowed this fate would never befall me, although it had, as surely and remorselessly as night follows day. I looked at the painting hanging on the living room wall of a bleak winter landscape with skeletal lifeless trees, standing dormant in barren unyielding earth. It was a scene reflecting the landscape of my soul, and it made me shudder.

OK, so I was depressed. I needed treatment, not tranquillizers but cognitive therapy, somebody I could talk to so I could get things in perspective. I warmed to the idea of opening up to a complete stranger as I began to wonder whether our health insurance would entitle me to therapy. So I went upstairs and started searching through a drawer packed full of important documents – passports, birth certificates, real estate insurance – you know the kind of thing. And boy did I find what I was looking for, and more besides, because wedged down the back of the drawer I discovered a handwritten letter.

Why had he kept it, this love letter from his ex-girlfriend, Britney? He must have deliberately hidden it there, knowing I was the least likely person to look through this particular drawer, as I left that kind of thing to Greg.

Sure it made me want to hurl, this sensual swamp of totally embarrassing declarations – I was surprised to learn that I had been sharing a bed with Valley Stream's answer to Christian Grey. She must have had a great imagination, this girl. However, it was nothing that I couldn't handle.

Until I read: 'when you said you loved me, my heart skipped a beat'.

When you said you loved me, my heart skipped a beat.

I read that sentence over and over again, and it didn't get any better.

So amid the confusion there were two glasses, one green, one blue. One promising life, however imperfect, the other death, complete, utter and consummate. I screwed up my list, throwing it into the trash can, concluding that fortune would decide whether I was to live or die in a deadly kitchen-based version of Russian Roulette. If I lived, fate would have decreed that I must find the wherewithal to carry on, or alternatively, I would entrust my life to death. Insane I know, but reading that declaration of love by my husband had finally pushed me over the edge.

Green. That was my name and it was as good a reason as any, I surmised, to drink out of the green glass as if it was meant to be, swallowing the contents in one gulp before I had time to change my mind. It seemed to tasted bitter, so I prepared for oblivion, curling up foetally to watch Angelina Jolie on TV receiving an award for acting beautifully in a mesmerising film, looking so adorable you could have licked her face.

I felt fatigue weigh heavily upon me, and much as I tried to resist sleep, fearing it could be of the big variety, I couldn't fight it any longer.

I needn't have worried. When I awoke later I was still in Valley Stream. I hadn't died and gone to heaven - I'd survived. And what's more, how could I have been so irresponsible as to even think of leaving a trail of despair behind me by taking my life? In truth, I could have choked on my self-disgust. I vowed to pull myself up by my bra straps and do what I should have done years ago – leave home and start a new life, on my own.

In haste, I packed a small case with essentials, jumped into my car and drove downtown at speed. I parked outside Forever Young, a beauty parlour I had once visited in the vain hope that I could turn back time, and headed towards the mall to buy a few last-minute necessities before driving north, properly north, maybe as far as Canada. In my head I needed to speak French with strangers.

As I walked around town none of the people around would have guessed that I, prosperous, admired, even respected Jennifer Green, was about to disappear without trace.

None of them, that is, except one.

CHAPTER TWO

It was just another day in Valley Stream, although it was a day I would never have seen had fate not conspired to save me. Everything seemed refreshingly ordinary, but made extraordinary by the fact I was still alive. I would never take anything for granted again and the word "bored" would be permanently deleted from my spell check. Truly today was the first day of the rest of my life, when it could so easily have been my last.

Amid all the familiar sights in the mall, only the handsome thirty-something artist at work behind his easel stood out as unusual, a brush in one hand as he ran the other through his long mane of lightly greying hair. OK, so he intrigued me. Valley Stream? Hardly Venice, was it? I was wondering why he'd chosen somewhere as achingly ordinary as this place instead of somewhere more blessed with beauty or history.

Predictably, he failed to acknowledge my hesitant smile, and I wasn't surprised, because I was one of those parts of the scenery which never catch the eye. Whatever, I was alive. I strained to identify the source of a maniacal voice, which I instantly recognised as the ramblings of a homeless or dispossessed person. I soon located a mad-eyed man in the distance, sitting on a bench opposite the fountain, shouting alarmingly, incessantly and to nobody in particular.

"There's no gain without pain!" he hollered, inviting hostile looks from two interested security guards who had him under ever-increasing surveillance. Shoppers looked away, painstakingly ignoring his manic cries by pretending to deny his existence, whereas I had been trained to embrace his reality, assessing he must be new in town, given my extensive knowledge of all the usual drifters who sometimes passed that way.

"Hi. Are you in need of refreshment?" I tentatively enquired of him. He mumbled incoherently in reply. I tried again, once more to be on the receiving end of a stream of indecipherable language, apart from the occasional clear swear word, neither shocking nor unfamiliar to me through my work at the shelter.

"Slowly. Speak slowly," I counselled him softly, as he looked up and stared a little disturbingly into my eyes.

"I've been waiting for you for so long", he replied, surprisingly now speaking in crystal-clear English, both perfectly pronounced and beautifully formed, in such contrast to the voice of only a few seconds earlier.

While others hurried by, as if social disconnection could be contagious, I stood transfixed, momentarily overwhelmed by this ridiculous declaration that our random meeting could somehow have been planned. And when common sense reclaimed me, I sensibly enquired whether he had checked in to the town's hostel for the homeless, a simple enough question which deserved a straightforward reply.

"If music be the food of love, play on", he screamed insanely, causing me to rear back in shocked surprise, presenting the security guards with all the excuse they needed to intervene.

"Leave him be!" I yelled at them, shoving one guy with all the force of Wonderwoman. I shocked the security man into relinquishing his grip on the hobo, which enabled me to grab the vagrant by the arm and escort him to a place of safety. There we sat on a bench on the other side of the fountain, onlookers bewildered by this strange combination of respectable middle-aged woman and disreputable down-and-out, a couple of invisibles both made visible by this unlikely union.

"Be calm" I consoled him.

"I've been sent to save you" he replied.

So where were you when I really needed you, I wanted to say.

"I've always been there for you" he replied regardless.

I scrutinised the hobo for clues. How old? He could have been anything between thirty and fifty years old, I surmised, rendering it impossible to categorise him, both infuriating and disconcerting for inhabitants of the normal sane world given our innate human need to pin labels on everybody we meet.

I reasoned he must be in need of food, although his stomach, distorted by drink and drugs, probably told him otherwise.

He didn't decline my offer of a lunch date though, agreeing to accompany me to a downtown diner where the staff and customers barely bothered to disguise their suspicion of us. OK, he was hardly the dining companion of a girl's dreams.

I doubt he would have gained access without me, although I provoked nearly as much curiosity as the down-and-out himself. Why should she choose to waste her valuable time with a mad guy from the streets? They could go to hell. I was in charge of my own destiny now.

We took our seats at a table by the window, a mistake on reflection, as we became the object of interest for people both inside and outside the diner.

"Regrets, I've had a few..." he sang in a demented groan.

"Is that absolutely necessary?" I challenged him, expecting us to be thrown out at any moment.

"I give them what they want" he knowingly replied.

I smiled, but the smile suddenly rearranged itself into a grimace as a sharp stab of pain hit the pit of my stomach. I gasped out loud.

"Embrace life, not death" he advised in that

incongruous, precisely pronounced delivery. Was I dying? Had I drunk the wrong glass after all?

"Come on, eat up" I encouraged him, dismissing both the possibility that I was about to drop dead and the idea that he might know it.

"There is a better way." He continued to persuade me that he had all the answers to my woes, while a cold-hearted waitress slammed a jug of coffee and two mugs down upon the table without words, her actions eloquent enough.

"Service with a smile", the hobo observed, "I'm minded to shout something insane."

"I'd rather you didn't", I gently cautioned him, knowing we were already about as welcome as a vegetarian in a French restaurant.

"I am not the man I once was", he said, chicken escaping from his inhospitable mouth into his welcoming but disgusting beard. "I once played a leading role in the great drama of life, but now I am forced to take a bit part, reduced to lurking in the wings."

"People fall on hard times. Shit happens".

"In my previous life…" he persisted.

"When you were young" I corrected him.

"I have lived many lives" said the hobo, maintaining his preposterous pretence, "and maybe you can too."

Absurd, I know. As if this ramshackle mess of a man could possibly help me. Surely I shouldn't have been fooled by his trick of sounding deep and meaningful while talking garbage. He could have run for President – all he needed was a makeover.

And yet however hard I tried to counter his arguments with rational explanations, a small part of me began to wonder whether there was more to this man than ranting at strangers. Maybe it was desperation, or could it have been I was losing my mind? Either way, I seriously started to believe he could save me; nothing more than any port in a storm I know, so how ridiculous was I, when all around me people looked disdainfully down upon this loser. Experience at the Shelter had taught me that I wouldn't be exactly immune to their disrespect or contempt either.

She ought to know better, I could almost hear the elderly lady with heavy blue-framed spectacles and a shock of white hair thinking, *imposing this unkempt vagrant upon decent folk going about their everyday lives.*

Regardless of what others thought, I would redirect my concerns from me to him as surely I would have died by now had I drunk the poisoned glass.

"Have you booked into a hostel for tonight?" I enquired of him.

"It's you who needs helping," he rambled on, and in the silence between our words I visualised the man he once could have been. In truth, he could have been handsome, many years ago.

"Sure, I've had my moments. You would have struggled

to resist me", he teased me, erupting into a throaty laugh, redolent of strong tobacco and cheap spirits, as if he could read my innermost thoughts, only to mock them.

You wish, I thought, my hollow laugh indicative of my discomfort.

Weirdly, his pronouncements, at first without rhyme or reason, gradually began to make sense to me. And yet I wanted to deny them, like an unwilling subject attempting to resist a hypnotist's influence, refusing to go under but anticipating relief should I submit to his will.

"So many regrets, yet deep down, still you yearn to make a difference. Why make lists when even at this late hour you can have it all?"

Dismiss those demented ramblings by bestowing advice upon him about where to get a hot shower and a clean bed for the night I lectured myself, until I was again mugged by pain, reeling from the shock of it, my head spinning, my guts heaving, my body preparing to shut down.

"I'll get the check" I said.

Hanging on to consciousness by a thread - so how long did it take to die? – I became consumed by the desire to hold on to everything I had. I felt driven to call a cab and head directly to ER, where they would flush out the poison and so hand me back that most precious of gifts, the gift of life, in all its knife-wielding hoodlum, hot-headed daughter, no-good cheating husband type glory.

"I know you, who you are and everything about you", he said, the stalker now inside my head.

"I'm running out of time. I need to leave" I replied, fumbling to collect my belongings.

"A second chance – that is my gift to you. To live your life in the glorious, wide-screen high definition colour of the here and now as a twenty first century young woman in her prime, in possession of a divine young face complemented by a delectable young body to sigh for, yet still retaining all your grown-up wisdom accrued in lessons learnt in decades gone by."

"It sure as hell sounds better than death" I said, grimacing.

"And it beats being cheated on too."

"You really do seem to know me."

"Comprehensively" he replied, smiling.

"And since when?"

"Forever" he replied.

So there I was standing on a precipice, peering over at what might befall me, comprehending the craziness of it all yet irrationally drawn to the edge. It must be my destiny.

"If only I knew then what I know now" he said, mimicking my voice surprisingly well. "Now you can have it all. Youth is wasted on the young? You betcha! So why not choose to be new? Go on! Just take it. It's yours." He made a sweep of his arm, like a salesman on TV highlighting his beguiling offer.

"What have I got to lose?" I replied.

"No more if onlys. Say goodbye to regrets."

"So how do I get there?"

"You simply kiss me."

Yuk! Suddenly, being dead didn't seem such a bad idea after all, until I was forced to acknowledge that kissing the hobo was the only game in town. I was caught between a rock and a hard face. I scrutinised him closely, those weather-beaten features with their ingrained dirt and remnants of rotting food surrounding his grizzly mouth, while inside were those yellowing teeth, a mouth of golden daffodils yet nowhere near as fragrant. Where was the heroine inside me when I needed her? Gone shopping, knowing my luck. So I had to be brave, as the elderly woman with the shock of white hair, who had been eavesdropping on our conversation bridled in disgust at the hobo's bizarre suggestion.

While it might seem impossible for you to understand even contemplating such a grotesque act, then please consider this – after what I'd believed was a failed suicide attempt my body was now telling me otherwise, and here was some random guy posing as my saviour proving that he knew everything about me, and could not only save me but deliver me to a better life. It's called survival. And if that wasn't enough, then along came the clincher.

"And you get to meet your dream man too", he taunted me. "Latino dark, WASP tall and worldwide handsome, as I believe you are known to describe him".

It was a done deal.

Had I taken leave of my senses? Obviously I had. I planted my lips on the hobo's, as if to prove the point.

I'd had better experiences – in fact I can't recall a worse one. His cracked lips pressed disgustingly against mine, his unkempt beard scratching nauseatingly against my skin, yet still I persisted with the kiss, my stomach churning. "Oh, gross!" I heard a nearby customer say.

The hobo let go, and that was when the nausea began to make way for wonder. "Wish for what you want", he said, already retreating from view.

I did not reply. I had already embarked on a voyage. I was sailing weightless to a bright, pink place where everything was pure, scented and serene.

CHAPTER THREE

You know that expression, 'have I died and gone to heaven?' I guess nobody, dead or alive, could have had more justification than me to ask it.

"Entrez" said an alluring but disembodied female voice. She was inviting me into a room in which unfeasibly gorgeous young women in dazzling white smocks and short black skirts awaited my presence. They beckoned me towards them, their incandescent loveliness beyond my comprehension. Then they unthreateningly encircled me and began tenderly to undress me until I was naked. Under normal circumstances this would have been my idea of hell, and yet like Eve before the Fall I felt no shame or embarrassment whatsoever as they lifted my feather-light body aloft, then let go, watching me drift gently downwards, settling snow white and naked on a luxurious bed of down.

"Think beautiful thoughts", one heavenly creature whispered sweetly into my ear, the scent of her breath pure Chanel No. 5.

"And wish for what you want", said another, echoing the hobo's earlier instructions.

At first my mind went blank. Nothing in my life could possibly have prepared me for it. I was utterly overwhelmed and entirely bewildered by the extraordinary situation I found myself in.

"You must tell us what you want", one purred pleadingly.

"I want…" I said, hesitant at the thought of articulating my innermost secrets.

"Go on, say it".

"I want to… I want to live. And not just to live, but to live a fulfilling and fascinating life."

"And?"

"And, I want to be beautiful again - that's if I ever was.

"As you are on the inside, so shall you be on the outside", said the foremost heavenly creature. She clapped her hands twice, in what amounted to a call to arms for a hundred little hands to set about remoulding my tired body and weary face, as if they were sculptors intent on creating their masterpiece from my suddenly and astonishingly pliant form.

I was about to be rebuilt according to my own specifications, hard though that might be for you to comprehend. The beautiful creatures were cognisant of my every wish, lengthening my legs, compressing my waist, sculpting my neck, uplifting my breasts, heightening my cheekbones, inflating my lips, softening my skin, sweetening my voice, lifting my bottom, zapping my cellulite, enlarging my eyes…

"More?" the heavenly creature enquired. Shamelessly, I nodded my assent. Thinning my thighs, softening my hands, tightening my sex, shrinking my ears, enlarging my breasts, refining my nose and emboldening my heart, giving me everything I had ever wished for.

"Enough!" I cried, sounding sweet yet feeling spent. A heavenly creature led me by the hand into a startling white space where the scent of lavender pervaded the air.

"You like?" the heavenly creature enquired, gesturing towards a full length mirror, when upon seeing the reflection in it, for once, I didn't recoil.

"Ta-da! What's not to like?" I gleefully exclaimed. I had always wanted to be a natural blonde, only on reflection mournfully adding, "But is it really me?"

"It's you as you were always intended", said a voice so awe-inspiringly masculine that I nearly turned to liquid.

And there he stood – Latino dark, WASP tall and worldwide handsome bare chest in tight-fitting jeans, the guy who'd kissed me on my wedding day, the ultimate man of my dreams, dispensing advice oblivious of his semi-nudity.

"Beauty is both a blessing and a curse. Use it wisely", he cautioned me as he walked towards me, looking so gorgeous I couldn't take my eyes off him. But where to look? His glistening muscular chest, or his absolutely fabulous abs, or his impressively packed jeans?

"Look into his eyes", one of the heavenly creatures advised.

I focused upwards, more than happy to alight upon his soulful deep brown eyes, the femininity of his extravagantly long eye lashes in stridently sharp contrast to his abundant masculinity. What bliss, falling effortlessly into his embrace as he held my almost comically tiny waist with his sure, firm grip. Whether I had just conjured up my best fantasy imaginable or was simply losing my mind as a prelude to the end of life – and oh boy, what a way to go – I couldn't be sure.

"Kiss me", he said in a voice so arousing that it could have corrupted angels.

As if I needed an invitation! Anyway, all this was unreal, wasn't it, my redeeming reason for my wanton ways? Otherwise, I would be no better than my husband. And please don't imagine that I would stoop so low as to seek revenge on my cheating husband by submitting to the charms of a beautiful semi-naked man. Nothing to do with that, in any way, whatsoever, at all.

So in this strange, twilight, blame-free world, I willingly obliged. Yet frustratingly, just at that holy, heavenly and heart-stopping point when our lips should have met, my body ablaze with the need for him, I began to swoon in the manner of a nineteenth-century romantic heroine, drifting in and out of consciousness. My sense of him began to fade - surely, this must be my punishment for surrendering to him so willingly – as he tantalisingly slipped away. I was now in a formless, unfamiliar place where my fantasy man was nowhere to be seen.

CHAPTER THREE

"Where am I?" I begged of somebody, anybody, who might be listening. Disappointingly, it was the hobo who replied. I was thinking I had seen and heard the last of him.

"You are where you are supposed to be", he explained, his voice disembodied but reassuringly recognisable. "The old you is safely back home in Valley Stream with Greg, who remains blissfully ignorant of what has befallen his Jennifer. Take a look." He referred me to a picture on a plasma television screen where everyday domestic life was being played out, carrying on regardless without me.

It may not surprise you to learn that I didn't quite get it at first. There I was watching this picture on a screen of me back home with Greg. I then looked down at the new me I had become. How could this woman pictured in Valley Stream be me too? I had already become somebody else who was beyond recognition, yet was also undeniably me, if only in personality, not looks?

Boy did I need clarification. Thankfully, the hobo duly obliged.

"One has become two. The new you has been extracted from the person you used to be, yet she still exists too."

OK, here comes the science, if that's what it was. As I understood it, it was as if I'd been cloned, the real me seeming to reside in the person I'd become, although I looked nothing like her, whereas the old me, a mirror image of myself, appeared to be somebody else entirely.

Is your head hurting? Think what mine was going

through. Yet it all made perfect sense to the hobo, who continued to advise.

"Don't think too hard about it, just live it, but first you must sleep" he advised me, like a doctor addressing a patient who had just undergone a particularly arduous surgical procedure.

I had been reprieved, given a licence to live. But first sleep took me, taking me so far out of consciousness that I could have drowned in dreams. Heaven knows how long I had slept for before I awoke later unscathed, apparently returned to reality. I slowly established that I was lying in a giant double bed in an upmarket hotel room, far away from imagined worlds.

People in crisis these days go on journeys. Mine was crazy enough to threaten my sanity, while my destination was no less mad.

Where was I? Who was I? And who the hell were they? I speculated as I became conscious of two fit young specimens of manhood, one either side of me, both of them fast asleep. What sort of woman have I become, I asked myself, precariously stepping over two slumbering bodies, one white, one black. A young woman's clothes were strewn tellingly across the bedroom floor. I supposed they must belong to me, or at least the person I had recently become.

I dressed hurriedly in those clothes, which were way too young for a middle-aged American housewife, anxious to exit before either of the guys should awake. I was relieved yet intrigued that the Agent Provocateur silk lingerie, the black and white checked Dior scoop top, the black Stella McCartney pencil skirt and the black and white Jimmy Choo shoes should fit me perfectly. I suspected that it must all be part of the hobo's prêt-a-porter plan.

Oh, how I froze when the naked white guy let forth a heartfelt sigh, screwing up his eyes and then yawning while throwing his arm around the black guy, presumably thinking it was me, having just disentangled myself from them.

"Ah, so that's who I am", I said softly under my breath, having opened a monochrome Prada handbag to discover the name Jennifer Gold inscribed on a credit card within. From Green to Gold – It's alchemy, I mused, exhilarated yet perturbed by being both astonishingly alive and miraculously transformed. I was guessing that it would take time to lay claim to this gorgeous stranger who I had adopted as myself.

"Byeee boys. Have fun!" I said *sotto voce*, gently clicking the door behind me and stepping out into Mid Town Manhattan, where beautiful young women are not unknown. So will you please forgive me when I write that heads turned as I hit the sidewalk? They just did, OK? Although believe me, I wanted to hide, to disappear, to be invisible again. I was nowhere near ready to enjoy this level of attention.

Wherever I went eyes followed me, and I was bowing my head to repel admirers. Evidently I had become that part of the scenery which did catch the eye.

As I was walking down Madison, a group of smokers exiled from their offices almost inhaled me as I passed by. I walked on relentlessly, having no destination in mind, alighting upon the Rockefeller Centre, where I had once taken my then twelve-year-old daughter to the NBC experience, inspiring her lifelong ambition to pursue a career in television.

I surveyed the scene around me. Tourists held sway in this part of town, sucking up the sights on open-topped red buses while vendors on the sidewalks pleaded with passers-by to liberate their dollars for postcards and the same six paintings on sale wherever you turned. I felt like I belonged there too, an existential tourist being whoever I wanted to be in a city where your history was irrelevant and reinventing yourself was obligatory.

Even here in this more family friendly environment I continued to be an object of fascination – *there she goes again* – wondering what the *American Vogue* had I done to deserve this level of attention.

"You better get used to it", said a down-and-out, unexpectedly holding out a begging bowl to my face.

"Pardon me?" I said, taken aback by his presence.

"The heat", he replied. "I can see it's bothering you. You better get used to it."

So, not every hobo was a magic one. It's not that far, I mused as I caught a fading echo of what I sensed was his once glorious past. A life on the streets could befall anybody, if this softly spoken, educated sounding guy was anything to go by.

I deposited a ten-dollar bill on his plate – strictly against Shelter rules – getting a gracious "too kind" in return, the hobo's presence a stark reminder that I too was homeless, the light already fading on that first new day.

I recalled Greg treating me to a luxury weekend at the Carlyle Hotel – the gift of a man with a guilty conscience no doubt – chosen by me after reading in the *New Yorker* that my one-time heroine, Princess Diana, usually stayed there when visiting Manhattan. It would have been 'have credit card will travel', had I not further explored my Prada handbag to discover a Trump Hotel key card and reservation slip hiding under lipstick, mascara and breath freshener, suggesting I already had a place to stay.

What a relief to know where I was going. I flagged down a taxi after several had already sped by, only to be greeted by the standard New York cab driver's weary indifference - *where to?* - until he saw my reflection in his rear-view mirror. Modesty forbids me from going on about the re-energising effect I appeared to have upon him, except to state that had he been a puppy dog he would have been rolling over on his back and waiting to be tickled on his tummy.

"Omigod," I exclaimed in desperation upon discovering I had no money in my purse.

"Everythink all right?" he enquired from the other side of his head.

"I've left home without any money. How could I be so blonde?"

"Money, schmoney," he reassured me. "What's a few dollars between friends? So ver to? You name it, I'll drive there."

Beauty is the strongest currency in the world.

"Trump Tower, if you would be so kind."

"That's easy. So you here on businezz or pleazure?"

"Pleasure, I guess."

"So pleazure is your buzinezz," he replied, highly amused by his own joke. I joined in a little more flirtatiously than I had intended with his laughter.

As the taxi negotiated Columbus Circle, Trump International loomed down above us, making me feel infinitesimal. My doubts were multiplying as to whether I should abandon this course of action until I realised I had already passed the point of no return and that in reality, there was nowhere else to go.

I felt such a fraud, masquerading as this glamorous young woman in the most exciting city on earth when I should have been at home preparing Greg's dinner, asking him how his day had been and working to get our marriage back on track.

The opulence of the hotel's reception area did little to restore my calm. Everything was designed to impress, or in my case, overwhelm.

"Will you be dining in our acclaimed Jean George's restaurant this evening?" the haughty manager on reception disdainfully enquired, reducing me to a vacant stare as if I had just been asked to explain the meaning of Stephen Hawking's *A Brief History Of Time*. I eventually nodded my assent, then smiled appreciatively at the Trump attaché who had been assigned to escort me to my suite as he explained how to employ my key card to activate the elevator, ascending us to the 14th floor in as many seconds.

"Nice uniform," I lamely observed, fearful of saying anything which would blow my cover and expose me as a suburban middle-aged housewife on the run. "And how do you get those shoes of yours so shiny?" I enquired, instantly blowing said cover. Surprisingly, the Trump attaché declined from calling security. He accompanied me into my suite and began acquainting me with all the domestic gadgets at my disposal.

"I can also arrange your business appointments, book you a massage or arrange a flight," he announced, momentarily making me feel like a princess.

As the attaché continued his well-rehearsed spiel I took in the wonders of the tastefully-appointed suite which surrounded me. I was impressed by its ultra-contemporary style with clean lined furniture, fabulous fabrics and soothing Tuscan tones. Standing handsomely at the far side was a dazzling white grand piano, which he must have realised had caught my eye.

"Do you play?" the young man enquired, pointing to the impressive Steinway.

"The piano is not my forte," I quipped. He did not smile.

"I see" he said. "Well, if you should require it, just dial extension 4306 and a pianist will be sent directly to your suite," he announced, pronouncing pianist a little like penis, leaving me attempting to stifle inappropriate laughter.

"Now that's what I call impressive. It's amazing what room service can serve up these days" I said.

"Glad to be of service," he spluttered, departing the room awkwardly, an incriminating blush blighting his face.

Alone at last, I ran to the bathroom, tearing off my clothes like a child on Christmas morning desperate to rip open their most longed-for present to behold the wonders inside. I stared into the full-length mirror, and for once it didn't disappoint. So this was the shape of things to come. I knew of films where ludicrously glamorous women became aroused by the very sight of themselves. OK, so I'd watched one once, Greg's attempt to resurrect our ailing sex life – it hadn't worked, by the way. So as I waited for my reflection to arouse and overwhelm me, instead I laughed out loud. Everything appearing to be designed to amuse and entertain, more Jessica Rabbit than Gwyneth Paltrow.

Take my breasts – and trust me, you would. They were so pert and upright they positively screamed out, 'Look at me, look at me, look at me!' Under-wired bras? Who needs them!

And my waist, so tiny a grown man's hand could almost encompass it, just made me want to giggle, as did my provocative bottom, which was of J-Lo booty shaking proportions. Nobody was ever going to believe I had a brain ever again.

So this was the pneumatic new creation I had become; more like Hugh Hefner's handiwork than mine. With one or two exceptions, this wasn't what I would have chosen; I'd have gone for something much more subtle and understated if I could have been transformed again.

Only my never-ending legs impressed me at first, especially as I'd always been cursed with chunky ice hockey players' calves. And I did have a sneaking regard for my new cute little feet, having always believed that the words 'beautiful' and 'feet' could never co-exist in the same sentence. Yet evidently there I was, calendar girl for foot fetishists everywhere.

Sure, I admired my perfect, youthful skin, but I drew even more comfort from discovering a familiar mole underneath my left rib cage, a remnant of my old self and a reminder of who I once used to be. You could say it was benign to me.

Anyway, medical examination over – I hear you breathe a sigh of relief – as I slipped on some fresh knickers, draping myself in the hotel's complimentary white bath robe. Curiously, I was reminded that I still had to eat, the first pangs of hunger beginning to strike. I called Room Service, firstly to order a Waldorf Salad and half a bottle of Chardonnay, and then, as advised, a pianist, to complement my dining experience.

While I was brushing my lustrous honey blonde hair the doorbell chimed, heralding the arrival of my meal. Then within minutes I discovered another visitor at my door, who I guessed must be the piano player.

"If music be the food of love, come in", I said – another of my cheesy jokes. At least he possessed the politeness to smile an appreciative crooked smile, which relaxed me, having the effect of making me feel instantly at home in his company. I suppose being a single young woman alone in a hotel room with a complete stranger, albeit an employee of the hotel, might appear a little inappropriate. He was young and not entirely unappealing instead of the ancient cocktail bar crooner I had somehow been expecting, yet I felt safe with him. He was that kinda guy.

I did sense he was intrigued by me. He was probably glad to have a client who was female and under the age of fifty.

"Any requests, or shall I surprise you?" he asked me, placing what I judged to be an agreeably cute bottom on the piano stool, then playfully affecting the manner of a concert pianist by clasping his hands and flexing them back and forth in preparation for performance.

"Can we talk first?" I asked.

"That costs extra", he replied.

"So put it on the account", I advised him, patting the sofa, signalling for him to come and sit alongside me as if I was summoning a pet dog. And since you ask, no I'm not proud. Obediently, he obeyed.

"I'll start", I said. "So what's a nice young boy like you doing in a place like this, entertaining women of uncertain virtue in their rooms late at night?"

"You speak so old for a girl so young", he observed.

He had spirit this boy, daring to tease me about my style of speech, risky for an employee to his client. He explained that he worked at the Trump Hotel as a means to fund his way through music college, and more crucially, to give him the time and the space to write his own songs.

"A composer? How cool is that?" I responded in language more appropriate for my years.

I observed his long, elegant fingers with fascination, and mischievously imagined them playing a sensual sonata on my ridiculously curvaceous body. Whoa there, I counselled myself, disturbed by how easily I could succumb to inappropriate thoughts whenever an unsuitably young man came into view. It was as if my transformation had an unexpected side effect, heightening my appreciation of the opposite sex to levels unbeknown to me. I had to get a grip on it, as I didn't want to do something I'd later regret.

"Let me play for you", he insisted, once more taking his position at the piano – cute bum in view again, stop it! – as the familiar chords of Billy Joel's *Just The Way You Are* washed over me. "Don't go changing" he sang sweetly, a sentiment too late for me, "I love you just the way you are". I was seriously impressed, moved by the warmth and purity inherent in the singer's surprisingly haunting voice.

"Bravo! Being serenaded is so sweet", I said, clapping appreciatively. The boy rose to his feet and performed an extravagant bow in return.

"So glad you approve", he said while gathering his sheet music in pointed preparation for departure.

"What? No encore?" I protested, wanting to stamp my feet in the manner of a spoilt child, furious at not getting its own way.

"My public awaits", he patiently explained regarding his residency in the bar downstairs, driving me to contemplate doing something desperate, like accidentally on purpose untying the cord on my bathrobe – and no, I'm not proud of that either.

"So go, see if I care", I taunted him.

"You could always come to the show." Bravely for him, he continued to persuade me, promising to find a suitably discreet table for me, away from prying eyes.

"I want to be inconspicuous" I begged of him.

"I guess nature decided otherwise. I'm Marty", he announced, smiling his crooked smile.

"I'll have to get changed, I said, referring to my bathrobe.

"No need. I love you just the way you are", he endearingly replied.

CHAPTER FOUR

Marty was true to his word. He had found a place for me partly obscured by a pillar from where I could watch him perform without being stared at, the fate of any single woman who has the nerve to sit in a bar alone.

While I sipped my Cosmopolitan, Marty checked me out between verses, smiling crookedly and addressing the most heartfelt of lyrics especially to me, just me, singing to the room yet continuing to serenade me, mostly me. I won't lie; I absolutely adored it. In fact, I hadn't felt this special in years. You are the sunshine of my life, he sang, and I felt the warmth of his song on my skin.

He was a sweet boy, yet I didn't want to lead him on. I suppose wearing a thigh-skimming black lace mini dress on skyscraper heels – please, I only had the wardrobe of a harlot to choose from at this stage – could have given him the wrong idea. But it wasn't just the dress to blame. The pillar was not quite substantial enough that I couldn't be seen from the far end of the bar, where a dashing and distinguished middle-aged man with greying temples and a defiantly retro Tom Selleck-style moustache was hunting me down with his eyes.

OK, this is where I have to make a confession; I flicked my hair flirtatiously in response. How wrong was I, and to do such a thing whilst Marty continued to sing his heart out to me on the other side of the room? Look, it was simply a reflex reaction, you tap a knee and a leg springs into the air, an intriguing middle-aged guy looks at you knowingly, and you flick your hair; a simple matter of quantum mechanics. He should have understood that. Instead he cast more commanding glances, the king of all he surveyed. In his head I had given him the green light. He was biding his time until he hit on me.

At first the prospect terrified me. I just didn't have the wherewithal to deal with hot guys hitting on me in bars. How could I possibly be expected to remember the etiquette of how to behave in pick-up joints? The rules had probably changed beyond all recognition since my day anyway. And then I recalled the hobo's words, reminding that nobody was better equipped than me, with my unique combination of mature mind and youthful body, to wrap this experienced, middle-aged Lothario around my little finger.

I would play him for sport, if for no other reason than just to see what happened. And yet I was terrified that he might make a move.

As I nervously awaited this inappropriate encounter, on the other side of the room a pretty girl intervened, brazenly approaching the middle-aged guy at the bar, shamelessly propositioning him, and then accepting his invitation to sit alongside him while nodding her assent to his offer of a drink. I watched this intruder go about her business with high indignation, unjustifiably resenting her interference. The man was now solely focused on the girl – how fickle men can be!

I turned my attention to the intruder again, who in spite of her sluttish behaviour had the appearance of a well-brought-up girl. She was attractively but modestly dressed, very much in the style of my daughter Elaine. In so many ways she could have been Elaine, and the longer I looked at her the more it dawned upon me that that's exactly who she was. She was not some random lookalike but my own one and only daughter, unaccountably propositioning a sleazy, past his prime, middle-aged guy in a hotel bar.

How I had to restrain myself from crashing in upon their cosy little scenario with all the delicacy of Naomi Campbell trashing a VIP airport lounge. God, I so wanted to bawl her out, accusing her, demanding of her, asking her, did she really believe that I had devoted all that time and money on her education and upbringing only to see her behave like a harlot? This was my daughter I was fuming about. She appeared to be operating as a prostitute in an uptown bar, albeit a smart one, and where was the consolation in that?

One small problem though – I'd conveniently overlooked the little matter of not looking or sounding anything like her mother any more. I could hardly break up their little party to give Elaine a stern telling off as her Mom when dressed up in a figure-hugging, thigh-skimming short dress. Not to mention that I appeared to be barely 21 myself.

In disbelief, I continued to watch events unfold powerless as smiles were exchanged, laughter shared and eye contact made, together with touching of forearms, then hands, climaxing with the guy writing down his room number, I assumed, on the back of a business card before handing it to Elaine, who deposited it in her purse, while he, no doubt, made his way back to his room. And worst of all, I was sure that I had seen him offer her some money.

Regardless of my radical transformation, maternal concern overwhelmed me. The urge both to protect and reprimand Elaine for her wanton ways was impossible to resist. Marty winked at me sweetly, oblivious to my distress, but I barely acknowledged him, my mind elsewhere, both confused and bewildered that Elaine, who had appeared to be so blissfully happy when last seen together with her young man Brad, should be acting in this immoral way.

Eventually emboldened by the knowledge that I would be unrecognisable to her, I emerged from the shadow of my discreet table to confront my daughter at the bar. I overheard her snatched cellphone conversation as I approached, although it made no sense to me whatsoever.

“He’s bought it, like a lamb to the slaughter, and I have incriminating evidence”, I heard her say.

"Don't do it", I begged of her. "He's old enough to be your father."

"Oh purlease. And who are you? My mother? I don't think so", she sneered after scrutinising me carefully.

I cringed a little, mostly inside.

"I suppose you probably think this is none of my business..."

"You suppose right."

"But I couldn't just sit there and watch you throw your life away. To sleep with a middle-aged man for the sake of a few bucks..."

"It's not what it seems", Elaine protested wearily, looking at her watch.

"You see, I've been watching you."

"My own personal stalker... great!"

"And what would your parents think? I doubt they would approve, would they?"

"And I've been watching you too" said Elaine belligerently, "making eyes at the cute piano player, not to mention hair flicks at our mutual middle-aged friend."

I wanted to shout, *don't do as I do, do as I say*, as I had on more than one occasion during those difficult teenage years.

"The piano player... well, he's my boyfriend," I said, struggling to concoct a credible explanation, "and the middle aged guy... well... I think you must be mistaken..."

"You don't owe me any explanations, nor me you" said Elaine, grabbing her purse, intent on quitting the bar.

"Let me stop you right there", I said, unashamedly holding up the palm of my hand to Elaine's face. "I demand an explanation."

"Are you for real?"

"I'm only trying to help."

"So why are you, a complete stranger, so concerned about me? Are you born again?"

"In a manner of speaking, yes."

"OK. Let me put you out of your misery. I'm not, and repeat not, nor have I ever been, a hooker."

"So what are you then?"

"Seeing as you ask, I'm a honey trap."

"And that's better?"

"Look, don't touch, that's our mantra", Elaine answered. "Look… I'll try to explain."

"I'm all ears."

She elaborated further about the role of the honey trap, hired by suspicious wives and girlfriends who have nagging doubts about their man's fidelity to see if they might succumb to temptation, collecting evidence and then presenting it to clients, either dismissing or more usually confirming their concern.

With foreboding, like a nervous gardener preparing to lift up a rock under which disgusting, wriggling creatures inevitably must lie, I hesitantly enquired about the nature of the evidence to prove guilt or otherwise.

"Something like this", said Elaine waving the middle

aged guy's business card with his room number and a message, 'don't be long' scribbled on the reverse side in his distinctive handwriting, then producing her digital recorder as back-up.

"That's more than enough to prove his guilt. He's toast", Elaine concluded, her mission evidently accomplished.

"So you won't be joining him in his room?"

"What kinda girl do you think I am? No, don't answer that", said Elaine, giggling conspiratorially.

"And is this what you might call your career?"

"No way. It's just a means to an end while I work unpaid as an intern on the Melissa Parker Show."

"But there must be a better way? Haven't you ever considered working as a waitress, or even behind a bar, to supplement your funds? Then there's your mom and dad. I'm sure they would have been only too happy to have helped out."

"Like getting blood from a stone" was Elaine's caustic response. How unfair was that? "A girl's gotta earn a living".

"And your boyfriend?"

"I prefer not to trouble him with it", Elaine reluctantly admitted.

"So you treat him like a mushroom?"

"I'm sorry?"

"You keep him in the dark."

"But he wouldn't understand. What man would?" she said, opening up. "Don't imagine for one moment that I'm entirely happy about what I do. It was only meant to be temporary until I landed a job in television. Now I feel trapped there. It's like blackmail, with my boss threatening to tell Groucho TV everything if I quit honey trapping."

"That's immoral and downright illegal," I railed. "You should be free to leave whenever you want."

"You haven't met old Alice, my boss", Elaine replied ominously.

"Maybe you should. You'd be dynamite at this game", said Elaine, surveying my absurd Jessica Rabbit body.

I heard her suggestion first as a joke, but as our conversation began to flow after what had been an arid beginning, the thought of becoming a honey trap myself exercised an almost mystical pull upon me. I was somehow sensing that it was my destiny, the reason for having been sent there in the first place, to liberate Elaine from her shameful occupation by offering myself as her replacement; a human sacrifice, if you will.

"Maybe I should make an appointment with this Alice." The flippancy of my remark betrayed a serious intent.

"Well, you're a fine one. One moment you're ranting on about my immoral occupation, and then you want to sign up to the trade yourself. You are decidedly weird," Elaine observed as I applauded Marty for his rendition of the *The More I See You*, while he smiled his crooked smile appreciatively in return.

"He's cute. How romantic to have a musician as a boyfriend," she speculated.

Don't even go there, I decided, and continued to pursue the history of her honey trap career instead.

"I booked Alice as Director of Truth Will Out to appear on an edition of Melissa's show entitled Is Your Man Programmed To Cheat," Elaine explained in response to my probing. "It was my responsibility to look after Alice at the studio, and although she condescended to me throughout, as she was leaving she handed me her card, announcing 'you might have what it takes to be a honey trap, call me.' Of course, I totally dismissed the idea at first – although I have to admit to being a little bit flattered – and as the bills began to stack up, and no salary was forthcoming from Groucho Productions, reluctantly I called Alice and enlisted for Truth soon after."

"You should have called your Mom and Dad instead", I reprimanded her.

"You would have thought so, except things haven't been too good between them since I left home and the last thing I wanted to do was worry them further."

"What a considerate daughter", I observed sarcastically. "And confidentially", I said posing a question, of course in no way inspired by my passing susceptibility to the charms of that middle-aged guy, "have you ever been tempted by one of your targets?"

"No way! It's strictly laugh out loud at their jokes, be mightily impressed by their careers, and nod supportively at their endless excuses for cheating on their wives, usually encapsulated by their one all-purpose explanation, 'my wife doesn't understand me'. Being a honey trap could put you off men for life."

"It's a risk I'm willing to take," I bravely volunteered. "I intend to have a word with this Alice, and if replacing you is what it takes to get you out of there, then I'll do it."

"Exchanging me for you? I'm as good as liberated."

"Don't count on it just yet."

"You're unreal," she said. "You'd do all this for me? That's awesome. I'm Elaine by the way, but only my mother calls me that. My friends call me Ellie."

"Hello Ellie," I greeted her with a formal handshake, as an audible upsurge in applause signified the end of Marty's set. He walked purposefully towards me, blissfully unaware that in the time it had taken him to sing six songs he had become my devoted boyfriend and I would be expected to greet him accordingly. How the Justin Bieber was I supposed to do that?

"Hey", I addressed him uncertainly at first, Elaine looking on fondly nevertheless.

"Hey", he replied cautiously back, happy to let me set the pace.

"You were fabulous, hon", I said, my prelude to showering him with kisses, an extravagant show of affection exclusively designed to convince Elaine that we were beyond any doubt a couple.

"That good eh? If only all of my customers were that appreciative", he said in shock.

Undeterred I grabbed his hand, presuming it to be a girlfriend kinda thing to do, if my memory served me well. He sat alongside me blissfully bewildered, lost in the moment, unaware of the disgruntled Tom Selleck lookalike who had returned from his room looking mean, infuriated by Elaine's failure to show and slapping his key card on the bar.

"Hey, what's keeping you?" he barked at Elaine while eyeing Marty suspiciously.

I couldn't begin to tell you how much I resented this revolting sleazebag speaking to my daughter like she was a two-bit hooker, except to decide that castrating him figured high on my list of things to do. OK, call me fickle if you must, but maternal concern sure as hell beats lusting after smooth guys in bars every time.

"You're too late", I said parking myself between him and Elaine. "Unfortunately for you the special offer has just expired. You are seriously past your sell-by date."

You would have thought I had just made myself abundantly clear, but apparently not. My meaning just didn't fit in with this ridiculous new body of mine.

"I don't suppose a piece of two-girl action would be out of the question?" the unreconstructed man enquired.

I threatened to call security, and the guy wisely exited at speed with his tail between his legs.

Marty, poor boy, watched these events unfold with incomprehension, yet I detected a trace of a crooked smile too. I guess we were the type of girls his mother had always warned him against, and this was making us utterly compelling to him. He continued to watch us intently as we exchanged cellphone numbers, Elaine expressing her surprise that I was actually a resident in the Trump Hotel, and questioning my need for meaningful employment with the Truth Agency, or anybody else for that matter if I could afford to stay in a luxury five-star hotel.

I assured her that my stay at the Trump was only temporary, and an income an imminent necessity, so we arranged to meet outside Truth HQ at ten o'clock the next morning. Then I could finally release Elaine from her honey trap hell. And should she go short of funds as a consequence, I even promised to lend her money.

"So why would you do that?" Elaine enquired. "You're seriously disturbing me now."

"I recently inherited a small amount from an elderly aunt," I lied. "It's just a short-term loan, until you can pay me back."

How could I not help her by whatever means possible? It was a matter of destiny you see. My sole reason for having been sent on this bizarre adventure was to rescue my daughter from the slippery slope that is honey trap. What other purpose could there have been?

We hugged one another warmly, having created a bond between us which defied explanation for two girls who had only known each other for a matter of minutes. Of course, I knew better.

And then there was Marty, having seen his relationship with me fast forwarded so rapidly – easily bypassing first and second date status – that he must have thought he was about to enter the promised land.

"Would you like me to play you to sleep in your room?" he asked me sweetly, while unsuccessfully attempting to reclaim my left hand, which I needed to stifle a yawn instead.

"Forgive me Marty, but it's been a long, tiring day."

"Then what better reason for me to sing you a lullaby?"

"But you wouldn't believe how tired I am."

"In the city that never sleeps? No way", he teased me, smiling his crooked smile. It would have been beguiling enough to break my resolve, had I not been overwhelmed by fatigue.

CHAPTER FIVE

Eve Couture wouldn't have looked out of place in the locale of Fifth Avenue and 57th Street, amid a glamorous collection of equally chic clothes stores selling iconic designer brands, had it not been for the frequent visits from people wearing worried and often haunted expressions. They would browse a while but rarely try anything on, not because of the high prices or the preponderance of classic evening wear but because they weren't really there to shop at all.

Of course, I didn't quite get it either when asked by Elaine to meet her in this haute couture designer boutique for my interview with Alice, until she explained that the shop served primarily as a front for the honey trap agency up above.

As I joined Elaine in a little pretend shopping – a requirement for honey traps and customers alike before entering into Truth – I noticed how the assistants acknowledge Elaine with a knowing smile, being familiar with her regular visits to the shop.

"I called Alice this morning about leaving," Elaine told

me while flicking through the dresses on the rails. "She hit the roof, but once I'd finished describing my replacement – that's you, in case you've forgotten - she accused me of exaggerating, although I knew I had her hooked."

"Oh dear. I do hope you haven't oversold me."

"What is it with you uberbabes? Do you really have no idea just how gorgeous you are, or is it just an act? Anyway, Alice is so going to hit on you. If you really want this job, at least give her hope." Elaine giggled.

After spending the obligatory time rustling through dresses, Elaine led me towards a back room, just like one of those old black-and-white movies where customers were escorted through fake businesses into speakeasies to drink illegal booze, only this establishment served up betrayal and revenge instead. Upon reaching the top of the stairs, a striking and distinctly attractive young woman looked down upon us as we emerged into her apartment, which doubled as the headquarters of Truth Will Out.

"So what have we got here?" said Alice as I nervously offered my hand to greet the intimidating yet alluring agency boss, with her black-haired bob, Chanel suit and Manolo Blahnik high-heeled shoes. "Could it be the answer to all my prayers? Come on through, and leave Elaine behind."

When Elaine had dismissively made reference to 'old Alice' the previous night at the Trump Hotel bar I would never have conceived of the modishly-coiffured, elegantly-manicured young business woman who sat imperiously behind her desk.

She's so going to hit on you. At least allow her hope, Elaine had advised me, the words now echoing in my lightly-blushing ears.

"So you're God's gift to men?" Alice taunted me.

"I wish," I replied, then quickly correcting myself, remembering both my reason for being there and my transformation from plain to glamorous.

"I wish sometimes I wasn't so, er, noticeable, but yes, guys do seem to notice me, which I guess, must be a requirement of the job."

"What a waste. And you? You notice them back?"

"I'm drawn to beauty, regardless of gender", I replied, remembering Elaine's earlier advice about giving her hope.

"And yet I am told you have a boyfriend. How does that happen?" bemoaned Alice.

"He's so talented. His name is Marty and he sings and plays piano at the Trump Hotel, but only until he makes it as a singer-songwriter in his own right", I confided. It sounded remarkably believable. How useful was that boy.

"Too much information", said Alice, "although we prefer our girls to be in relationships. Less likely to be tempted when out on a hit than single girls. Look don't touch is our mantra." She began to detail the dos and don'ts of the honey trap trade as if it were a wholly legitimate service. I learned of the overarching objective of a honey trap – to collect sufficient evidence to expose the man as a proven cheat, whether an invitation to a guy's room, an incriminating recording or a revealing photograph.

"Tempt but don't be tempted," Alice warned me. "This agency is about honey trapping, not prostitution. Our reputation is everything," she grandly proclaimed, causing me to smile inside at Alice's crazy notion that honey trapping was somehow a virtuous trade. Regardless, I adopted a sincerely concerned expression as I listened with all the intensity of a grade A student to the telltale signs which gave rise to a woman's suspicion of betrayal.

"Over-attentive behaviour, buying her flowers, jewellery, or god forbid chocolates, remembering anniversaries – that's a sure sign – and escorting her to candlelit restaurants while coming up with unbelievable explanations for absences – shall I go on?"

I nodded.

"Forever attending late night business meetings, being unexpectedly called away on long-distance trips while dressing unfeasibly young – then it's guilty as charged. Just a matter of backing it up with evidence. And that's when I call you, to see how long it takes for him to fall for your charms."

If only I'd known these things when Greg began to behave strangely a couple of years ago, I'd have called Alice and had him put to the test.

"When a woman suspects, she is right to be suspicious", Alice maintained, "and it's your job to justify the client's fears, giving her grounds, because that's what she's paid for."

"But what if the man shouldn't even give me a second look?"

"How adorable. That's never going to happen with irresistible bait like you. After all, every man's predisposition is to cheat whenever the opportunity presents itself."

I should have kept my mouth shut – hardly the time or place to question the principles of a business I was attempting to join, yet I couldn't suppress my instinct to challenge injustice whenever it stared me in the face.

"But not all men are the same, and let's be honest, women cheat too," I said, regretting it within seconds of the words having left my lips.

"Only restricted opportunity, illness or being hideously ugly will prevent the male of the species from doing what for them comes naturally", Alice maintained. "And as for women cheating on men? Well, who could possibly blame them? For women, an affair is never lightly undertaken, and almost always justifiable."

Let me count the holes in Alice's argument. Much as I wanted to raise the issue of just how fair was it to expose a man to manufactured temptation, I had a job to get. Besides I would do whatever it took to save my daughter, and compromise my principles if needs be. It's called being a mother.

While Alice briefly disappeared to take a call I allowed my mind to wander, wondering how I was being represented back home with Greg in Valley Stream, and which of these two women, middle-aged housewife or aspiring honey trap, was the real me. At this particular point my brain appeared to shut down, thereby preserving my sanity.

"Am I keeping you awake?" said Alice on her return. "I said, I'm offering you a trial as a trainee honey trap, subject to the usual conditions."

"That's cool," I said, trying to act young.

"And you will release Elaine without contacting her employer," I had the presence of mind to ask.

"As long as you don't screw up, although why you should be so concerned about that girl I can't imagine," she mused, arising, to signify that only she would decide when the meeting was over.

Being unused to skyscraper shoes, I struggled miserably to match Alice's effortless style, toppling awkwardly as I got up, less a honey trap on high heels and more an elephant on roller skates. How embarrassed was I when while attempting to regain my balance I grabbed hold of the nearest thing that came to hand, my new employer's waist. She looked me in the eye, and smirked, before teasingly reciprocating. We became loosely entwined. I was stunned into silence by our unexpected embrace.

"Are you going to let go first or shall I?" Alice eventually asked, amused by the turmoil she had unleashed in my mind.

"It's your call", I said, submissively enough to satisfy Alice's apparent interest in me as something other than an employee.

"You're so hired. I will be forwarding you details of your first hit within days." She lazily let go of me, obviously confident that I would be drawn back to Truth again and again until she decided it was time for me to go.

I couldn't wait to escape from her office, although as I was emerging from Alice's lair a blush splashed tellingly across my face, there for Elaine to see as she sat waiting outside, nervously fidgeting, anxiously awaiting my fate, and in consequence, hers too.

"How scary was that!" I announced.

"Don't tell me, you've backed out. I wouldn't blame you if you had."

"I'm not that much of a wuss", I reassured her. "You're free at last. Now go and get yourself a proper job."

"How can I ever repay you?" she asked while hugging me appreciatively.

And when it later emerged that I was searching for a place to live – the Trump Hotel being little more than a costly temporary refuge – Elaine conjured up a solution decidedly close to home to resolve my plight of homelessness. However, my heart went down like the

Titanic upon learning that I would have to submit to another interview, this time to gain the approval of Elaine's remaining room-mate, Hannah, who was reportedly only marginally less scary than Alice.

According to Elaine, ever since the departure of her previous roomie, Wendy, a vivacious brunette and aspiring actress who she sorely missed, Hannah appeared significantly less bearable than when the three of them had shared their apartment. Her cut-glass English accent, which had once used to delight, had become a source of irritation, while her hostile attitude to Elaine's involvement in the honey trap trade was unrelenting. She only reluctantly agreed to keep it secret from Elaine's boyfriend and frequent visitor, Brad. As a gifted and respected young scientist who worked at the American Museum of Natural History, Hannah aspired to high standards, whether it be in her professional life or how to conduct herself in the apartment. So the interview, organised primarily for Hannah's benefit, was arranged for the following day.

As I tried to make sense of unfolding events, I calculated that this apartment-sharing opportunity must represent the second base of the hobo's grand game plan. He had presented me with the ideal opportunity to keep a close eye on my sometime impressionable daughter to ensure her safety, and to guide her wisely in the pursuit of a life and a career in the city – in essence, to have influence, when as her mother, I would have been totally ignored.

I would be that little voice of sanity whispering into her ear, as I had in the Trump Hotel bar, where I had already successfully altered her ways. And how could she possibly ignore me now, her totally hot, exceedingly young, clued-up friend?

I had inadvertently wandered into every slightly possessive mother's perfect dream scenario, to be the invisible woman in their grown-up son or daughter's apartment, to see stuff normally denied to the maternal eye. And as Elaine had always been more of a Daddy's girl, maybe I wanted to shift her parental compass ever so slightly away from father to mother; for her to be guided a little by my achievements, and even more by my mistakes. Amateur psychologists, make of that what you will.

Elaine hugged me appreciatively, and having wished her a fond farewell I walked the last few hundred yards to my hotel, where nearby a bunch of builders perched eight storeys high whistled at me lasciviously, shouting lewd comments. I struggled to remember the last time I'd been whistled at by builders, or anybody else for that matter. OK, so I own up, I'd enjoyed it, just a little more than I'd been embarrassed by them, yet I really don't think that's what they'd intended.

"You come down here and say that", I yelled up to them, my hand forming an imaginary bullhorn, my defiance greeted by a loud supportive cheer from two female office workers on the other side of the street.

Suddenly I began to feel better about myself; I was becoming Jennifer Gold.

★★★

As arranged, I showed up at the apartment block situated in Houston Street, East Village, reprimanding myself that I had never visited before, unlike Greg, who had already viewed and approved the place when Elaine first came to the City. Parental responsibility, you see – high time I played my part. As if giving birth wasn't enough.

I climbed two flights of stairs, encountering an exotic mixture of sounds and smells sourced from every continent in the world. Undoubtedly bohemian, just a step up from student chic, a place where young professionals getting their first foot on the career ladder could live alongside old Russian émigrés, exotic cross dressers and young, aspiring artists.

When Elaine answered the apartment door she wore an exaggerated smile, the kind used by nurses and doctors to distract nervous patients from impending pain. In this instance the pain was Hannah, the hard-hearted room-mate.

"Jennifer, meet Hannah," she said. "You remember, I told you all about Jen and how she helped me to escape from Alice by volunteering to take my place."

"How heroic of you," she said in her cut-glass English accent. "Nothing to do with the money whatsoever."

"A girl's got to earn a living" I said, trying to lighten the atmosphere by repeating Elaine's line.

"I deeply disprove of your chosen career" she said, sucking any lightness left out of the room.

"And I approve of your disapproval," I replied, eager to placate Hannah by arguing that it was only a temporary position until I secured something more appropriate.

"Now where have I heard that before?" Hannah cast an accusing look at her roommate. Then she began to mock my resolution that entrapping men was only a short-term solution, maintaining that once a girl succumbs to the lure of easy money she will never go back to working nine to five. However much Elaine continued to stress my so-called sacrifice, which she repeatedly emphasised had enabled her to quit the Truth Agency, everything about Hannah indicated that she judged me to be more of an opportunist than a Good Samaritan.

"Surely what matters most is that I'm honest, I don't do drugs and I will pay my rent on time. And I love tidying up," I added, plumping up a cushion as if to prove the point.

"And she's got a lovely boyfriend too. He's a musician you know", Elaine intervened. Hannah betrayed only a glimmer of interest before reverting to type. Eventually a vote was called for, Elaine registering a yes and Hannah an equally predictable no. The stalemate was resolved by the handsome young man who had just entered the apartment unannounced, as if he belonged there. Brad. I watched my daughter's boyfriend make himself at home. He seemed unusually happy to make my acquaintance. I wonder why?

"I propose Brad should have the deciding vote", Elaine declared.

"Well, seeing as you virtually live here", said Hannah pointedly.

"Excellent! So Brad, is there anything you would like to ask Jennifer?" Elaine enquired of him, in a concession to democratic debate.

Brad paused a while, looking searchingly into my eyes, alarming me somewhat as if he knew something of the truth of me, until what appeared to be a spark of recognition failed to ignite.

"Yankees or Mets?" he demanded.

"Mets", I replied without hesitation, although really wanting to say Red Sox.

"Cut yourself a key, you're in", he pronounced, rendering Elaine beside herself with joy.

CHAPTER SIX

Brad couldn't do enough for me, and I truly wanted to believe it was simple politeness rather than being driven by anything else. It certainly felt different from the days when he came to visit in Valley Stream. He was more eager than I'd ever remembered him, his metaphorical tail now wagging enthusiastically whenever I walked through the door. I wanted to tame him, and refocus his attentions back towards Elaine, my reason for rejecting his offer of help to assist me in my move from Trump Tower.

"I'm travelling light," I explained, which only succeeded in raising more questions from Elaine and Hannah about how come I appeared to have all my worldly possessions in one Louis Vuitton suitcase.

So I concocted a story about being forced to flee my small town home in a great hurry to escape an insanely jealous boyfriend. My explanation was good enough to satisfy Elaine and Brad, although Hannah looked less convinced, screwing up her eyes and furrowing her brow as I spoke. "Unbelievable", was all she would say - not in the way most people would use that word, meaning amazing, but more like, I don't believe you. So unlike Elaine, who trusted me implicitly.

"I bless the day you came into my life", she announced one evening after her second glass of Californian Pinot, claiming to be amazed by all the stuff I supposedly knew, marvelling at what she described as my "unfeasibly large general knowledge" and acclaiming my insights into "what it was to be alive."

She would listen in awe when I explained that Brazil was the fifth largest country in the world both by geographical area and population – some 192 million people – or that you burn 26 calories in a one-minute kiss, and to never, ever forget that you were born an original, so don't die a copy.

I simply loved getting the undivided attention of my daughter and watching her listening intently to just about everything I said. In fact she was hanging on to my every word, when back home she would have given me thirty seconds maximum before delivering her familiar cry of "Oh Mother", her cue for me to be quiet.

"Do you think this dress is too short?" she would now ask me.

"Perhaps just a shade", I would reply, and incredibly she would act on it as if my opinion really mattered.

I would have loved to have spent even more quality time alone with her had Brad's visits not become ever more frequent. Not that he had much to say for himself, as I now had the debilitating effect of striking him speechless whenever he came near me, making me feel a touch uncomfortable in his presence.

"You must meet Jen's boyfriend, Marty", Elaine pointedly suggested to Brad. "He's such a talented guy. You'd love him", Brad greeting her suggestion with extreme indifference.

While others worked during the day I languished alone in the apartment, awaiting the call which would activate my honey trap career, a prospect I both dreaded and desired. Although the phone had occasionally rung, Alice had yet to call, until one day I picked up in anticipation and was horrified to hear Greg's familiar voice on the line instead. Panic ensued – that's Greg, my husband in case you'd forgotten. As you can imagine, I hadn't.

Sure I'd missed him, in the way you miss that old familiar threadbare sweater, except sweaters don't cheat on you, and are honest and faithful to the end.

And regarding my old life as a whole, it appeared like a blur on the horizon. Whenever I reflected on what I'd left behind, it was as if the sun had set on my thoughts, my brain effectively shutting that side of my existence down, re-classifying it as restricted information. And yet there I was, forced to deal with my past.

"Can I speak to Elaine, please?" I heard his voice as daylight began to flood in on my previous life.

"Sorry, she's out", I replied, hoping that would be the

end of it, assuming he would go away, not being a conversational kinda guy.

"So who are you?" he replied. How to answer?

"I'm Elaine's new roommate. My name's Jen", I said, deliberately using a version of my name which he rarely used.

"Oh that's strange. My wife's a Jennifer too."

"It's a fairly common name."

"And how are you settling in? All human life is there in that apartment block", he said, his way of letting me know that he wasn't a stranger there.

"Oh typical East Village. I love it."

"So I guess we might bump into each other next time I call?"

"That would be nice. Maybe", I said correcting myself after appearing to be too familiar by far.

"Would it be possible for you to give Elaine a message for me?" he enquired. He always had impeccable manners, my husband.

"You betcha", I replied, desperate to sound young.

"Can you ask her to ring her mom?"

"Why? Is everything OK?" I just couldn't help myself asking. It silenced him for a short while until he hesitantly resumed our conversation.

"Well seeing as you ask, tell her it's nothing to worry about, but she does seem a little bit low – not at all like her old self – although I'm sure a call from Elaine would really cheer her up."

"I'll tell her. Trust me Greg, I really will tell her" I promised him, inadvertently using his first name.

"OK" he said, "but don't alarm her. I'm sure it's just a passing phase." He never wanted to make a crisis out of a crisis, my Greg. "But I do worry about Elaine being away from home in the big city", he unexpectedly added.

"That's only natural, Mr Green. I won't let her come to any harm. You can be so sure of that."

And then the darndest thing happened. Neither of us wanted to be the first to hang up - nothing untoward or inappropriate, just a friendly conversation. We talked a little more about the area, the weather, and daytime television, but nothing that really mattered. If only we could have had meandering conversations like this at home.

"It's been a real pleasure talking to you", he finally said. "I look forward to meeting you."

Oh, I bet you do, I thought, slamming the phone down on the hook, my resentment ignited by imagining similar declarations to his twenty-three year old Britney as he stepped unknowingly on an emotional land mine.

I blamed it on a faulty line when he called back – what else could I do? – because he truly hadn't deserved my anger when talking on the phone. So I wished him a polite goodbye and breathed a sigh of relief upon ending the call. When two worlds collide, or what?

Caught in a whirlwind of conflicting emotions, I once

more allowed my mind to go blank by watching daytime television, regularly making an appointment to catch what I considered to be Elaine's Melissa Parker Show.

"Melly! Melly! Melly!" an audience of apparently demented people chanted as the self-same Melissa sailed elegantly across the set, docking centre stage to launch the latest edition of her show.

"Torn between two lovers, which one should she choose? You decide!" she provocatively announced, concern and a hint of mischief evident in her delivery.

So this was how Elaine spent her day, populating the studio with the extremes of human existence who were happy to expose their innermost secrets to millions of strangers in return for the obligatory fifteen minutes of fame and a subsidised hotel room in New York City.

"Meet Ava, a girl in demand who has a big decision to make", said Melissa on TV. "Two guys, both with strengths and weaknesses, but only one can be chosen. Which one shall it be?"

"Can you believe these people? Have they no shame?" said Hannah, back from work unexpectedly early. She was quick to disapprove but slow to turn away.

"Hey! I didn't hear you come in. Did you have a good day at the museum?" I enquired, conscious of how unintentionally dumb my question sounded, even as it was leaving my lips.

Hannah declined to answer, preferring instead to pour scorn on the girl's suitors.

"That's what we in England would call Hobson's Choice. In other words, no choice at all."

"Between the devil and the deep blue sea."

We continued to watch, occasionally open mouthed, as the guys traded verbal insults, a sad indictment Hannah proposed of television, society and the human condition itself. Now I knew the meaning of car crash television.

While one guy appeared deathly dull, a trainee financial advisor destined to be forever unexciting, the other was a strikingly suave smooth operator with the morals of an alley cat, the type who was genetically programmed to break a girl's heart.

Compounding the felony, the show's resident relationship counsellor, Barbara Boulay, only succeeded in generating more heat than light by showering the girl with platitudes such as 'follow your heart', arousing my anger – what an incredibly short fuse I had these days – as I shouted at the screen, "Dump them both!" I turned away. "Why should she have to compromise and settle for second best?" I protested.

"As Barbara Boulay might say, that was one from the heart", said Hannah, evidently intrigued by the intensity of my response.

CHAPTER SEVEN

When the call eventually came from Alice greenlighting my honey trap career I thanked her kindly, replaced the receiver and yelled, 'bring it on!' Not that I wasn't ready to hurl at the prospect of my first hit, but only by succeeding would I liberate Elaine from the agency for all time, my sole purpose for being there. But then I would become enslaved myself - except that that wasn't going to happen as, unlike Elaine, I could handle Alice. I wasn't some young girl who could be bossed around. And maybe with my unique combination of mature mind and youthful body I could become a player in this honey trap game, even if I hadn't quite yet taken ownership of the new me yet. In my eyes I was nowhere near clever enough, funny enough, or pretty enough, so why would a man ever want to hit on me?

And then I caught a glimpse of myself in the mirror and I thought, that girl's dynamite, but she sure as hell ain't me. And why would I want to excel at honey trapping anyway, apart from the simple, no-nonsense joy of actually being good at something?

So I showed up at her apartment after a little mandatory shopping in Eve Couture, exchanging small talk with a shop assistant until Alice announced that she was ready to see me, as daunting second time around as first.

She threw me a sly smile upon entering her office, obviously enjoying the disturbing effect she had upon me, knowing that I was both intimidated and intrigued by her.

She soon got down to business – what a relief, not referring directly to our previous little incident in the office – and handed me a comprehensive file about 'the target'. I flicked through the pages as Alice spoke, a catalogue of crime, betraying all the usual signs of infidelity, while his unflattering photo suggested dishonesty and deceit.

"He's a liar and a cheat, and if you need any further proof then look no further than his birth certificate under the heading, gender male," said Alice triumphantly. I let that one pass.

And where was my training? I'd somehow imagined I would be sent on a course, or at the very least to shadow an experienced honey trapper in the field, as if I'd been awarded an apprenticeship with General Motors instead of a trial with a disreputable man-trapping agency.

Alice handed me a single sheet of typed dos and don'ts for honey trapping – what amounted to training at the Truth Agency – as I read a selection of them out loud.

"Look, Don't Touch, and Tempt But Don't be Tempted." Absolutely no problem for me whatsoever. I'm in a relationship of course.

"Never Put Yourself In Danger" – a fine regard for health and safety. I approve of that.

"Dress Sexy" – is there any other way? – a requirement, I suppose.

"Assume The Target Is Guilty." I struggled with that one, so I let Alice talk instead.

"Every honey trapper develops their own style, some loud and brash, others coy and winsome, depending on the guy and the situation she finds herself in" Alice advised. "It will be fascinating to see how you evolve", she said, smirking at me provocatively.

"And if you could only give me one piece of advice?"

"Always remain in control."

"Except with you?"

"You're learning fast."

She sent me on my way as I had to act fast in order to track down my first target – a guy called George who'd been frequenting a mystery location in Manhattan sometimes twice a week, and was due in town the next day. Alice had enclosed details of his mid-town hotel where he was supposedly attending a business meeting, his business being shoot 'em up computer games. I hated him already.

However much I would have liked to have asked Elaine's opinion on what to wear, how to attract and when to engage – given she had accomplished almost 20 successful hits in her time working for Alice – it would have felt fundamentally wrong to seek advice from my daughter on something so disreputable as waylaying strange men in bars, clearly not an appropriate thing for a mother to do.

So as Alice had earlier suggested I would need to develop my own style. I would dress sexy as instructed, but classy too, a smart black business suit with the top button undone, having once read that a man could spot a woman's cleavage from over thirty feet away. And courtesy of my transformation, he would have struggled to have missed mine at sixty.

Of course, I guessed I would be nervous, but not so badly afflicted that I couldn't speak - hardly the ideal condition for a honey trap on active service.

Unconvincingly I affected nonchalance, sitting in the corner of the hotel lobby pretending to read *Vanity Fair*. Every guy who walked by could have been him. I referred surreptitiously time and time again to the victim's photograph before concluding each time that he was not the one – not tall enough, not dark enough, not old enough, just not him.

And then nausea struck, compelling me to rush to the ladies' rest room, where I prepared to hurl, although nothing was forthcoming. In panic I returned to the lobby just in time to see the hunted man, evidently in a hurry, rushing to catch a cab. I would have to act decisively.

"Would you like to share?" I asked him, referring to the lone cab parked outside.

"Only if you can dance", he replied.

"Just call me Ginger".

"Ginger?"

"As in Rogers."

"Jump in", he agreed, instructing the driver to transport us to the Lexington Dance Academy – beginners welcome – where we were soon salsa-dancing the night away. It couldn't have been more innocent. It was not at all what Alice had had in mind when she had sent me out on my mission, her face dropping as I reported back that this genuine guy was only intending to surprise his wife in the most charming and thoughtful of ways by taking secret dance lessons, so he could sweep her off her feet at their forthcoming anniversary party.

"Ah, how sweet", Alice sarcastically replied, adamant that the guy must have propositioned me, regardless of his admirable plan.

"What man wouldn't?" she maintained. "And he danced with you, and what is dancing but a vertical expression of a horizontal desire?"

"He was the perfect gentleman. And as far as the dancing – there was no hidden agenda, He was doing it for his wife."

I would have carried on, quoting this as proof that not all men were bastards, had Alice's mood not darkened considerably as I pleaded with her to withhold the information regarding the secret dancing classes from his wife until the anniversary had passed.

"What do you think this is? Marriage guidance?" she said. She warned me that she had expected a much better outcome to the hit than this, especially as clients were offered a partial refund if their partners were proven to be innocent.

"I've got a business to run. You, Miss Gold, are paid to corrupt the incorruptible – and if you should fail, I will show you the door, and reinstate Elaine."

"You can't do that. That's illegal."

"Try me" Alice challenged me. I couldn't risk it.

With stakes that high I guess the next hit never stood a chance, regardless of whether he was innocent or guilty, such was my single-minded determination to stop Elaine being forced back into the honey trap trade.

His name was Guy, which according to Alice meant that he embodied all the sins of the male gender. "A typical guy", she observed. In pursuit of him, I persuaded myself to already dislike him deeply, judging him guilty as charged. His ever-increasing number of business trips, regularly staying at a four-star hotel in Manhattan, must surely be a cover for something irredeemably sleazy.

It was as if I had swallowed Alice's views and opinions whole, purely to sustain me in my immoral quest. In perfect harmony we devised a plan whereby I would pose as a market researcher for an upmarket lingerie company, enquiring into the likes and dislikes of husbands when buying underwear for their wives. The things we do for love.

And if you'd ever wondered what it might be like to spring a honey trap, I suspect you might imagine it's slightly exotic, just a little bit exciting and possibly glamorous too, when in truth it was fear, above all else, which defined a hit.

So once more I fought to keep my nerves under control, my resolve strengthened by my grim determination to succeed at all costs. Armed with an album of partially-naked young women dressed in designer lingerie, I positioned myself strategically in the lobby at the Holiday Inn, Wall Street, attempting to appear businesslike yet alluring.

In a nightmare opening, I mistakenly approached the wrong man, who annoyingly persisted in following me around the hotel lobby until I was forced into telling him "get lost, creep", which he obediently did.

Having refreshed my memory by once again consulting the agency's official photograph, I breathed in deeply and approached another besuited businessman who also closely resembled Guy, this time answering not only his description but his name too. I'd got my Guy.

He enthusiastically agreed to participate in my survey, sitting alongside me like teacher and pupil as we flicked through page after page of voluptuous sexy young women and rated them, or supposedly their underwear, out of ten for my so-called research.

That was the easy part. The next step would be

horrendous for me. Running away suddenly seemed more tempting than spreading strawberry jam on Brad Pitt's abs and then eating him as a sandwich, even if it meant incurring the wrath of Alice.

"Allow me to introduce our new line", I said breathily, "although as we don't have any pictures of models wearing it yet, you'll just have to use your imagination." I produced a sparkly bra and spangled knickers from my executive bag.

Guy handled the garments warily, unsure, as I'd rightly suspected, how to rate the wrapping without seeing the parcel.

"I must have a score, otherwise my boss will murder me for not completing the survey and I can't afford to lose my job, but why should I burden you with my problems?" I gabbled on. "I know" I said, enacting a brainwave of Einstein proportions, "why don't I model the lingerie for you, and then I might just still have a career?"

"If you want to."

"Omigod! You'd do that for me? What an adorable man you are" I said, lightly touching his forearm, thereby breaking the first rule of Truth. I quickly withdrew my touch while suggesting he write down his name and room number, where I would meet him for a private showing just as soon as I had phoned my office. He obligingly agreed, and as soon as he was out of sight I excitedly called Alice.

CHAPTER SEVEN

"Got him", I said triumphantly to my unimpressed boss.

And yet when I presented her with the details of what had occurred she totally blew her top. She stridently maintained that she must have a compromising picture of me and Guy if we were truly to convince the man's wife.

"But I've got his name and room number written down, condemning himself in his own handwriting, plus everything's recorded too", I assured her.

"You just don't have enough evidence."

"So you expect me to join him, wearing only skimpy underwear, alone in his hotel room? Elaine never had to go this far, so why should I?"

"Because she always followed proper honey trap procedures. I could always demand that she rejoined the Agency if you'd prefer it."

Alice had discovered exactly where my one great weakness lay. That compelled me to march into the bar, first ordering and then downing a large vodka and tonic before riding the elevator to the fourteenth floor.

"Hi, I'm here to complete my survey. Do you still want to partake?" I purred to him provocatively at the door.

"I'm a man of my word. Anything to help", he said, gesturing me in. He had the look of a Guy for whom Thanksgiving, Christmas and the Superbowl had all arrived on the same day.

"Don't go away", I said teasingly as I disappeared into

the bathroom to strip and then slip into a luxurious bra and briefs.

My heart beating alarmingly fast, I remained incredulous about what I was about to do, wondering if the alcohol would ever begin to ease my nerves. I stole a little peek at the mirror to behold the vision that was about to greet him, seriously dreading the response I might provoke in him.

How I look back and cringe as I recall sashaying back into the room on my Manolo Blahniks, tossing my hair back coquettishly and challenging him provocatively by looking him straight between the eyes, having already pre-announced my arrival by whispering seductively from behind the door, "Prepare to mark out of 10."

"You like?" I breathily enquired.

It was only then when I properly began to notice that with his ice-cool blue eyes, dark lustrous hair and broad, manly shoulders, Guy was not unattractive to the eye.

"God, you look fabulous", he said, his eyes greedily consuming me.

"Lingerie naughty, not me" I said, playfully reprimanding him by lightly slapping him on his BTM.

When I should have felt vulnerable I did in fact feel empowered, completely in control. I was manipulating Guy as I wished, having the confidence to demand that we should share a photograph together without giving him a reason why.

"A perfect ten", he said as I slipped my arm around his waist. Then he reciprocated when I suggested he did likewise, and I held my smartphone at arm's length to photograph us in a sexually-charged embrace.

"It's fine, but I have to say you do look a bit overdressed", I said teasingly, surveying the shot. He accepted my challenge, undressing right down to his Calvin Kleins, and then graciously accepted my invitation to embrace me.

"Smile," I said as I greedily gathered more photographic evidence on my iPhone. I held him close, feeling his arousal pressed urgently against me. I can't deny I had feelings – my libido having become strangely supercharged since my transformation, constantly reminding me to temper my inappropriate moments at every turn. This was a highly charged erotic situation I'd got myself into, but I wasn't about to mess up by messing around on my first real deal hit, and besides, Elaine would suffer if I did. And it was hardly acceptable behaviour, was it – to get intimate with a guy you'd only just picked up in a hotel lobby?

"Oh, is that the time," I said looking nowhere in particular, "I must go. Thank you for completing the survey," I said like a cold caller concluding their script.

"And what am I supposed to do with this?" said Guy pointing to his inflated Calvin Kleins.

"I'm sure you'll think of something", I replied. "And

then why not enter our on line competition when you could win a holiday for two to Hawaii?" I retreated to the bathroom, where I hastily slipped back into my clothes. "Ciao for now," I said upon my return, placing my folder in my executive case, relieved to see that he had dressed too.

"Nice meeting you," Guy replied. He was scratching his head, as if waiting for a celebrity to pop up from nowhere to announce that he had been the good-natured victim of a reality TV hoax.

So I returned to Truth on a high, elated that I had collected more evidence than Monica Lewinsky's dress and feeling like a fully-fledged, real deal, honey trap. Maybe Alice would shake me warmly by the hand, or perhaps even give me a hug, or possibly a kiss on the cheek; I would let her decide.

I rang the bell of her apartment, access via Eve Couture denied during evening hours. Alice's greeting on the intercom, "Oh it's you", was a little less fulsome than I had expected.

"I trust you'll approve," I declared upon meeting her. I dug out my evidence for her to peruse, especially the compromising photograph, which I couldn't help but notice she savoured with her eyes.

"Omigod, you ought to be illegal", said Alice upon seeing the photo. "You know, I never thought you'd actually do it. I wouldn't normally expect one of my girls to go into a guy's room and strip off. I only wanted to see how far you would go."

"Oh great" I replied, meaning exactly the opposite, and not bothering to disguise it either.

Had it not been for my focus on Elaine and keeping her out of harm's way from Alice, I would have resigned there and then.

"You did well enough though," said Alice, the closest she could get to a compliment, and then undoing it all by criticising me for not waiting for Guy himself to propose that I should model the lingerie.

"The man must always condemn himself by his own words. Get his admission on digital and then you've got all the ammunition you need, no visiting men's rooms or stripping required."

It came as a great relief to know that I wouldn't have to place myself in danger again, assuming I'd secured a position at Truth, but Alice was keeping me in suspense longer than that guy on American Idol.

"OK, you'll do", she finally announced.

"And Elaine?"

"She's history. I never want to see her again" she said. Then she dismissed me as you would a servant.

Regardless of this I was elated, and felt a warm glow on the cab journey home, knowing that Elaine was finally free and out of Alice's clutches forever. But then one or two doubts gradually began to trouble me, reflecting uncomfortably on my role in the pain which was about to be inflicted on Guy and his wife, when in truth, he really didn't deserve it. Within two blocks I went from exhilaration to shame, and as my taxi negotiated the rain-splattered streets of Manhattan I vowed to operate more fairly in future, only reporting guys who condemned themselves as cheats, however much Alice might disapprove.

I was thankful to discover on entering the apartment that Elaine and Hannah had already gone to bed. I fixed myself a coffee and stretched out on the sofa to consider my day further. In the midst of near darkness a bedroom door opened and out stepped a bleary-eyed Brad, his naked torso compellingly visible in the half light.

"A dime for your thoughts" he said, yawning.

"I've decided to be a better person", I replied, averting my eyes from the boy as if to prove my point.

"Shame", said Brad. "I like you just the way you are".

CHAPTER EIGHT

With experience I became an accomplished honey trapper, even Alice grudgingly admitting that I was "good enough" – high praise indeed, coming from her. OK, I did occasionally incur her displeasure for not being ruthless enough, striving to behave as morally as I could within her immoral universe and always endeavouring to cut the guy some slack by at least giving him the benefit of the doubt. If he didn't hit on me straight away after a little gentle provocation I wouldn't chase him further, as I had with Guy. Depressingly, most guys still came on strong given the merest hint of encouragement, so in my eyes, they deserved everything they got. *Take that, Greg!* I sometimes fantasised.

Sure, I continued to have more than one sleepless night about the legitimacy of what I was being asked to do. If I could have left Truth there and then, you wouldn't have seen me for eye dust. I was only kept there by the fear that Alice might force Elaine back by threatening to expose her honey trapping past to the Melissa Parker Show. Just how long would it take before I could quit? I decided to give Alice six months, and then I would be ready to walk whether she liked it or not.

CHAPTER EIGHT

I dreaded becoming irreplaceable to Alice's agency, her secret weapon in her war against cheating men – an unlikely position for me, especially for someone as unnoticeable as I once used to be – except what was the purpose of being that attractive, if only to inflict pain by destroying relationships and ruining lives? I began to feel ashamed of myself, whereas unbelievably Alice wanted me to think I'd signed up to a noble cause. I just didn't buy it.

At first, Elaine regularly interrogated me about my earliest hits – natural enough, I suppose, since she'd only recently been a honey trapper herself – but thankfully she soon lost interest, and was now more concerned with making it in TV. She had recently confided in me about a guy at Groucho TV, a producer called Kyle, who'd been relentlessly giving her a tough time, always belittling her work, usually without reason, and she didn't know why.

"One day I'm going to explode and say something I might regret," she'd forewarned me.

"Then ask him around for coffee and cupcakes," I advised her.

"Clever. I see what you're doing there. I like it" she said. At home she would have pronounced me insane.

"Let's make it a dinner party. Kyle would be a great match for Hannah. And you are so invited," Elaine declared.

Marty, who had only ever been a pretend boyfriend, was invited along too. My lame excuses that he would be far too busy playing his piano at the Trump bar were rejected out of hand.

It's not that I didn't like Marty – in fact he had a certain style – only he was so incredibly young, or that's how he appeared to me. I hadn't dated a guy that young since junior high, and I wasn't sure I should be starting again now.

However, I had to approach Marty, as I couldn't see a way out of this dinner party dilemma. I had steadfastly ignored his calls and messages for nearly a month, so he was bound to be angry with me, wasn't he? Or maybe he would reject my call – and who could possibly blame him?

He did seem a little surprised when I first called, then somewhat surly, until he softened upon hearing I wanted to see him.

"It's a long story, but would you be willing to pretend to be my boyfriend, if that's OK?" I begged him without frills.

"No need to pretend. It's a role that could have been written for me," he charmingly replied when he could have told me to go take a hike. He agreed to meet me outside the apartment prior to joining the other guests.

Of course I felt dreadful about using him, but still I somehow explained to Marty as we stood on the noisy sidewalk that I needed him to pose as my date for the night, and then like Cinderfella he would leave at midnight and go home like nothing had ever happened, although I suspected he had other plans.

We entered the building and climbed the stairs in silence until we reached the front door of my apartment, when an idea sparked in my mind as I rang the front door bell.

"For the purposes of this evening, prepare to be kissed" I said. I swooped upon Marty's lips as the door opened to reveal Elaine.

"Hey you two, get a room!" she said, before enthusiastically inviting us both in.

"You must be Marty. I've heard so little about you", said Hannah as Marty was introduced one by one to the assembled guests. "More's the pity. Where's she been hiding you?" Hannah positively purred, her flirtatiousness detonating an unexpected shot of jealousy within me.

I hadn't known that Elaine considered herself to be something of a matchmaker – the things you learn about your kids when you're in disguise! I watched her reluctantly return to the kitchen, where she put the finishing touches to her culinary creation while her friend sipped cocktails in the room next door, forming what she would have considered to have been inappropriate relationships in her absence. Not only had Hannah – who had been earmarked for Kyle, the pushy TV producer from Groucho Productions – become significantly drawn to Marty, but Kyle began hitting on me, irrespective of the fact that I took an instant dislike to him, a dislike which only intensified as the evening progressed.

Popping her head around the door to monitor all these

mismatches, Elaine quickly returned crestfallen to her cooking, joined first by me and then Brad, her boyfriend administering a reassuring hug to her, then dipping his finger into something simmering aromatically on the stove.

"Mmm! Delicious!" he declared, amplifying his enjoyment with unfeasible enthusiasm to boost Elaine's fragile belief in her culinary skills.

"Smells good" I said, having followed a scented trail across the entire length of our apartment.

"And what brings you in here?" Elaine demanded of me.

"I'm escaping Kyle's attentions. What a total sleazebag. He just told me that he could fix it for me to get my big break in television if I should be nice to him."

"Well, it was your idea to invite him", she rightly reminded me. "Anyway, get back in there and separate Hannah from Marty and then get Kyle to appreciate Hannah."

"Whoa there! People will go where they want to go", I admonished her.

"Such defeatist talk. Go sort things out!"

Having been persuaded to return to the fray, I was once more forced to endure Kyle and his ludicrously inflated descriptions of his allegedly crucial role in the miracle of giving birth to an hour of "must see" television. As he droned endlessly on, my eyes became inexorably drawn towards the continuing and growing intimacy between my Marty – OK, I owned him now – and the frosty English girl, who was perceptibly thawing.

And from a distance, mistakenly believing he was unobserved, I caught sight of Brad out of the corner of my eye, unzipping me with his eyes, giving me cause to seriously question whether this handsome young man with his wandering eyes was a suitable match for my daughter.

"And your favourite song?" Kyle enquired of me, digressing for a moment from making grandiose statements about his brilliant career.

"Oh - *Just The Way You Are*", I replied distractedly, my mind elsewhere, much more focused on monitoring Hannah's pursuit of Marty with mounting irritation than answering his annoying questions.

"How uncool is that", proclaimed Kyle, now the self-appointed arbiter of good taste. "Billy Joel is pure cheese. And that song gives mediocrity a bad name."

His ludicrous critique acted as a wake-up call for me to act my age. I back-tracked rapidly by claiming that I had only enjoyed it in a post-modern ironic kind of way, scared that I should blow my cover and be exposed as a respectable Valley Stream housewife on vacation from middle age.

I needn't have worried – Kyle had eyes only for himself. How could I have possibly suggested inviting him? Still, I hoped his presence would create a connection between him and Elaine, strictly for work purposes only. I would have hated her to like him for any other reason than that of necessity.

I sought out distractions to cleanse my mind of him. Elaine's first course of salmon en croute was diverting enough, far exceeding our expectations of a girl who professed to be to cuisine what Simon Cowell was to diplomacy.

"Are you pining for your English rose?" I whispered mischievously into Marty's ear, having noted a marked decline in his effervescence since Hannah had been persuaded by Elaine to sit next to Kyle.

"My god, you're jealous. You're so jealous. Girls like you just don't do jealousy with boys like me", he said disbelievingly. Maybe he had got a little under my skin.

Back on planet Kyle, his righteousness droned remorselessly on, firing off opinions like a one-eyed gunman at a turkey shoot as Hannah struggled to stifle a yawn.

"Of course, television is the new rock and roll", he grandly pronounced. "If you're not on TV, you might as well be dead."

I watched Marty clench his fists, keeping it all in. Then finally he could contain it no more.

"Rock and Roll is the new, old, forever and always rock and roll", he declared. "Nothing – and when I say nothing, I mean nothing – can compare to the emotional impact of a well-crafted song. Nobody would ever choose a David Letterman monologue to walk down the aisle to on their wedding day or a Tina Fey sketch to perform at their funeral. You see, music feeds the soul whereas television only wallpapers it."

I adored Marty more at that precise moment than any other mortal man alive – OK, how fickle am I? I was curiously moved by his bravery in defence of his art. Before Kyle, he was just that sweet boy who came to play piano in my room. After Kyle he had been transformed into a hero, possessing both grace and strength when under attack.

Pictures of Marty permeated my thoughts as I retreated to the rest room, where there came a knock on the door. It could only be Marty. Our emotions were now in perfect harmony.

"Entrez" I said, attempting a voice as sultry as Singapore. The door opened and to my horror in crashed Kyle, lunging clumsily towards me, the sheer force of him propelling me backwards as I slipped back against the bathroom wall. I struggled to repel him in vain. His superior strength was rendering me helpless, until I rallied with a strategically-placed knee in his groin. That took the desire out of his pants, the bastard.

"What gives you the right?" I demanded of him in barely a whisper as I attempted to compose myself, my quietness more menacing to him than a shout or a scream.

He recoiled from me, rapidly backing off, intimidated by my control and bemused by my calm.

"You gave me all the signals. What else was I supposed to think?" he spluttered through gritted teeth, doubled up in pain.

"You confuse being listened to, which I guess for you must have been a new and novel experience, with being found attractive."

He sneered, not bothering to reply, just adjusting his clothing instead.

"Let's pretend it never happened, shall we?"

I returned to the dining table trying too hard to be nonchalant, whereas Kyle had time to compose himself, eventually returning all guns blazing when not pointedly sucking up to Hannah.

"You're so middle-aged in your thinking," he accused me as we discussed our favourite movies of all time. So what was wrong with *Mamma Mia*?

"If you were a swimming pool you'd only have one end, the shallow one", Marty mocked Kyle, rallying gallantly to my cause.

"Boys! Boys!" Elaine cried, her soirée slowly sinking under the weight of so much misdirected passion. I however was positively bathing in the glow of Marty's chivalrous defence.

At long last Kyle mercifully announced he had to go – something to do with an early morning edit.

"Oh please don't leave us without giving us another one of your fascinating theories", Hannah teased him.

"I suppose I could stay just a little bit longer if you really wanted it."

"I wouldn't even hear of it. Of course you must go" she said, virtually pushing him out of the door. "The nuts and the sluts are depending on you."

At his departure they all breathed a collective sigh of relief, whereas I apologised profusely to Elaine for getting that particular invitation so profoundly wrong.

"Next time, I'll invite Hannibal Lecter instead" she said. "I hadn't realised how totally obnoxious he is to absolutely everybody – not just me. I won't take anything he says at work to me personally ever again. Another life lesson learned." She gave me a warm hug of appreciation, although surely, I hadn't deserved it.

After a brief burst of exuberance inspired by the departure of our totally annoying guest, the party slowly began to run out of gas. First Elaine and Brad, and then Hannah, retired for the night, leaving Marty and me alone on the sofa resembling a couple of embarrassed teenagers wondering what to do next.

"That Kyle, eh?" said Marty, softening the silence.

"I really appreciated you coming to my rescue like that. I'm not worthy."

I sincerely meant it, having used Marty when it suited me almost from the day we first met.

"He'd really got it in for you. What could you have possible done to rile him so badly?"

"I kicked him in the balls."

"OK" he replied quizzically.

"You see, he hit on me big time."

"Shame. I was thinking of doing the same thing. So if I should happen to lean forward, like this, and kiss you on the lips, would I suffer a similar fate?"

"Only one way to find out".

I watched him weigh up the likely consequences then tentatively move a shade closer. I met him halfway, his lips relishing mine, and I was welcoming it.

I arose and held out my hand to him to lead him into my bedroom. I sensed not only his excitement but his trepidation.

"Your first time?" I said, gently probing him while unbuttoning his shirt to reveal his silky-skinned, downy, almost boyish chest.

He nodded, shamefaced.

"Me too" I replied.

"No way!"

"In this life, yes."

"I can't even begin to understand that", he replied, before I rendered his incomprehension irrelevant by stroking him intimately, possessing him in pleasure, then inviting him into my scented bed.

He was spent in seconds, but I encouraged him not to lose heart. "That was lovely" I reassured him, dismissing his need for an apology and doing everything I could to build him right back up.

And he proved to be a willing pupil, as we became one again - and again, and again - each time lasting longer than the last, until finally he was seduced from me by sleep. I watched him dream his sweet dreams, amazed and astonished by his youth, yet not feeling guilty that he should be sharing my bed.

I was beginning to act my age.

CHAPTER NINE

I know what you're probably thinking – did I give any thought whatsoever to my old life back in Valley Stream while I was busy going to bed with a guy half my age? I really tried, for as my new life evolved so the memory of my other existence began to fade – not in the normal way where recall becomes hazy as the months and years progress, but more like amnesia; forgetting something, then being totally unable to recall it.

Even though there were times when I did wonder about Greg – more often than not, inspired by some innocent remark by Elaine about her father's absent mindedness or his workaholic tendencies – whenever I tried to imagine him at home with that remnant of me, his wife, my mind simply seized up again, impairing my memory further, so that the only guarantee I had of being able to recall him again was not to think about him at all.

All very convenient, I'm sure you will agree when dealing with the consequences of sleeping with another guy. However, just think about it for a moment – in my new life Marty was only eighteen months younger than me, me being 21 or thereabouts, and in a sense, I was single too, wasn't I? Or was it more a case of what happens in the new life, stays in the new life? Regardless, my relationship with Marty had evolved to that point of no return where sleeping together seemed almost inevitable, or otherwise we would have to part. And I had become drawn to him as the evening progressed, listening to him defending my honour, admiring him for his devotion to me when I truly hadn't deserved it.

My discovery that he was a virgin had placed a certain responsibility upon me, just like that record *Summer The First Time*, initiating him in the ways of physical love – but how he'd never managed to get laid when he could play the piano, talk cleverly and smile crookedly was beyond me. OK, so it wasn't that passionate night of wild abandon I had longed for; I was too much in control for that, more teacher than lover. But it was kinda sweet – a word I believe every man dreads hearing – and I felt honoured that he had chosen me to be the one. So I chose to make his position as boyfriend official. And I should be so fortunate after the way I had used him, but he was happy to have me, and I was happy to be had.

Of course, I wasn't the only one to have admired Marty on the night of the dinner party.

"You're so lucky to have him as a boyfriend. Marty's adorable", Hannah had once said to me after she had uncharacteristically poured her heart out to me following a dreadful argument between us. It had begun upon arriving back in the apartment laden down with shopping late one afternoon, the perfect opportunity for her to deride me for my part in the honey trap trade.

"Been spending your ill-gotten gains?" she had said accusingly.

"I hope you don't judge yourself as harshly as you judge others, or you would never get out of bed in the morning", I had retaliated.

And that triggered a torrent of tears to flow from Hannah, who encouraged by my gentle probing seriously unburdened herself, confessing a past cataclysmic event. It emerged that she had been cruelly left standing at the altar, jilted on her wedding day by her fiancé who had failed to show at church. Humiliated, she had quit England in one hell of a hurry to attempt a fresh start in New York. Yet still her past continued to haunt her, making it impossible for her to declare peace with the world, her anger never more than a mildly inconsiderate remark away.

"The trouble is, he's still in your life" I said. "You're thinking about him every single day. Don't give him the satisfaction of continuing to ruin you for a second longer. You've left London behind, now let him go too."

As if to prove it, we caught a cab to JFK airport, and amid the happy hellos and sad farewells of assorted passengers we symbolically waved her ex-fiancé good riddance and then embraced in celebration of his virtual departure. And on the way home we began to talk about Marty, our former distance replaced by a rapidly rising friendship.

"I want to be a happier person, and by being happy, hopefully make others happy too," Hannah proclaimed.

It was as if Pollyanna herself had taken Hannah over. No wonder Elaine struggled to recognise the open-minded, warm-hearted person her roommate had become.

"You should be a therapist. Freud's got nothing on you," Elaine teased me, even if Hannah still drew the line at accompanying me to a recording of the Melissa Parker Show.

"I'd rather stick pins in my eyes," Hannah reassuringly confirmed.

★★★

Outside the uptown television studios, a long line of pilgrims waited with eager-eyed anticipation, ready to worship in the temple of their goddess, the blessed Melissa Parker. Head buried, I self-consciously pushed my way through the crowd, the faithful eyeing me enviously as I waved my temporary pass to attract the attention of Security.

"Hey, over here!" Elaine called over to me, clutching a clipboard in one hand and a cellphone in the other.

"If looks could kill, I thought I was going to get lynched", I said, referring to the fans outside, the majority of them having been on a waiting list for nearly two years, such was their devotion to the show.

"So what delights do you have in store for us today?" I enquired as we strode purposefully down the neon-lit corridor towards Studio A.

"My Mother Won't Act Her Age", Elaine replied.

How appropriate, I thought. "How interesting" I said.

"Welcome to my world", Elaine announced, hauling open the cumbersome soundproofed studio door and escorting me into the instantly recognisable surroundings of the Melissa Parker Show. The set appeared reassuringly familiar, although much smaller than I had anticipated.

"The cameras make everything look bigger – people too – and that includes poor Melissa", Elaine explained.

I remembered the talk show star's well-publicised struggle against fluctuating weight. I didn't envy her at all, forced to live her private life in the public gaze.

I had been reserved a prime seat from which I could watch the human drama unfold.

"Enjoy", said Elaine, a smile playing mischievously on her lips, "and of course, if the mood takes you, feel free to testify at the microphone over there", she said, pointing towards the aisle.

"I'd rather have root canal surgery", I replied.

Happy to hide away under cover of the audience, I'd leave the talking to those who were either brave or foolish enough to try and resolve their fractured relationships on national television.

While Elaine retreated backstage to keep the warring

mothers and daughters at bay, those of us in the audience were subjected to a wisecracking compere with slicked-back hair and a hideous tangerine-coloured shirt who teased and cajoled us into a state of mild frenzy, bringing us to the boil just in time for Melissa's eagerly-awaited entrance.

"Go wild in the aisles", he hollered like a man possessed, "for the doyenne of discussion… the one… the only…the First Lady of Television… Miss Melissa Parker!"

The crowd reacted as if they were about to witness the Second Coming.

"Melly! Melly! Melly!" they chanted in time to a pulsating beat, everybody, including me, rising to our feet to pay homage to the Special One.

"I'm not worthy", she gently admonished us, holding her arms out wide for a symbolic hug. Unbelievably there she was, standing right there in front of us in all her glory, in 3D without us needing glasses, the woman who had lived her entire adult life under the glare of the spotlight – the failed marriages, the multiple diets, the battle against the booze. What you see is what you get, she seemed to be saying, disarming even the most militant of hearts. Through her transparency she had won our respect, thereby creating a connection, conjuring up an illusion that she was "one of us", a victim turned victor who had become a role model for millions of women across the globe.

As Melissa began what I imagined must have been a well-rehearsed routine designed to put the audience at their ease, I spotted Kyle and felt my skin crawl. The self-important producer had been ominously lurking in the background. Now he took centre stage, shouting, “Silence. Run to record.”

In swept the sound of the familiar theme tune and without prompting the audience began clapping and chanting, “Yo Melly!”, with all the fervour of disciples at a revivalist meeting.

In this strange and exhilarating place I watched Melissa exercise absolute control with awe and respect, her followers quick to obey.

“Which mother hasn’t been driven to yell ‘grow up!’ at her impossible teenage daughter?” she began. “But here’s the twist for today. We meet girls who are so embarrassed by their mothers that they have been driven to say, ‘Mom, Please, Act Your Age!’”

On trooped the disaffected daughters. The first to be featured was a hard-faced young woman who didn’t endear herself to the audience with her sarcastic reaction to her mother dating a guy she described as “a kid young enough to be my brother”.

“They only want her for one thing”, she sneeringly said, “and that’s for her money – so they can go and buy candy with it.”

The crowd around me erupted with jeers, laughter and catcalls while I continued to hold my counsel, disapproving of the girl but wanting to see the mother before talking sides.

"Why else would a young guy want to make out with an old woman? It's so unnatural", the daughter argued with gross insensitivity. The rage was rising within me. As you can probably appreciate, I had a vested interest in the arguments going down.

"Let's meet Mom", said Melissa. The crowd licked their lips at the prospect.

The mother duly entered, taking a seat alongside her belligerent daughter. I later learned from Elaine that Mom had been manipulated by Kyle to dress to excess, showing a little too much of everything, a look specifically designed by him to increase viewer ratings by confirming that the older woman was most definitely behaving inappropriately.

"See what I mean?" said the girl, referring dismissively to her mother's disappearance. "How embarrassing is that?"

Jeers descended upon them both.

"Poor woman, imagine giving birth to that", I said to the audience member sitting to the left of me.

"Your daughter Charlene accuses you of inappropriate behaviour. What have you got to say for yourself?" Melissa challenged her.

The mother dealt her daughter a withering stare.

"Ever since your father walked out on me for a girl not much older than you I have always put you first – rightly so. Now it's my time. Get over it."

"Go girl!" I yelled like you're supposed to on a television talk show, yet meaning it nevertheless.

I wasn't alone in my backing of her. The mother's testimony was triggering a tidal wave of support, drowning out the few dissenters who sank without trace. Amid this feeding frenzy posing as a television show, insults and arguments were hurled back and forth, the debate generating more heat than clarity, until the daughter inadvertently and outrageously admitted that her mother's boyfriend was undeniably hot.

"Ah, the green-eyed monster. Or let me put it another way - you are, in fact, jealous of your mother."

The girl screamed curses in response, her over-elaborate, ear-shattering denial a sure sign that the Queen of Talk had once again touched a raw nerve. However, when the so-called 'relationship expert' Barbara Boulay was finally called upon to dispense her alleged wisdom, I watched in disbelief as the show took an unexpected turn. She started lambasting the mother for "flying in the face of nature", being an "irreprehensible role model" for her daughter and acting like a "hormonally-charged teenager." Her observations sucked the spirit out of the audience and a resentful silence settled upon us, although a part of me wanted to spring to my feet and throw my shoes at her, had they not been so expensive.

She admonished the crushed mother in a final flurry of bigotry.

"Shame on you. It's high time you acted your age", she raged. Even Melissa was taken aback. Inevitably, her consummate professionalism kicked back in, helping to steady the ship and to navigate the show towards its next port of call, the commercial break.

During this short pause in the proceedings, Kyle the creepy producer added insult to injury by emerging from the darkness to congratulate Barbara on her contribution to the debate before appealing for anybody in the audience who wished to participate in the discussion to head towards the microphone stand. I didn't need to be asked twice, least of all by that self-satisfied excuse for a human being. I would not be silenced any longer.

"Oh please God, not her", I watched Kyle mouth towards Elaine. "Get that bitch off!" I distinctly heard him say, but too late. The theme music came crashing back in, signalling the start of the next phase of the show.

"A young woman wants to speak" said Melissa.

"Where is it written" I said, almost breathless with emotion, "that meeting new people, exploring relationships and enjoying sex is the sole prerogative of the young?"

I wrongfooted them at first. I suspect the audience had expected me to support the daughter, given my apparent youth, but they roared their approval upon realising that I was backing the mother all the way.

"Everybody deserves a second time around. It's out there if you want it", I concluded, the crowd rising to their feet as one to express their unconditional support.

"Go girl!" said Melissa. The victimised mother was

dabbing her red eyes, kindness rather than hostility always more likely to elicit tears.

"Well I bet you didn't expect that", said Melissa. "Let's take a break. Don't go flicking."

Had the show peaked too soon? But all was not totally lost. They had more crazy people in fraught situations up their sleeves to keep the audience entertained, although I wasn't alone in noticing a slight sense of anti-climax pervading the proceedings after the excesses of Part One. If Kyle had hated me before, he certainly must have loathed me after, as the Star of The Show returned to deliver Melissa's Last Thought by quoting neither Sigmund Freud nor even Doctor Phil but me – yes, me – in support of her conclusion.

"Listen to what the girl said", Melissa declared, looking unerringly down the lens of the camera. "Who decided that what is carefree when you are young becomes irresponsible when you are old? Having a life should never be the exclusive preserve of the young, and so, as our young friend magnificently proclaimed, everybody deserves a second time around. Go grab it!"

"It's a wrap!" Kyle yelled once the recording had been cleared for technical faults. That was the starting signal for Elaine to sprint up the bleachers at breakneck speed to smother me with praise for my part in the show.

"You were awesome. Where did that passion come from?" Elaine squealed, a question best left unanswered, considering my unique and extraordinary circumstances.

How Kyle must have resented my intervention. He found consolation by comforting his protégée Barbara Boulay, who stared at me accusingly.

"Step this way to hospitality," Elaine instructed me. "It's time to meet the team."

I didn't want to be ungracious, although judging by the glares from Kyle and Miss Boulay I would be about as welcome as Barack Obama at a Tea Party.

"Thanks, but no thanks," I explained.

"Oh pur*lease*," Elaine whined in that irritating and ingratiating voice specifically designed to get me to do things that I don't want to do. And it worked. I instantly regretted my decision to go backstage upon seeing Barbara Boulay now scowling at me from the other side of the room.

It didn't help that well-wishers gathered around me, every one of them representing a knife in the heart of an infuriated agony aunt.

"You have such empathy, showing real concern for a woman twice your age" one of these admirers congratulated me.

Like a wounded porcupine prickling with indignation, Barbara Boulay moved menacingly towards me. Elaine was helpless to intervene, already laden down with a plate of chicken salad and glass of white wine about six yards away. I greeted her politely, which seemed to inflame her further.

"Come back when you've grown up and got something to say!" she hollered at me, pushing through my admirers to confront me head on. "Wisdom comes with age!"

Of course, I should have known better.

"Well looking at you, you must be very wise indeed" I said. I shouldn't have said it, but I did. She launched herself at me and began slapping me about the head – ouch! I didn't deserve that, did I? Finally she was restrained by a couple of astonished scriptwriters.

"Are you happy now?" snarled Kyle, taking Miss Boulay lightly by the arm to escort her out of hospitality before she could embarrass herself further.

"Oh dear God, what have I done?" I said to Elaine.

I was utterly mortified that my words should have provoked such mayhem in my daughter's workplace. I should have listened to my own advice and quit while I was ahead.

"I can't take you anywhere" Elaine joked.

As you would expect, after such an outrage the room came alive with speculation, the common consensus being that Boulay was television toast, largely due to the presence of a tabloid journalist who had gleefully witnessed the caring sharing people person raining punches down on me, an unsuspecting member of the audience. No sooner had the journalist been politely but firmly encouraged to leave than the word was out that Melissa would be joining her team imminently to address staff, when she would be making a highly significant announcement. And as I was preparing to leave, judging that I ought not to intrude upon a family argument, a smart willowy girl placed her hand firmly on my shoulder and politely but forcefully suggested that I was going nowhere.

"Who was that girl?" I enquired of Elaine.

"You've just been visited by Kate, our Senior Producer. Congratulations, you live to tell the tale."

Evidently, this world of television could be a scary place, increasingly so as Melissa finally materialised, as grand as she had been earlier in the studio yet much more formidable when shorn of razzmatazz. She exuded power, her manner one of smiley steeliness.

"Barbara will be taking a well-deserved vacation," she announced. "In the meantime, I will be searching for a short-term replacement." This was a cue for a cascade of whispers about the identity of the likely candidates to flow surreptitiously across the room.

"And even more happily", Melissa continued, "I am delighted to announce that Elaine, everybody's favourite intern, is to join the staff as assistant producer with immediate effect. OK Elaine" she said, gesturing for her to join her for one of her legendary hugs, "You're hired".

Without prompting, an ear-shattering, spontaneous cheer greeted news of the appointment.

"Every office should have somebody like Elaine", Melissa declared, draping her arm around her new assistant producer's shoulder, "a hugely likeable, talented and genuinely warm person. Unlike those – and you know who you are – who prefer to gripe, bitch and backstab at one another's expense, she remains above the petty jealousies which can ever so occasionally affect our office life. So meet our new role model."

Her colleagues could have hated her for having just been crowned Little Miss Goody Two Shoes by Melissa. On the contrary, they seemed to love her even more, cheering her appointment to the skyscrapers.

"I'm so proud of you", I told her.

She appeared a little taken aback by the depth of my reaction. My eyes were moistening, blinded to the presence of the television legend who had joined us unannounced.

"So what do you know? It's the girl who hijacked my show", said Melissa, radiating good humour above an undercurrent of threat.

"What can I say? I guess I got a bit carried away."

"False modesty – who needs it? You were sensational and you know you were. In fact, you blew everybody away, especially me" said Melissa.

I blushed away the praise. Still, I didn't want to stop the sun from shining on Elaine's parade – this had to be her special time, the day she first got herself a career, to be remembered and cherished for years to come, I sincerely hoped. So I switched the spotlight back on to Elaine, congratulating Melissa on her decision to employ this remarkable girl.

"She'll go far", said Melissa, happy at least to acknowledge Elaine's innate professionalism. "But do tell me" she said, bringing the subject unerringly back to me, "how come one so young is so wise?"

"Not so wise that I know how to answer your question" I honestly said.

"Another smart reply" said Melissa. "Give me a call, and make it soon." She handed me a card inscribed with Melissa's precious, private cellphone number. "Don't be a stranger" was her parting comment as she was ushered away by Kyle.

No sooner had Melissa departed the room than the team erupted. People were busy analysing, debating and dissecting her words, searching for the hidden meaning cunningly concealed in her apparently upbeat announcement.

Amid the general speculation I couldn't help but notice that Elaine's manner towards me had cooled. Like any mother, in my head I thought I knew my daughter better than she knew herself. I could read her mind, sensing that she was secretly envious that a passer-by like me should get Melissa's secret cellphone number, then beating herself up for thinking the worst of me. She could never hold a grudge for long. If only I could say the same.

Loving her as they did, Elaine's work colleagues insisted that she should join them on a night on the town to celebrate her success. I was invited to accompany them too. In fact however much I protested that I wanted to go home, wash my hair and finish reading my book they insisted on it, teasingly claiming that they would be honoured to have a 'celebrity' in their midst.

Hesitant at first, I gave way under duress and accepted, ultimately feeling privileged to be included among these shiny, bright people, all of them plugged into the electricity of existence, wired up, switched on, neon young. I belonged, I guess.

As one village bar morphed into another, we talked, drank and flirted the hours away, Elaine's straight colleagues competing to impress me. Harmless fun, or so I'd intended, so best blame the booze, or maybe the corrosive effect of my honey trap career as things started to get a little out of hand.

"I so want to know you better," this one guy whispered into my ear, his girlfriend only a slap on the face away.

"And you must meet her boyfriend Marty too", said Elaine, intervening as my unofficial chaperone.

"I've never ever wanted to cheat on anybody until I met you" he claimed, undeterred. "You make me want to do bad things", he slurred. But he was overheard by Kyle as he brushed past us carrying a tray full of drinks.

"Have you no shame?" Kyle sneeringly enquired of me.

"None whatsoever, except where you're concerned. A girl's got to draw the line somewhere."

***

As our night wound down, Elaine dispersed my admirers by issuing vile threats while the remainder drifted away to their respective beds. However, I could see she didn't want the night to end. She was pleading with me to join her at her favourite all night Italian restaurant, mischievously known locally as Is the Pope Catholic? I didn't want to disappoint her, and contrary to the song, I'd always maintained that Italian restaurants, not diamonds, were a girl's best friend, boasting pasta, pizza and handsome waiters in figure-hugging black pants wielding ridiculously large pepper mills.

"Can I interest you in something hot and spicy?" the head waiter enquired of us.

"No, I would prefer something long and stimulating - like a nice cool glass of Frascati" I replied. I turned to Elaine. "I'm only flirting. There's no harm in it", I assured her.

"I truly believe you. In fact, I would trust you with my Brad."

I really wanted to change the subject, as she was confidentially speculating that her Brad might be working towards a proposal of marriage, although she sounded oddly alarmed by the prospect.

"And that's a good thing", I reminded her.

"Without doubt. Bring it on. What's not to like?" she said unconvincingly.

"And yet, I sense a 'but' coming."

"But can I really trust him?"

Good question, I thought.

"So why would you ever doubt him?" I said.

"I've seen the way he looks at you, although I'm not for one moment suggesting you're to blame."

I put on my poker face, not wanting to betray anything, and dreading where this might be leading.

"I began to wonder – how could I ever consider marrying him if I can't be a hundred per cent sure that he will remain faithful to me? And then it dawned on me, if he can resist you, he can resist anybody." My poker face slipped as the ghastly implications of Elaine's meanderings began to hit home. So she wanted me to perform a honey trap hit - on Brad!

I searched in vain for clues, still hoping that I might be the victim of a cruel practical joke.

"You know, I don't really think this is such a great plan", I gently admonished her.

"So you do think Brad wants to hit on you?"

"Of course I don't."

"Or perhaps you are susceptible to Brad after all."

"I'm so not!"

"Then do this one thing for me and if everything goes well, as I know it will, I will be free to accept his proposal and live happily ever after with the man I love."

"Insanity."

"I know you wouldn't want to deny me the chance of

having peace of mind. Only you can help me. Is that too much to ask of a friend?"

She was fundamentally a sensible girl who occasionally did ridiculous things. And that's where I had come in - to stop her doing ridiculous things. Yet suddenly she had stopped listening to me.

"Don't even go there, because no good will come of it," I pleaded with her, yet whenever I objected to her crazy plan I was as good as accused of having untoward feelings for her Brad. It was as if I had become her mother again, having lost my influence over her.

I was caught in a lose/lose situation. My only hope of a way out was Elaine sobering up in the morning and wondering how she could ever have devised such a crazy scheme.

CHAPTER TEN

Sadly time did not mellow Elaine, and even in the hard-hearted cold light of day, a thousand universes away from the intoxicating atmosphere of the post-show party, she remained hell bent on executing her insane plan.

I tried every which way to make her see sense, but I always hit the same brick wall as she resorted to equating my reluctance to seduce Brad with proof that I nursed inappropriate feelings for him. Of course, I rejected that outright, and by so doing, was obliged to support her plan. She calmly discussed logistics, proposing that the best time for me to strike would be when she was away visiting her mom and dad in Valley Stream for the weekend, leaving the way clear for me to encounter Brad.

"Dad said Mom hasn't been her usual self these last few months," Elaine had explained. "He reckons that a visit on my own might help lift her spirits."

Don't even go there, my poor befuddled mind warned me, so I did what any mature, sensible, grown-up person does in these circumstances – I went into denial, and phoned an iconic, global megastar instead. Not that I was in the habit of calling show business royalty, expecting my call to be declined, yet Melissa accepted my call with a curt "yes", as I attempted to explain exactly who I was in a confused and slightly manic manner.

"Let's do lunch", she instantly replied, so I accepted her invitation to join her the next day at the 21 Club in West 52nd Street, a favoured haunt of show business icons.

"I guess it must be something to do with audience research," I speculated to Elaine.

"At the 21 Club? I don't think so!" she said, with a hint of resentment that only I as her mother could have detected.

As nobody ever kept Melissa waiting, I arrived unfashionably early at the restaurant and was escorted to a holding area by an obliging waiter, who became even more obliging upon being informed that I was a guest of the esteemed Melissa Parker.

"Would you like to order a drink, Miss?" he solicitously enquired.

How I loved that word Miss.

If they could see me now, I reflected. I recalled drinking cappuccinos with pampered, cynical, middle-aged friends in Valley Stream and discussing the previous night's episode of *Desperate Housewives.* I had been living life second hand, an existence which had been so far removed from my table at the 21 Club as I eagerly awaited the arrival of an American icon.

I have to admit to being nervous, both at the prospect of meeting a television legend and the fear of being interrogated by her razor-sharp skills when I had so much to hide. Elaine had advised, "Just be yourself" - whoever that might be, I wondered as I sipped my sparkling mineral water with a lemon slice.

"Miss Parker is prone to being somewhat tardy", the waiter informed me with old-world courtesy, handing me the menu for me to peruse. I was relieved to have it as a shield to hide behind, as I had noticed a former honey trap victim of mine, deep in conversation at a neighbouring table with his respectable wife. Panic undid him when he caught sight of me, and he suddenly got to his feet and disappeared towards the sanctuary of the men's room at speed. As he rushed out, Melissa marched in, having to take evasive action to avoid being bowled over.

"What's with that guy? Good to see you", she said, offering her outstretched hand to me.

I was lost for words. Melissa, familiar with people being rendered speechless when coming into contact with her, expertly put me at me ease. Then she wasted no time in getting down to business.

"I don't do false modesty. It was a stunning performance, so much wisdom in one so young. So tell me about yourself."

"I'm a runaway, escaping a possessive boyfriend and a bad case of the small town blues, desperate to find fulfilment in Manhattan because life is for living, or so my grandma used to tell me."

She fell for it. Even America's most perceptive interviewer was susceptible to hearing what she wanted to hear.

"So what do you think of the show?" Melissa enquired over her smoked salmon entrée.

"Honestly?"

"I don't do bull", Melissa replied.

"It's not that I don't enjoy the show", I said warily.

"Please! Speak your mind. I don't need my ego massaging. I've got Kyle for that."

"But I do feel it could be a little - er... better", I hesitantly and somewhat vaguely proposed. She cocked an eyebrow.

"OK then, here goes" I said, inhaling deeply. "Too many Springer-style debates like 'I cheated on my boyfriend with his brother, father, horse' type of thing."

I paused just long enough to give Melissa the chance to storm out if she wished, but she didn't.

"What makes the show special is you, and the strength we can all draw from your success in winning against all odds in a man's world" I went on.

"So your solution is?" Melissa enquired.

"Make it real. Ring bells, strike chords, hit nerves. Do stuff an audience can really relate to, like 'my husband diminishes me', 'I won't take it any more'. Inspire downtrodden women everywhere to rebuild their self-esteem. Show them, step by step, how it can be achieved."

Melissa remained stonily silent. By refraining from any kind of comment she was inducing a sense of foreboding within me. Had I fatally overstepped the mark?

"There's a guy over there waving at you", I observed. I was saying something, anything, absolutely anything at all to deflect from my previous rant. It was a late-night talk show host called Johnny Mailman.

"That man!" said an exasperated Melissa, returning the man's greeting with a regal wave and smiling graciously as she did so. "He ridicules me every night in his hilarious monologues, yet he expects me to react like I'm his bosom buddy."

"You could always ignore him."

"I wouldn't give him the satisfaction."

And then the Mailman bestowed a wave upon me, which I tentatively acknowledged by waving half-heartedly in return. That reduced the other three men on the talk show host's table to unfeasibly loud gales of laughter and an exchange of fifty-dollar bills.

"Don't encourage them. It looks like he's won a bet" said Melissa.

"Men will be boys" I observed.

"And girls will be women" said Melissa, "If your perceptive observations about the state of my show are anything to go by."

And so I listened wide-eyed as Melissa explained how pressure from the network had forced the show towards sensation and controversy in its quest for ratings, which even she had struggled to resist. The time had come to make a stand, she declared, and now that Barbara Boulay had been 'encouraged' to take an extended holiday, what better moment could there be for her to announce a significant development?

"I want you to replace Barbara Boulay on the show", said Melissa, as casually as if she was offering me a pair of audience tickets.

"Pardon me?"

"On a trial basis of course", she added, as if that made it more believable. "Although I only ever back winners, so you will succeed regardless."

She sealed the deal with a formal handshake, suggesting that I should call into the office tomorrow, when I would be officially introduced to the team.

"Must fly", said the American icon, already an angel in my estimation, albeit without wings.

I sat there in my little bubble, oblivious to the sophisticated diners around me. Astonished, amazed and bewildered didn't come close to it as I struggled to come to terms with Melissa's fantastic offer. Sure, I was delighted, yet troubled too. I was worrying exactly what being Melissa's People Person could do to help shape my ultimate destiny.

The honey trap? That could easily be explained, saving Elaine from her disreputable way of earning a living. And getting a room in her apartment? A chance for me to watch over her and at least try to encourage her to do the right thing.

So maybe Melissa represented the next stage – a bigger stage in fact – my chance to reach a much wider audience, forsaking sleaze and sensation for intelligent debate, taking the Talk Show to higher ground, and by so doing, improving peoples' lives in the process. A touch pretentious I admit, but how else could I possibly explain it?

And I would still be there for Elaine. Yet how the Ricki Lake would she react to my elevation to People Person on the show?

And then somebody interrupted my thoughts.

"Can I join you?" Johnny Mailman enquired.

"So you can win another bet? I don't think so."

"Ouch!" he responded. "I guess I should try and make amends. And please don't think I have any hidden agenda, but I couldn't help but notice that you are exceptionally easy on the eye. Permit me to offer you a job as one of my Mailman girls, delivering me on stage at the top of the show."

I nearly choked on my Perrier.

"There's nothing to it. No need to talk – just grab hold of my arm, get walking and smile sweetly and for that, I will pay you handsomely."

So where was the harm in his suggestion? Just because a girl looks pretty doesn't mean she's stupid – I'd seen *Legally Blonde* - and yet one offer from Melissa and I became a total diva.

"Nice try" I derided him, "But you're too late. You see, I've just been signed up by Melissa and astonishingly, she even trusts me to open my mouth." I flounced out with a flourish, leaving the late night TV star to return red-faced to his friends.

***

I didn't walk so much as float home, taking a detour through Central Park, the world now decidedly on my side. It was with a happy heart I came upon Strawberry Fields, the garden memorial to the late John Lennon which his wife, Yoko, had donated to the people of New York, the city where he had lived for so many years.

"How extraordinary! Melissa chose me", I said, absent-mindedly articulating my expression of joy out loud. I was overheard by a follically-challenged hippie of 1960s vintage who was sitting on a park bench, contemplating the lyrics of his hero's most famous song, *Imagine*.

"Anything's possible man", he said, having invited me to sit next to him. I was happy to while away a few minutes.

"You'll have to excuse me. I'm on a high" I explained.

"Welcome to my world" he slurred.

"I loved the Beatles, although Paul was always my favourite."

"I would have thought you would be more American Idol than Fab Four."

"Great music is timeless. You should listen to Paul's song *Here Today*. It's all about John. Paul loved him too."

"Cool", he replied, offering me a smoke on his joint, which I politely declined. How I dreaded returning to the apartment, where I would be invited by Elaine to deliver my news. I couldn't conceive of any palatable way of presenting it without causing her resentment. I preferred instead to stay in Strawberry Fields forever. I was now accompanied by a blue-eyed, blond-haired Danish tourist called Kurt and the lovely Lorraine, his sweet-voiced, English girlfriend, who'd joined us, strumming *Yellow Submarine* on their guitar.

"All we are saying", we then all sang, "Is give peace a chance". We moved on to more thought-provoking material, until I eventually ran out of songs and had to go home.

"You're never going to believe…" I said to Elaine upon taking my key out of the door to deliver the amazing news, and for a split second, upon revealing that I had been appointed trainee People Person, I could have sworn she hated me.

CHAPTER ELEVEN

As I'd expected, Elaine had returned to her sweet-natured self by the next day. I appreciated that accompanying me to Groucho Productions on my first day in the office as a budding agony aunt couldn't have been easy for her, but she dealt with it brilliantly. She smiled at me supportively as I strode purposefully alongside her in the early morning sunshine on a New York sidewalk, where smart-suited, sharply-dressed men and women were preparing to pursue their daily mission to make the world a more successful and shiny place.

"Nervous?" she enquired of me.

"I would be, except I feel like I'm in a dream."

A new job, one of life's most intimidating yet exhilarating rites of passage, a daunting mixture of anticipation and dread – and how I embraced it. I'd always wanted to be part of something bigger and more momentous than myself, although doubts remained.

"That's not work," Greg used to say, mocking my hours spent at the homeless shelter. "You'd never survive in the commercial world," he once said derisively. That was all the motivation I needed to prove I could succeed in a business environment, and of course to repay Melissa for showing such exceptional faith in me.

"You'll never ever guess", I said to Elaine above the cacophony of the city's early bird overture. "No sooner had Melissa left than Mailman appeared at my table – no shame whatsoever – propositioning me to be one of those brain-dead girls who escort him on stage at the top of the show."

"How amazing is that?" said Elaine without wonder.

"I should have told him, don't judge a book by its cover, but I did tell him exactly what he could do with his offer."

"Was that wise?"

I'd only gone and done it again, apparently showing off when I'd assumed we would unite in condemning what I perceived to be Mailman's sexist behaviour. Of course I could sympathise with how she must have felt about my rapid rise from nowhere when compared to her long apprenticeship, having only just become employed after months of unpaid hard work behind the scenes. So I avoided the subject of Melissa and my new job for the remainder of our journey, hard to ignore though when confronted by pictures of my new show business friend everywhere the eye could see in the foyer of Groucho productions.

"Are these guys in mourning?" I quizzed Elaine, perplexed by the preponderance of black worn by the young men and women who inhabited the entrance to the building.

"It's a fashion thing," Elaine explained.

I was only half listening, distracted as I inspected my new company identity card. I belonged to Groucho now.

As we progressed further inside the building you could sense the energy positively bouncing off every wall as Elaine exchanged greetings with a procession of eager young things, most of them carrying clipboards.

"This is where we part company. Here is strictly for the drones." Elaine gestured to the massive open-plan office, inside which shiny bright young people tapped lightly on keyboards or spoke persuasively into phones.

"The talent hangs out through there" she said, pointing to a security enhanced door. "You and I inhabit different planets from this day on." She told me I would be in the care of Kate Benetto, Executive Producer, Groucho Productions.

I hesitated at the door, disappointed that we would be working in separate offices. I had imagined we would be together as a team.

"Hi, I'm Jennifer" I said, introducing myself to Kate, who I guessed was in her early thirties – and that was old for round these parts - while Elaine had quietly retreated to her office, knowing her place in the order of things.

"No need for introductions", Kate briskly observed. "How could I possibly forget your show-stopping contribution to the mothers and daughters debate?"

"I was just speaking my mind."

"But what a mind!"

"And what a body too," I overheard a passing young guy pushing a trolley full of letters say.

"Ignore him", said Kate, miming a slap on the young man's head. "I'll speak to his manager later."

In the meantime she escorted me to a conference room where a group of switched-on people sat lounging around a table, the majority of them appearing much too young to justify the group's title, Senior Editorial Team.

"I believe you two have already met," said Kate, indicating a figure who was depressingly recognisable as Kyle.

"Whatever", he replied under his breath, smiling maliciously. I knew I could handle Kyle, although I did have to pinch myself. I was astonished to be sitting in the engine room of America's Number One Talk Show. It was all I could do to smile as Kate formally welcomed me before she began the painstaking process of compiling the schedules for the next two weeks.

"Now here's the thing," said Kyle, charging in mouth first to verbally assault the meeting. "My husband became my wife", he announced, his chest puffed out, swelling under the influence of his own imagined brilliance.

"There's this husband who's had his dick chopped off..."

"I believe the proper technical term is gender reassignment", I corrected him.

"As I was saying, there's this guy who's had the ch…"

"Gender reassignment", Melissa intervened, having slipped into the room unannounced.

"Precisely", said Kyle, willing to take the correction from Melissa. "And then, he and his wife adapt so well to the new circumstances sharing not only eye shadow, dresses and moisturiser but the same guy too, a muscle-bound builder from Oregon who came to install more than just a new bathroom."

Melissa struggled to stifle a yawn. Even Kyle was not so insensitive that he couldn't detect which way the wind was blowing.

"Perhaps this might be more to your tastes" said Kyle, a note of desperation creeping into his voice. "Now That's What I Call Education", he boldly proclaimed.

"Sounds a touch more interesting. Tell me more, tell me more," she said, quoting a line from the musical *Grease*, in which she had once famously appeared.

"A thirty-five year old female teacher who's having a full-on affair with one of her eighteen-year-old male students. It's legal, but is it right?"

Melissa slapped the palm of her hand against her forehead to register despair. Then she nodded to me to give her assent for me to address the meeting.

I really had intended to keep quiet, yet there was something about Kyle which brought out the fighter in me – well, he had the bruises on his groin to prove it.

"Surely Melissa is worthy of better than this", I said breathlessly.

"Is that so?" said Kyle, slamming his folder upon the desk. "Now tell me, how many awards have you ever won? Oh, that's right. Exactly none!"

"Hear her out, Kyle," said Melissa.

"Think of me as your typical viewer", I continued, Kyle's intervention had given me time to compose myself and speak normally again. "That's what gives me the right to have an opinion. I speak on behalf of the audience, and they deserve something more uplifting. Inspire them with stories which can encourage viewers to lead better lives, rather than constantly rubbing their noses in the worst aspects of human behaviour."

"Well hello Mary Poppins," exclaimed an exasperated Kyle, scanning around the table in vain for any signs of support for his sleazy ideas.

"That's enough, Kyle", Melissa warned him.

She now announced the launch of a new editorial policy which would see a significant shift away from Jerry Springer-style sensationalism to more inspirational shows. "It's time to get back to basics – to do what I do best – to challenge, to entertain and inspire," she decreed.

Kyle winced as if in pain, although not yet fatally wounded.

"While respecting your sentiments, Melissa" he said unconvincingly, "I doubt very much whether the Head of

Network would ever agree, as Angelo Ramirez is known to prefer controversy to caring/sharing TV."

That name - Angelo Ramirez. It struck me like a kiss. How could anybody with such a poetic name be opposed to our enlightened approach?

"You can leave Ramirez to me," Melissa assured Kyle. After all, she was a TV legend, whereas this Angelo had only been in the top job for a matter of weeks, being something of a mystery having made his name in Europe – and yet he held our fate in his hands.

"So can you please explain", Kyle demanded, once more directing his ire exclusively towards me, "how you would set about raising the tone of Melissa's Show? And be specific please."

"Don't feel you have to answer", Melissa cautioned me.

"It's a fair question which deserves a comprehensive answer," I replied, knowing exactly what I wanted to say.

"Men Who Bring Women Down. Sounds familiar Kyle? Well it oughta. Shine a light on husbands who undermine their wives by constantly demeaning them, gnawing away at their self-confidence until they feel utterly worthless and unable to go on. Confront control freaks – boyfriends who destroy their partners' self-esteem by criticising them night and day, and challenge bosses who keep their poorly-paid female employees under their thumbs, paying them less than their male counterparts."

"Shall I count the ways I love this? Let's do it," Melissa decreed.

And as if that wasn't amazing enough, the group's surprise escalated to astonishment as she announced her decision to cast me as on screen People Person and relationship advisor, with none other than Kyle overseeing the project.

"Why him?" I enquired of Kate once Melissa had departed the room, the meeting having run its course.

"You're thinking it's a little like putting Dracula in charge of the blood bank," Kate guessed, correctly. "Let me put your mind at rest. Melissa chose Kyle because quite simply, he's the best."

Obviously making television shows was a strange and mysterious business, as I would later discover when I visited Kyle's desk.

Truly, anywhere within a hundred miles radius of Kyle was a place I didn't want to be, let alone standing right next to him, where I watched him tapping relentlessly on his keyboard, more likely to be composing his letter of resignation than ideas for my show.

So I had been placed in a predicament where my success depended on Kyle being totally committed to the project, whatever my reservations.

"I guess I'm not your favourite person right now", I said with a conciliatory air.

"Oh that," he said dismissively. "The bottom line is,

I'm a professional and regardless of how I might feel about you personally you can be certain that you will have the finest guests, the most thorough research and cleverest questions to help make your show fly."

My, was he believable. Having read of warring producers and directors who still manage to make great movies together, or musicians who shamelessly hate one another yet compose classic songs in partnership, I nervously decided to put my faith in him.

"The show will open with an inferior and less qualified guy promoted at the expense of a more talented junior female executive, followed by a control freak boyfriend dictating what his partner should not wear, ending with a manipulative husband guilty of ridiculing his wife's tentative attempts to get back into employment," he said, explaining his proposed running order to me.

"I could have written that myself, except nowhere near as well," I congratulated him. "Obviously I have much to learn." I was shamelessly sucking up to him.

"Trust me, I'm a producer. I will deliver a great show for you," he promised me once more.

"And I know we have history – that night at Elaine's – but I really do appreciate your professional attitude, so let's keep the two things separate."

"That's cool by me," he confirmed, as I left him to type scripts, or so I'd assumed.

Leaving the editorial content of the show in his hands,

I was spirited away to be introduced to a bewildering number of team members who all facilitated the show in various ways, including a fast-talking, sharply-dressed publicity officer who spoke beguilingly of a forthcoming photo shoot for *Vanity Fair* and an eccentrically-attired costume designer, Posy, who I sincerely hoped had better taste when it came to choosing clothes for people other than herself.

"Lacroix, Versace, McCartney, all the usual suspects," Posy trilled, eagerly anticipating our shopping spree, which she promised would create a unique and cutting-edge look for my appearances on Melissa's show.

CHAPTER TWELVE

When the wind changes direction a clear blue sky can quickly become filled with clouds. In my case one was one Brad-shaped, while the other that was scudding towards me looking alarmingly like Alice. They were both storms waiting to happen. I had to find shelter from my relationship with Alice and end it before the press got wind of my inappropriate past.

I resolutely vowed to confront Alice, demanding that she cut all ties with both me and Elaine. I would remind her that we were employees, not slaves, and therefore free to go on whenever and wherever we wanted. I would have acted straight away had Elaine not called to say that I should cancel everything and prepare to hit on Brad. Still I pleaded with Elaine to see sense and to abandon this madness without success. My infuriating daughter remained resolute regarding her plan, and adamant that only by putting Brad's loyalty to the test could she ever commit to marrying him.

"Everything will be just fine. I trust you implicitly", said Elaine.

"In Brad you should trust," I advised, once more imploring her to call the whole thing off, but my words fell on unreceptive ears.

So much urgency to report, a window having opened, and in order to facilitate her plan Elaine had phoned Brad to inform him that she'd been called away at short notice to visit her mom at her dad's insistence. He was concerned about his wife's depressed mental state – and that was me – or the me I used to be, in case you'd forgotten.

Elaine had asked Brad whether he would mind calling at the apartment to pick up her contacts book, which she needed for a phone call she had promised to make on behalf of Melissa. Agreeing to her request, Brad arranged to visit the apartment early Saturday evening, a perfect time to call as Hannah would be safely out of the way in Boston, Mass., where she would be attending an international convention of palaeontologists.

A little later Elaine contacted me, like a spymaster, to relay Brad's estimated time of arrival, while I in turn made an excuse to Marty that I had a horrible headache, and so would be unable to see him. He bore it bravely, sweet boy that he was.

And yet, how could I have possibly got myself into this dangerous situation? I was supposed to be the responsible one, steering Elaine away from madness like this, so how come I was waiting apprehensively in the apartment preparing to seduce my daughter's boyfriend – and at her request?

CHAPTER TWELVE

It was time to reclaim my maturity. I would do the absolute bare minimum when it came to Brad's hit, perhaps a desultory flutter of the eyelashes, a little hair tossing maybe and not a hint of promise in the way I dressed.

There then followed a succession of failed attempts to strike the right balance, and as one fashion disaster followed another, every one of those clothes catastrophes was punctuated by a large consoling glass of white wine, leading to me drinking myself inadvertently into an alcoholic daze. I had brilliantly suppressed my gut-wrenching fear about this weekend hit, although compromising my judgement in the process. Three more glasses of Pinot following in rapid succession unhelpfully sent me to sleep.

When I awoke in a heap on hearing the front door opening – reasoning that it must be Brad – I stumbled awkwardly, my inebriation taking me by surprise. It anaesthetised my nervousness but rendered me clumsy, verging on incoherent.

"Oh... hi," I said struggling to articulate. "What brings you here?" I just about enquired, feigning surprise at his supposedly unexpected presence.

"You look – er - different," he said, ignoring my question until he had finished savouring me with his eyes. "I'm on a mission for Elaine while she's away visiting her mom."

"Her mom?" I said quizzically. "We've never been properly acquainted. From everything Elaine's said, she sounds so sad. I really pity her."

"No way," she's middle-aged eye candy – hot in fact – yet she doesn't seem to know it herself."

"Then you should have told her," I said sliding back on the sofa, my tongue loosened by drink.

"Oh sure, like Mrs Green. I'm dating your daughter but you're a mother I would like to fuck. I don't think so!"

"You look nice, Mrs Green, would have been sufficient," I said before falling asleep where I lay.

Apparently, I was totally out for the count. Brad later claiming that he had gazed on fondly, passion kindling within him, and that even in my drunken state I had that rare gift of remaining what he described as "absolutely adorable". What rubbish men talk. He then drank himself into a stupor too, attempting to get on the same wavelength as me, hoping to achieve intimacy through inebriation; somewhat pointless, considering I was way too out of it to respond.

It must have been quite a dilemma for Brad, wondering what to do with this unconscious girl. Ultimately he decided to do the gentlemanly thing by lifting me aloft and carrying me into my bedroom. He laid me down tenderly on my bed, and I momentarily stirred.

"I was supposed to seduce you" I said, creating confusion within him.

"Well I appear to be in your bedroom. So far, so good," he said. It was the last thing I remember hearing before slipping into another booze-induced sleep.

I've often thought about it since. I have no reason whatsoever to disbelieve his absolute and definitive assurances that he really did place the duvet respectfully upon my sleeping form before reluctantly returning to the living room, demolishing what was left of the wine before clumsily divesting himself of shirt, socks and pants while stumbling fatally towards what he mistakenly thought was Elaine's empty room – so he would earnestly later claim – and innocently and unknowingly tumbling into my bed. At least, that's what I wanted to believe.

I could sense the heat of him, lying isolated alongside me. And then he threw his arms around me and my right hand fell upon his muscular inner thigh.

"Thank you for visiting," I sleepily welcomed him, automatically stroking his surprisingly silky-skinned bottom. He responded with an appreciative little growl which descended into a gently rhythmic snore.

"Go to sleep. We have nothing to be ashamed of." I half sighed it, half said it. "Not yet" he grunted, and I secretly hoped he meant it.

CHAPTER THIRTEEN

We could never have predicted that Hannah would have returned nearly twelve hours early from her weekend conference. The next morning, when she blundered into my bedroom talking animatedly about her time in Boston, she was at first blissfully ignorant of the visitor in my bed. We had that much in common at least, for I too had forgotten the goings-on of the previous night, initially insulated from it by the hangover in my head. But then as I squinted into the daylight, a cold chill progressed ominously up my spine. I slowly began to recall the presence of my sleeping partner with escalating horror. Thank god he was buried under the duvet.

'Don't move a muscle', I prayed to whoever it is you pray to when trying to hide boys in your bed. Hannah was going on about an email she had received from her brother in London regarding her soccer team Spurs and their most recent success in beating something called Arsenal. On and on she went. Just as I thought she was going to the kitchen to fix us both a coffee she launched into another tirade about all "the fossils" attending her conference and how she couldn't bear to stay there another day longer, so happy was she to be back home in the apartment. Still she remained oblivious, until a telltale yawn emanating from underneath the covers struck her dumb. On seeing Brad emerge like a hibernating animal greeting spring and then quickly wishing it was winter, she ran from the room, her hand to her mouth as if she was going to hurl.

We had been caught red-handed for doing next to nothing. Gripped by utter panic and sheer desperation, I shot out of bed and pursued her next door where Hannah stood-ashen faced with anger at what she had just witnessed.

"How could you?" she bawled at me.

"I know it looks bad but we simply slept, soundly and fast asleep."

Hannah chuckled mirthlessly.

"Believe me. I did not have sex with that man."

"Ah, the Bill Clinton defence. And we know how honest and truthful that proved to be," Hannah replied, spitting contempt.

"But I would never do anything to hurt Elaine," I protested. Just then a bleary-eyed Brad joined us to defend our innocence. "I just got into the wrong bed. I fucked up, that's all," he said unhelpfully.

"You must think I was born yesterday. I have no choice but to tell Elaine. I refuse to collaborate with your affair."

I was begging her to disbelieve the evidence of her own eyes. "To destroy Elaine's peace of mind for no discernible reason would be pointlessly cruel," I argued.

"She deserves to be told the truth. I refuse to keep her in the dark," said Hannah, unswayed.

"It's my responsibility, not yours," said Brad, intervening. "If there's anything to be said, I will say it to Ellie," he counselled us both, at last giving Hannah reason to re-evaluate her unyielding stance for the first time.

"If you don't tell Elaine the truth, I will. The clock is ticking," she threatened us both.

Maybe I should have revealed that Elaine had asked me to seduce Brad, but that would have been the most unbelievable excuse of them all.

I had thought long and hard about what might have happened had Hannah not come bursting in. I'm certain I would have woken up, horrified by the close proximity of Brad sleeping next to me, and escaped to the bathroom with a bundle of clothes under my arm to make myself decent. And then on to the kitchen to fix him a breakfast which I would have carried on a tray back into my bedroom with a jaunty air, to greet him a hearty good morning in the most wholesome, sexless way imaginable, implying, we've got nothing to be ashamed of, so eat up, get up and get over it.

So how would Brad have behaved if he had woken first? A perfect gentleman, averting his gaze, sensitively stepping over my slumbering body to make a discreet departure, mindful of his undying commitment to Elaine? Maybe. Although in Alice's eyes, as a man he would have inevitably made a pass, preceded by some predictable chat-up lines which I would have scornfully dismissed before storming out of bed in a rage.

And then I contemplated a third less wholesome scenario. What if I awoke first, quietly slipping away into the bathroom without waking him, a swift shower, then a light application of moisturiser, a dab of mascara and a slash of lipstick, followed by cleaning of teeth and a spray of breath freshener, deodorant sprayed under the arms and elsewhere and a dab of perfume behind the ears. Then a change of underwear (sexiest available), a brush of the lustrous blond hair and then creeping back into bed, as if I always woke up naturally resembling a goddess every morning, regardless of how much I had drunk the previous night. And when Brad awoke… then still I believe we would have come to our senses. I could never have betrayed Elaine, in this life, or the last.

***

Having secured Hannah's silence, I now had to convince Elaine. Although not exactly innocent – I should never have agreed to the hit in the first place - I didn't consider myself properly guilty either. Somewhere in between in fact, more about thought than action, and how heartless would it have been to have subjected Elaine to distressing images of me lying drunkenly in bed with Brad when nothing really happened? So I would give Elaine the answer she most wanted to hear, and to that end, I rehearsed for the moment when I would see her for the first time since returning from Valley Stream. I knew that words would be superfluous. My expression and posture would tell Elaine everything she needed to know about the outcome.

Think yourself blameless, I counselled myself at the bathroom mirror, and upon hearing the front door open I didn't rush to join her. I bided my time until it felt right to step out to greet her. My open and relaxed demeanour was winning enough to persuade Elaine that she had been worrying unnecessarily about Brad. I was living proof that in the hands of an accomplished practitioner, body language could lie too.

"So he passed then?"

"Absolutely. With honours."

"And you did come on strong, did you?"

"As strong as I needed to. I acted a little drunk, but not so much that he would be repelled by me."

"That was never going to happen."

"I guess he'll forgive me and assume it was just the booze talking."

"Although being a man, he's sure to feel a little bit flattered about being hit on."

"Although he most definitely pushed me away."

"I'm glad to know it."

"And do you want to know what I was wearing?"

"Maybe that's too much information – time to move on."

"So I guess you two can get married now?"

"Only if he should ask me."

"It's inevitable, isn't it?"

"So, do you want to be my bridesmaid?"

I would probably pass on that. I much preferred Mother of The Bride.

CHAPTER FOURTEEN

The shock of what might have been with Brad acted as my long overdue wake-up call. I really needed to get my act together, to re-establish order and to stop my hormones from ruling my head. How could I have got it so wrong – to claim to be teaching Elaine life lessons yet agreeing to hit in her boyfriend Brad?

I would get back to being my sensible old buttoned-up self and restore propriety in my life, however much this ridiculous body of mine yearned to contradict me. No more honey trap hits, Alice must be told. I would liberate myself from her. And I would set Marty free, too. He was a sweet boy, yet however hard I tried I didn't feel strongly enough towards him, while he appeared to be besotted with me. The imbalance of our respective feelings could only end in tears. He deserved better than me, and I would be doing him a favour by letting him go.

However he didn't quite see it like that. I genuinely tried to let him down gently, but every time I raised the subject of 'us' he would create a diversion. I dropped hints, but he refused to pick them up. And once when I called into the Trump Bar to talk about our future he first insisted on playing me a poignant song which he had composed in my honour called, *You're Everything To Me.* How could I possibly dump him after that?

I tried again a couple of days later. "Maybe we should take a holiday from each other," I suggested, and "It's not you, it's me." And yes, I really did say that.

"I know what this is about," he fought back. "I guess I'll be seeing less of you now that you're going to be on TV. That's OK. I can handle it." He was apparently happy to play Best Supporting Actor to me, his girlfriend.

Yet I refused to use him any longer. I accompanied him to a nearby Starbucks where I searched for my inner Cruella De Ville, and boy did I find her.

"You'll never be the one," I said, taking his heart and smashing it into a thousand pieces.

"But with this song," he said, handing me an A4 sheet of paper inscribed with both words and music, "I will make you immortal". A messianic glint flickered disturbingly in his eyes.

"This isn't me," I said, handing back his composition with a heavy heart. "The girl you describe is nothing more than an illusion. You should go find somebody real."

"I just knew it couldn't last, with every guy in the world wanting to hit on you. I've seen them looking at you. Can you imagine how that's made me feel?" he whined.

I watched as his once-adorable crooked smile mutated

into a jaded, derisory smirk, as if being rejected by me had unhinged him.

"I will never let you go. You can be sure of that," he promised, exuding menace.

He'd get over it, I then believed, refusing to accept I could have turned a good boy, bad.

If breaking away from Marty had been painful, divorcing Alice would be bloodier by far. It would be the difference between slapping away a poodle and freeing yourself from the jaws of a rottweiler. Having entered Eve Couture I didn't even wait for Alice to sanction my ascent upstairs.

"I don't recall inviting you in," said Alice when I presented myself unannounced in her office.

"I want out," I informed her.

"Yes, I was wondering when you would attempt to resign. I've already heard about your little foray into television with Melissa," she casually informed me.

"So you already know why I have to quit, and don't go thinking you can get Elaine back either," I warned her, still standing as I spoke.

"Hardly a replacement for you my dear," she said encircling me with her walk as she ran her silky little hand down my cheek. "I have unilaterally decided that I will only release you from service if you can find an equivalent replacement, and since in your case that's never going to happen then you will continue to stay with me until I decide you are finished here."

I then endeavoured to appeal to Alice's better nature – a doomed venture if ever there was one – but no amount of heartfelt pleas that this was my chance of a lifetime would soften her intransigence, driving me to despairingly declare that I would rather be exposed as a honey trap – if that's what she intended to do – and suffer rejection and dismissal by Melissa than be forced to carry on as an employee of Truth.

"Do your worst. I'm leaving you behind" I said, ablaze with righteousness. I turned my back on her and prepared to leave.

"Sit down. I have a proposal," she said, inviting me to reclaim my chair. She placed her hands on my compliant shoulders and began to massage them with a sure and sensual touch.

"So much tension," she whispered teasingly into my ear. "You will always belong to me, but caring for you as I do, and having your best interests at heart, I shall agree to let Melissa borrow you, if she so desires, until I demand that you return, whenever and however that might be."

There must be limits even to Alice's power and influence, I thought. I doubted that she could either own me or loan me in 21st century USA. Yet if agreeing to her demented compromise and humouring her into believing she still had some influence over me would enable me to escape from Truth unscathed, then it was a price worth paying. And surely, once safely installed in my new television career, fame would immunise me against my tormentor's threat to drag me back to honey trapping.

"Are you sure you won't tell Melissa, or anybody else at Groucho, about all this?" I demanded of her.

Alice nodded her assent. "The tension's easing," she said, her hands moving dangerously downwards, straying provocatively beneath my shoulders. "Do you still have that boyfriend of yours?" she asked disdainfully, both kneading and needing ever softer flesh.

"I dumped him."

"Good girl."

"I wish I was."

"Really?" asked Alice, "we'll see about that." She took me by the hand and led me into her private apartment, where I finally discovered what that tiny, most sensitive part of me was actually for.

CHAPTER FIFTEEN

So in attempting to de-clutter my life I had only gone and created a new intimate connection – well done Jennifer! Regardless of our night together, as far as I was concerned I had still utterly and completely severed my relationship with Alice, although why I had succumbed to her at all, God only knows. I wasn't even gay, or at least I hadn't thought I was. Sure, I admit to finding Angelina Jolie attractive – after all, female sexuality is everywhere you look, so how can you possibly avoid it? – but never had I seriously thought about sleeping with another woman, except in fantasies, and that involved a threesome where I would always cast a reassuring guy. Maybe I had imagined by agreeing to sleep with her that I would ensure my liberation from Truth, and yet deep down I knew I was fooling myself, somehow knowing that ever since meeting Alice I had gradually become more susceptible to her influence.

So how was it for you, I can imagine you asking? Mind your own business, I am tempted to reply, except to inform you that it was soft, luscious, fluffy, yielding, succulent and ecstatic, more female marshmallow than male hard candy. Following the hesitancy of Marty, how I relished being with someone who appeared to know my own body better than I did. And she was uncharacteristically tender too, making me wonder whether she might actually possess deeper and warmer feelings for me than could be explained by pure, unadulterated lust. A penis would have been nice, though.

At least I could keep this misdemeanour – if that's what it was – a secret from my roommates, relations in the apartment having cooled significantly since the honey trap hit on Brad, which had affected everybody detrimentally as I had originally feared. Brad betrayed telltale signs of guilt whenever he called or came to stay, purposefully avoiding me and diverting his eyes from me whenever we occupied the same room together, risking incriminating himself in the eyes of Elaine. And contrary to Elaine's expectations, no marriage proposal was forthcoming from Brad either, perhaps mercifully, as I had reason to believe that he was hardly husband material for my daughter.

Hannah meanwhile went about her business with simmering resentment, threatening to erupt at any moment and spew forth the lurid details of my supposed illicit intimacy with Brad.

So I lived in a state of perpetual dread of exposure at any single moment, driving me to flatter and humour her and cater for all of Hannah's whims. She in turn took full advantage of my precarious predicament. Once or twice while I was relaxing in our sitting room watching TV I became convinced she was about to reveal all to Elaine, following an appropriately relevant story line in a television drama or soap. She would smile knowingly in my direction. "Can I fix you a snack?" I would say and jump up. Anything to distract her from coughing up the truth.

"I would like to have a word," Hannah addressed me ominously one day when we were sitting alone in the flat together, setting alarm bells ringing in my head. Had there had been a recent devastating enclosure.

"I'm dating Marty. I trust you're OK with that," she brazenly announced.

I breathed in. Why, in a city of two million eligible men did Hannah have to choose this one?

"I'm cool with that," I said in a brittle voice. "In fact, you have my blessing."

I had hoped that my willingness to approve might gently persuade Hannah to turn a blind eye, yet no sign of forgiveness for my night with Brad was forthcoming. And if that wasn't uncomfortable enough, I wasn't exactly relishing the prospect of Marty visiting the apartment in the guise of Hannah's boyfriend.

I strove hard to create an air of normality when Marty visited, whereas he haughtily acknowledged me with a curt nod, and then demonstrated a complete lack of class by inappropriately snuggling up to Hannah on the sofa in a performance more designed to give me pain than Hannah pleasure.

Hannah couldn't have been lighter and frothier when in the presence of Marty, eagerly volunteering to go out and buy a replacement carton of milk to leave me worryingly alone with my ex-boyfriend, who instantly dropped his guard the moment Hannah had stepped out of the door.

"Well, this is strange. I'm so happy for you though," I said regardless.

Marty chuckled resentfully. "I don't believe that for a moment. You're furious."

"Surprised maybe, but glad nevertheless" I said, struggling to maintain the illusion that all was well, and smiling extravagantly to sustain it.

"Don't kid yourself. Underneath that smiley exterior you're actually seething – ready to explode in anger – that I'm already dating Hannah instead of serving the statutory sentence required of a grieving, jilted boyfriend, locked up, being miserable in his room."

"All I want is for you both to be happy" I protested.

"You want that about as much as I do. How else could I ever hope to stay in contact with you other than by dating your roommate?" he reasoned.

"No no no!" I vehemently protested. "Marty, what has become of you?" I took his face in my hands like a consoling mother who has only to kiss it to make the boy happy and reasonable again.

"You should know. It's you who made me like this. After all, it's you who created the new me," he berated me, immune to my soothing balm.

"But being rejected, and learning to get over it is part of growing up," I advised him.

"There you go again – talking like a woman twice your age when in fact you're no wiser than the rest of us," he taunted me. "And if you should ever consider revealing my true intentions, just remember, Hannah will never believe you. She will simply assume you've become bitter and twisted through jealousy."

The sound of a key in the door had the instant effect of restoring Marty to a version of his old self, although I could see right through his manufactured façade.

"It's so great to see you guys getting on as friends," said Hannah naively.

Of course I was sorely tempted me to unleash a tirade of truth about what had really passed between us.

Consider this; I was awash in a sea of turmoil I once used to refer to as the apartment, a haven turned hellish what with Marty stalking, Elaine suspecting and Hannah resenting me. For the first time since I had moved in I seriously contemplated finding a new home. My feelings were further heightened by the knowledge that Elaine no longer listened to a single word I said without questioning just about everything I ever proposed. Just like old times in fact, my purpose for being there now totally irrelevant.

CHAPTER FIFTEEN

As a temporary escape I sought sanctuary at work, spending more time at Groucho than was absolutely necessary. Look around any workplace and you will see them, forlorn people sitting at their desks in the twilight hours escaping unhappy marriages, failing relationships, annoying roommates or the agony of isolation in a safe, warm place where getting a salary was almost secondary.

For me too, going to work proved to be a merciful release from the stresses and strains of the apartment. I was always enjoying a momentary feeling of pride tinged with relief upon being waved through by the imposing security guards, reminding me that I belonged to something welcoming, warm and worthwhile. Once inside the gilded cage, I was almost always treated with politeness and respect – by everyone except Kyle of course.

And although I was always scrupulously polite, I began to detect a touch of resentment from Kate, our Senior Producer, who showed signs of becoming increasingly irritated by me as Melissa began bestowing projects upon me that would previously have been hers.

"Have you got a moment?" Kate briskly enquired, summoning me into her no nonsense, businesslike, minimalist office.

"Have I done something wrong?"

"On the contrary, Melissa has a little challenge for you."

Firstly, Kate apologised on behalf of Melissa for her

absence due to a prior commitment in LA, where she was presenting an award at the Women In Media Group.

"Angelo, the new Head of Network, claims to have received information through what we believe are unauthorised sources about our new plans to make a show which doesn't insult the viewers' intelligence."

"How disturbing is that?" I said, sighing.

"We suspect there might be a spy in the camp, and what is worse, Angelo is demanding that we throw your idea out with the trash."

Even without words, my sly smile betrayed my strong suspicion that Kyle was the one to blame.

"Don't even go there," said Kate reading my mind. "Kyle might have his faults, but disloyalty is not one of them."

There they go, television people, all of them wilfully deceived by Kyle, excusing every one of his serious character flaws as if they were nothing more than endearing little quirks you might find in some naughty but ultimately loveable teenage boy.

"If you say so," I said. I should have called the cops when he tried to molest me – that would have put an end to his vicious little games.

"Angelo wants to see Melissa ASAP to find out, in his words, 'what the fuck is going on'."

"Well, whoever this Angelo is, he'll be no match for Melissa."

"That would be true, except she's two and a half

thousand miles away on the coast and won't be back in time, which is where you come in," said Kate. She explained that in her absence Melissa had nominated me – yes, it's that girl again – to be the one to plead their case. Had Melissa taken leave of her senses?

"I know it might seem crazy, asking somebody like you to champion our cause…"

"Gee, thanks," I playfully interrupted her.

"But Melissa is renowned for her insane schemes, and yet 99 times out of 100 they play out brilliantly."

Maybe I would be the one who would fail; in fact, it was inevitable. Her tales of Angelo's incandescent anger and his demands to see a representative of Groucho that very day were producing panic within me. I had so little time to prepare a coherent case for my show on the theme 'Men Who Put Women Down'.

"Speak from the heart but engage your brain," Kate advised me succinctly, "just as you did when you first sold your idea to Melissa."

She made it sound so easy, as she rehearsed me on the main points justifying our new editorial agenda.

"I'll order you a limo. It will make you feel better about yourself."

It would take more than a fancy car to convince me that I had what it took to influence Angelo.

I searched for ways and means to revive my self-belief, eventually falling back on good old anger to fuel my resolve, both emboldened and enraged by Angelo's ruthless response to this ill-informed leak by a cowardly mole. My blood rush of rage, however, soon ran dry, only lasting as far as a one-mile drive down Broadway, my nerve having totally failed me upon reaching Network Centre as I instructed the chauffeur to go one more time around the block. Quite what might have happened had Melissa not called, Dr Phil only knows. She fortified my fragile confidence by assuring me that she would never have nominated me for the task if she had thought for one minute that I wasn't capable of closing a deal.

"Look, you believe in this idea with all your heart and soul, so there is no better person alive than you to sell it," Melissa enthused, inspiring me to believe that I really could persuade this Angelo to go with our plans.

Let me at him, I kind of thought, exuding a brittle brand of confidence as I stepped out of my limo and into the pristine, gleaming entrance hall of the Wolf Network HQ.

"I would like to see Angelo Ramirez," I said to the cool girl behind the desk.

"You mean Angelo Ramirez, the Head of the Wolf Network?" she queried me, as if I could have been referring to another Mr A. Ramirez, you know, the one who worked in the car pool.

"That's the guy. The head honcho. He's expecting me," I confirmed with exaggerated nonchalance.

"So you've got an appointment then?" the cool girl wearily enquired.

"You betcha," I said, rising to the full height delivered by my six-inch heels. "I am here on behalf of Melissa Parker and I should warn you that nobody, but nobody keeps Melissa waiting," I grandly proclaimed. Upon discovering that everything I had declared was true after all, she explained that a member of Angelo's personal staff would come to collect me shortly. She hardly bothered to disguise how happy she would be to hand me over to the care of somebody else.

As promised, within five minutes I was greeted by another identikit, uber-glamorous, super-efficient girl who acknowledged me formally and with as much warmth as an Alaskan winter. We rode the elevator together to the top floor in silence, exiting into a hallowed area where you could positively smell the power. It was populated by an overwhelming preponderance of super-efficient beautiful young women, all of them seriously devoted to making Angelo successful. As I patiently waited, sleek girls sashayed back and forth around me, occasionally firing contemptuous looks at me as if they were part of a gigantic, corporate conspiracy to make me feel as small and worthless as possible. I had to remind myself that I was as tall and eye-catching as they were.

"Will he be much longer?" I enquired of the gatekeeping girl who had overseen my entry to Angelo's offices, after another twenty minutes had elapsed.

"He is aware that you are waiting," she replied. Where did they find these people?

In my head I vowed to wait for only another five minutes, and once my self- imposed deadline had passed I arose from my chair, announcing that I refused to be kept waiting a single second longer. I fooled the smart girls into believing that I was about to quit the building. I watched them relax their guard, adeptly wrongfooting them, and charged directly past the gatekeeping girl to push open the heavy padded door and find myself in the heart of Angelo's office.

And then I stopped dead in my tracks.

"It's you," I said.

I was gazing up in wonder at him, my Latino dark, WASP tall, worldwide handsome man. You know, the stranger at my wedding who'd kissed me? In the intervening years he had become almost unreal to me, but now he looked more real than any supposed figment of the imagination had a right to be.

"What is the meaning of this?" he yelled at me.

It really was him. You know, the guy I told you about, first seen on the day of my wedding. I would have chased after him had I not been restrained by my mother. And thereafter I had visualised him in my thoughts, in my dreams and perhaps real life too. Always near, yet tantalisingly just out of reach. My ideal fantasy man had materialised in front of me. There he was, sitting behind a desk, purporting to be Angelo Ramirez, Head of the Wolf Network – and he didn't look a day older than on my wedding day either – and so unlikely to slip away, although my continued presence in his office was more under threat.

"I wish I knew. It's extremely hard to explain. Just something that has haunted me all of my life."

"Alert security," he shouted into the intercom. "There's a mad girl in my office."

"Sorry! Sorry! Sorry!" cried the gatekeeping girl, as she rushed in to attempt to rescue him from my unexpected invasion.

"Get your hands off me, right now," I demanded. "I'm here on behalf of Melissa, and nobody is going to throw Melissa out of the office." My absurd declaration elicited just a trace of a smile from Angelo.

"Let her stay," he decreed, and the gatekeeping girl reluctantly released her grip on me. "And stand down security. She's harmless."

"Harmless? I don't do harmless!" I raged at him.

"I only meant to assert that you are unlikely to murder me, unless of course Melissa has resorted to hiring beautiful female assassins, which I seriously doubt, considering her inclination to hold the human race in such high esteem."

He could have been reciting the New York Metropolitan Area Telephone Book for all I knew. His super seductive voice was transporting me to a tropical beach where we lay entwined together against the backdrop of an azure blue sea. However, I had a job to do.

"So, shoot", he commanded me.

"Well, it was you who demanded to see me."

"I don't recall requesting you in person. I was hoping to get Melissa. I guess I'll have to make do with Melissa's little helper instead." My anger at this was only marginally less strong than my desire for him.

"It is my duty to instruct you that you are entirely wrong in your opinion of our forthcoming show, Men Who Put Women Down. And therefore you must allow this show to proceed without interference."

"You're shitting me."

"Oh pur*lease*."

"I haven't got time for politeness," he cautioned me. "Especially when some mouthy young broad manages to get inside Melissa's head, filling it with garbage, and by so doing, jeopardizes jobs and threatens the existence of what once used to be this Network's top talk show."

I bit my lip so hard it nearly drew blood.

"Quality and popularity don't have to be mutually exclusive you know," I proclaimed. His chair vibrated to the sound if his own laughter.

"What grown-up words from one so young," he taunted me.

"Thank you so much for patronising me."

"Anytime. So how will this show work?" he asked.

"One of our very best producers is already on the case." He gave a knowing smile. "We'll shine a light on men who, knowingly or unknowingly, hold women back by underestimating or undermining them, and then confront the guys who bring them down and challenge them to change their ways. It'll be dynamite."

"As pitches go, not bad for a piece of eye candy," he continued, undeterred by my extravagant head shaking, "delivered to me perfectly gift wrapped by Melissa, who knows exactly what I like. She was hoping to distract me from what I have to do, and that's to kick this idea into the back row of the bleachers."

Boy, how I hated and despised and desired and lusted after him all at the same time, but not necessarily in that order.

He awaited my reply, but I rode the silence, pausing long enough to scrutinise him forensically. He certainly looked like the guy I'd kissed at my wedding and had fantasised about ever since, so much so that I'd began to think he was imaginary.

Whatever, I refused to speak first.

Oooh! Was that a spark of recognition? Or was I simply imagining it?

"As managing director of a multi-million dollar broadcasting empire" – Aha, he spoke first, fifteen love to me – "it is my job to deliver the largest possible audience, in order to attract the wealthiest blue chip companies to buy advertising time, thereby maximising profits and producing huge dividends for our shareholders. You dig?"

Maybe I was out of my depth there. Angelo was making no allowances whatsoever for my perceived youth or my actual inexperience in network economics. I think I preferred being patronised to emerging from the rubble of my collapsed arguments blinking in the sunlight, having been buried alive under the weight of Angelo's rhetoric, yet ready to confront him once more.

"Whatever you may have heard from your well-placed insider," I goaded him, "the last thing on our mind is to reduce the popularity of our show, not even by one person. On the contrary, by making it relevant to the lives of our viewers we can build on the foundation of our existing loyal audience by adding wealthier, more upmarket viewers, drawn in by a better quality show. That will impress both your advertisers and shareholders alike."

"You're good, surprisingly good. I can see why Melissa sent you to do her dirty work."

I hated myself for enjoying his praise.

"So go ahead and make your show, see if I care. But only on one condition," he challenged me.

"And that is?" I said scenting victory.

"That you will join me for dinner."

"Then you will have to eat alone," I said, refusing to believe that I had just declined an offer so exhilarating it should have sent me dancing into the street.

What the Jay Leno was I playing at? I had won a famous victory on behalf of Melissa and then rejected a date with Mr Impossibly Gorgeous himself. Maybe I just couldn't cope with that much happiness in my life.

"So be it. Meeting terminated at 13.14," he voiced into a Dictaphone, brutally ending our conversation like a slap in the face.

You've messed up again Jennifer, I thought, reflecting on my latest double whammy of despair, having only bad news to relay to Melissa whilst screwing up big time on the chance to date a guy I had been longing for throughout almost my entire adult life.

"Whoa! Stop right there. So what am I supposed to tell Melissa?" I said, just about remembering my one true reason for being there.

"Tell her she should only employ people who have the grace to accept an invitation in the spirit it was intended."

"And the show?"

"Men Who Put Women Down? Well just to prove I'm not one of those guys, do it anyway," he said, a smile surfacing ruefully upon his so-kissable lips.

And that made it doubly annoying. I'd turned down a date for no reason at all, yet it was mission accomplished for Melissa. OK, so what if I had seriously considered suggesting that he should re-issue his invitation to escort me to dinner?

While I still had a speck of self-respect left I acknowledged his business like shake of the hand, kissed him on the cheek and ran away.

CHAPTER SIXTEEN

"Awesome", said Kate when I returned as the homecoming heroine to Groucho Productions, although in all honesty I thought her congratulations came over as a little manufactured.

"I only did as you advised me," I said, trying so hard not to monopolise all of the praise.

"I guess I'll leave network politics to Melissa in future," I said.

And how I would have liked to have wiped the smirk off Kyle's face. He had already drawn his own base conclusions as to what it was about me that had led Angelo to change his mind.

"Was he super scary?" a young female intern enquired, evidently intrigued by the thought of so much power packed into Angelo's admirably-toned body and razor-sharp mind.

I chose my words carefully, hypersensitive about not wanting to betray the slightest suggestion of anything other than professional interest in this new Head of Network, and painfully aware that Kyle was waiting to pounce and misinterpret everything I said.

Oh, just your typical control freak, mesmerised by his own imagined brilliance, unused to being challenged yet intrigued that anyone should be crazy enough to question his supposed genius – that's what I should have said.

"Highly professional. A man who knows his own mind, yet is willing to listen to alternative opinions", I in fact replied.

"I think we can safely assume that it wasn't your intellect which persuaded him to change his mind," Kyle sneeringly observed.

"Thank you Kyle for comprehensively proving that being a bitch is not the sole prerogative of the female sex," I gave it to him, both barrels blazing.

Yet still he came back for more, like one of those apparently dead serial killers at the end of scary movies who just refuse to lie down and die.

"Negotiation is a matter of give and take," he said, adopting a misleadingly measured tone. "So what did you have to give up in return for Angelo backing your project?"

Nothing I didn't want to surrender, I mischievously thought.

"I gave him you, Kyle, and your brilliant production skills," I actually said, "which are guaranteed to make 'Men Who Put Women Down' a truly first class show."

The only event capable of silencing Kyle – a call from Melissa – ensured that he ground to an ungainly halt, while the American Icon showered me with superlatives, and in turn I thanked Melissa for having such an extraordinary level of faith in me. It was as if she had seen something in me that I didn't know I had myself.

I had no other alternative but to embrace this praise, more used to being taken for granted than being singled out for compliments. I do have to confess to experiencing relief when Melissa finally moved on to future projects, her voice adopting a more brisk and businesslike tone. She pointedly reminded me that the stakes were even higher now that Angelo had given the go ahead for the show.

"Maybe he's just given us enough rope to hang ourselves," she ominously speculated. "Failure will not be an option when we tape Men Who Put Women Down".

"No pressure then," I joked feebly.

"There's always pressure. It only ends when you're dead."

Melissa then confirmed that she would be back in the office the next day to discuss the choreography of our joint presentation.

After Kate had initially got the ball rolling with a gruelling hour-long session defining my on-screen relationship with Melissa, I was instructed to submit to some intensive retail therapy to be administered by Posy, the eccentric-looking Costume Designer who had been briefed to create a distinctive new image that would impress but not threaten Melissa's army of female fans.

Just picture that iconic scene from *Pretty Woman* when

Richard Gere takes Julia Roberts shopping in a designer boutique, orchestrating the assistants to cater for her every whim – well I had become Julia, while Posy adopted the Gere role, confidently whipping the staff into shape. I watched her issuing commands as assistants sprinted backwards and forwards laden down with a never-ending flow of designer creations, while departmental managers stood in line to have their respective labels adorned all over me, purely because I was destined to appear on a top-rated network television show. How could I not feel special having so much attention lavished upon me? The only comparable experience in my retail history had been being wedding shopping for something white and made of netting which had the effect of making me look like a giant meringue.

Contrary to what her appearance might suggest, Posy had surprisingly good taste, and as you would expect she had a keen and experienced eye for what worked well on television.

"I want you to represent the best of New York fashion today", she explained to me. "I'm talking a little bit hip while incorporating an older Oscar de la Renta kind of style to keep you accessible."

She strove to find me the clothes which would make me appear smart and in control while not so high fashion or high-powered business woman that I would alienate a housewife in Oklahoma.

"Melissa is very brave agreeing to appear alongside you," said Posy in between me trying on a succession of outfits, I suppose alluding to my perceived youth and beauty.

"Nobody could ever upstage Melissa. I must never get too big for my Jimmy Choos," I intoned reverentially.

We shopped until Posy dropped me back at the office where I checked my emails, a routine task, had it not been for a startling arrival in my inbox, screaming at me to click open. It read: *So you won't join me for dinner. Then would you at least consider a purely professional engagement and accompany me to a film premiere, which is something I have to do? It's my job. Strictly business, no pleasure whatsoever. Be there, Angelo.*

How I regretted my impetuous high-handedness in turning down his invitation to dinner in the first place. So here was my second chance - everybody deserves one after all – and maybe being with Angelo was where my destiny lay – the next, the final and the ultimate reason why I had been sent there, especially now that I had completed my mission of liberating Elaine from her honey trap hell.

Just as I had been given a second chance in my new life, Angelo had given me a second chance too. He could easily have thrown his executive toys out of the pram after I'd declined his invitation. Yet there he still was, continuing to consider me, finding time within his busy schedule to ask me out again. Thank heavens I'd kissed him in his office. Not so impetuous and stupid after all.

I struggled to find words which might not appear too

willing, in a style that was casual bordering on laid back. Never had being relaxed been so stressful.

If I must… I prepared to click reply, then thought better of it.

Never mix business with pleasure, I'd heard people say. So, of course I ought to inform Melissa first that I was about to go on a date with the man who held our business future in his hands. I would keep Melissa in the loop, regardless that everyone has a right to a private, personal life.

I'll sleep on it was the reply I eventually sent to Angelo. Hardly a romantic statement of intent, I admit. In spite of his onerous responsibilities at the Wolf Network Headquarters his reply took less than a minute to arrive, exuding irritation. Unused to being kept waiting, I guess.

I need an answer pretty darn quick so I can get security clearance in time for the upcoming deadline. Hesitation isn't for the likes of us, he wrote.

How I wished I had somebody to talk to, a friend who would listen to my dilemma and maybe offer advice. Sometimes, in spite of being surrounded by an array of fabulous people, I felt like the loneliest person on earth. I could hardly open up about Angelo to Elaine. When the opportunity came for me to inform Melissa of my invitation to attend the Premiere with him, my courage deserted me. Yet still Angelo continued to pursue me for an answer, his latest reminder an exquisitely-wrapped package, exciting the interest of the girls who sat behind the Groucho reception.

You see, ever since word had spread of my Davina versus Goliath triumph at Network HQ, interest in me among Groucho staff had grown somewhat embarrassingly. Every aspect of my life had become a matter of intense interest, as if I were a celebrity already.

So, I suppose there was a certain amount of inevitability that a package addressed for the attention of Ms Jennifer Gold would arouse heightened interest, especially when the name Armani was identified on the wrapper, bestowing iconic status upon it. In contrast, I couldn't have been less enthused, greeting the parcel like an unwelcome visitor, wanting to hide, just wishing it would go away.

"You are going to open it?" Posy posed. Her fashion radar could unerringly detect a designer label at distance.

"I never open packages I haven't ordered", I said, washing my hands of the offending article.

"I wonder who it could be from?" Posy speculated.

"Mark it return to sender," I decreed.

Posy's face dropped faster than the Stock Market after the collapse of Lehman Brothers. I didn't want to become one of those impossible prima donnas who make everybody around them suffer for their art while claiming all the good times and the glory for themselves – especially as I had yet to achieve anything at all, assuming I ever would.

"Open it if you want," I said casually.

"If you say so," said Posy affecting a tone of mock

weary indifference before discovering a handwritten note composed by Angelo inside.

God was showing off when he made you, Angelo had written in his spidery, untidy hand. *I hope this dress will do his work justice when you wear it to the premiere of Ravishing starring Brad Pitt and Angelina Jolie at Radio City on Thursday night.*

"Who does this man think is?" I fumed. I examined the dress as I would a dead dog. "Even if I were to accept, there's no way I would be able to squeeze into this." I was momentarily forgetting the shape I was now in. Posy lowered her head and averted her gaze in response.

"Trust me. I'm a designer. It will fit," Posy confessed. "His PA called requesting your measurements. I complied with his request. What else was I supposed to do?"

"But that's confidential information. How could you be so indiscreet?" I raged, reducing Posy to tears as she took flight to the rest room.

In Posy's absence I examined the dress in forensic detail. I was at first shocked and then seduced by this black floor-length Armani Privé gown which plunged almost to the navel at the front and scooped outrageously low at the back. It would take a far braver woman than me to face the world in that, yet the dress thought otherwise. It was screaming at me 'wear me, wear me, wear me!' Could I be that easily tempted by Angelo's bribes while dispensing with modesty too? Or was I just being annoyingly precious, as befitted my new status as a talk show presenter?

In turmoil I sought out Posy, who I discovered by a mirror in the ladies restroom, wiping away mascara from her tear-stained eyes. I wrapped my arm around her shoulder and expressed my sincere regret for my outburst, with Posy offering her remorse in return.

"It is such an amazing dress though," Posy added in mitigation.

"Is it? I hadn't even noticed," I said, smiling. "I suppose I could try it on when I get home – if there's nothing on TV. Which doesn't of course imply that I'm weakening or succumbing to that presumptuous man's charms in any way whatsoever."

"Obviously not" Posy replied.

Her eyes twinkled mischievously as she urged me to robe up without further delay under the expert supervision of the person she described as my Costume Consultant in the privacy of the Groucho dressing rooms. I duly obliged – well, what else could I do? – it was my duty to cheer the girl up. I underwent nearly as radical a transformation as I had experienced under the guidance of the hobo. It certainly felt as if a new layer of skin had gloriously enveloped me. It was even more shiny, silky and smooth than the previous one, re-energising me as I gazed at my reflection which radiated a provocative sensuality, appearing resplendent in my jaw-dropping gown.

"Ta da!" I sang to accompany my grand entrance while Posy, who thought she had seen it all before, was forced to think again.

"Senfuckingsational," she declared, "although it needs taking in a little around the waist." Her professional instincts began to resurface.

"It doesn't leave too much to the imagination," I said warily. "I could never be seen in public wearing something this daring."

"If you've got it…" said Posy, challenging me while miming the shape of an impossibly curvaceous woman to emphasise the point… "or shall I send it back?"

"Now let's think this thing through," I cautioned her. "OK, so I do need a dress worthy of the red carpet – assuming I accept Angelo's invitation anyway – although there's no way I'm going to reveal that much flesh, so prepare to make alterations, Posy".

"Assuming you go."

"Assume I will."

However, I never quite got round to telling Melissa. Surely she wouldn't want to be distracted by the trivial fine details of my personal life when a momentous show lay ahead of her. It wasn't the right time to be filling her head with such nonsense, was it? She wouldn't thank me for raising the issue of my date with Angelo, would she?

***

"I will ask the questions that matter, bringing you in for opinions only when I cue you," said Melissa, laying down the ground rules at our programme planning meeting in a manner which defied contradiction. “If you feel the need to interrupt, fight it!” she commanded me, reminding me of a mighty lioness marking out her territory. “Never forget that I’m in charge. The audience expect it of me and I will look most unfavourably upon you talking over my links, comments and questions.”

So this was the iron fist inside the velvet glove, a side of Melissa rarely seen by her adoring public yet widely suspected. Underneath her warm and welcoming exterior there lay a ruthless, driven woman.

As if that wasn’t terrifying enough, along came Kyle, detailing the case history of the control freaks he had lined up both to grace and deface the show. I can’t deny that I was mightily impressed with Kyle’s work in assembling a rogue’s gallery of apparently hateful men who had incredibly agreed to air their faults in front of ten million viewers, such was the lure of being on TV. Melissa, meanwhile, proved to be considerably more critical than me, turning Kyle’s running order upside down and decreeing among other things that the guy who dictates what his girlfriend wears would be allocated another two minutes, that the sexist boss who only promotes male colleagues should be relegated to item two and that the rich businessman who objects to his wife pursuing a career would be promoted to lead the show.

If Kyle had been hurt by the deconstruction of his perfect running order by Melissa then he certainly didn’t show it, except by venting his frustration on me.

"Is there anything you would like to change?" he asked of me, his tone noticeably less friendly than when enquiring of Melissa.

"I'll just go with the flow," I reassured him. "I reckon Melissa's got it just right."

When the day of the show finally dawned I awoke experiencing a curious mixture of eager-eyed anticipation and blind terror at the prospect of what lay ahead. I positively shuddered upon entering the television studio where only weeks earlier I had spoken as a carefree, if impassioned, member of the audience. I sat nervously in wait, so far out of my comfort zone I might as well have been in North Korea.

Even after a heavenly session of divine pampering from no less a person than award winning make-up artiste Charmaine Clemente, I remained resolutely unrelaxed.

"Chill out girl, you're making me nervous!" said Melissa.

"I'm trying really hard to get relaxed," I explained apologetically. "There's so much to take in. I feel like my head is about to explode." I flicked through my reams of notes.

"Let your mind go empty," Melissa intoned, coaxing me towards a state of karma. "And put those notes down and trust your instincts instead."

Easy for her to say, and besides, my nerves were so shot to pieces that I doubted I had any functioning instincts left. The more I tried to remain calm the more stressed I became, an ever-increasing vicious circle that would surely culminate in me suffering a complete on air nervous breakdown. Even Barbara Boulay would be preferable to a gibbering wreck.

"If you think you're nervous you should have seen me on my first-ever show," Melissa confided in me. "We used to go live in those days, so as I prepared to read my opening script I wasn't sure whether I would speak or hurl."

So Melissa was human after all, although my nerves still held sway.

"God, I could murder a drink," I admitted.

"And that's a feeling I get every day of my life," Melissa confessed. "I just take a slug of sparkling mineral water and dream that I'm drinking champagne."

Inspired by her honesty and restored by her soothing tones, I fell under the influence of Charmaine's healing hands, and as she deftly massaged Clarins moisturiser into my cheeks I actually managed to close my eyes and allow my thoughts to wander, recalling my earlier bright idea which had miraculously illuminated a whole new reason for me being there – my destiny – to present a national television show, spreading the word about such good old-fashioned values as forgiveness, fairness and taking responsibility. Suddenly, the realisation that presenting on Melissa was also meant to be gave me the confidence I needed to handle this daunting challenge. It was my new destiny, and not even

Kyle could undermine me as he knocked ferociously on the door, mangling our mellow mood by marching in without waiting for permission while issuing instructions to his studio director through his clip mike.

"Yes, they're nearly done," he informed his colleague, although the two of us were far from the finished article.

"How are we doing?" he enquired.

"We were doing just fine until you crashed in," Melissa blasted him. Kyle was more concerned with listening to the voices in his headphones. "Here are your last minute instructions," he announced regardless, handing me a folio of paper containing densely-printed notes.

"Give me those!" Melissa barked at him, snatching them and throwing them disdainfully into the nearest garbage bin.

"Everything we need is up here," said Melissa, pointedly tapping my forehead, spurring me on to believe I could succeed.

"Let's make television!" said Melissa. She removed the protective cape from her shoulders with a matador's flourish, outlining how she would have a brief talk with the studio audience before introducing me to the already hyped up crowd. And no sooner had she advised me to be "ready in five", than she was gone, a roar of appreciation perceptible in the distance as she once again connected with her adoring fans.

They shouldn't have left me alone. I was devising a

route to escape the building and become an agony aunt on the run. Yet Melissa had shown such faith in me. How could I possibly desert her now?

Successfully suppressing my instinct to take flight I joined her in the studio as instructed, marvelling as I stood in the wings at the star's consummate ability to coax, cajole and flirt with the studio audience, adeptly bring them to the boil and then let them simmer in a prolonged stew of excitement.

"You'll never be as good as Melissa," Kyle whispered into my ear, having slithered unexpectedly alongside me.

"And you will never get to have sex with me," I punched back.

In spite of feeling a little ashamed by my outburst I managed to savour the discomfort it produced in him. In fact I relished it so much that I missed the big introduction from Melissa and my cue to join her on set.

"She's playing hard to get," Melissa repeated, a hint of irritation discernible in her delivery.

"As I said earlier, she's an old head on young shoulders. Please welcome – once again – our new People Person, Jennifer Gold."

Sensory overload verging on total shutdown threatening to overwhelm me, I stepped out into the illuminated bear pit, bedazzled by lights and disorientated by applause, the audience greeting me as if I was somebody who mattered, their welcome reverberating in my head.

I waved and smiled, walking along the bank of cheering spectators in true First Lady style until I saw Marty and Hannah grinning disturbingly down on me.

"Hi guys. Enjoy", I mouthed, simultaneously thinking 'who the hell let them in?' I blew kisses to Melissa's disciples, eager to be accepted by the devoted followers of the Chat Show Queen.

"Silence in the studio. Ready to record," Kyle growled threateningly, always ready to cut me down to size whenever the opportunity presented itself.

When I heard the familiar theme tune it was as if I had just stepped on board a runaway train. I was terrified how the journey might end, yet knew that it was impossible to get off.

I became mesmerised by the crowd clapping in time chanting 'Yo Melly Go!' with pseudo-religious fervour and rising as one to acclaim Melissa as she gave herself to her fans, holding her arms out wide to symbolise a global group hug.

"Are you feeling good?" she half said, half sang in the style of a red hot soul diva.

"You betcha," they yelled back at her in the agreed manner, experiencing ecstasy simply by being in her presence.

"Well not for much longer," Melissa howled, because today you are about to meet Men Who Put Women Down."

Howls of protest rained down from the bleachers as I sat there in a trance, wearing an all-purpose smile, modifying my expression as required by shadowing Melissa's responses without really understanding them.

Subconsciously I could just about grasp something of the plight of Ellen Chernow, a middle-aged housewife married to a successful businessman who was accused of neglecting her while developing a flourishing chain of egg-based fast food restaurants. With Melissa prompting her expertly, Ellen cautiously recounted what she considered to be her tale of woe, failing at first to gain the sympathy of those listening who judged her to be just another stereotypical rich, desperate housewife.

"You've gotten a fabulous lifestyle and a husband who works night and day to keep you in the manner to which you have obviously become accustomed, so tell me, what's your problem?"

"He makes me feel like I don't know who I am," I distinctly heard her say.

The crowd in the studio were however unmoved. They were yet to be convinced that they should waste any of their sympathy – a precious commodity at the best of times – on this pampered woman, and warmly welcomed her husband Joe instead as he entered to make his case.

"What more could I have done?" he pleaded, endearing himself to them further. "If working all the hours God sends to provide Ellen with a dream home, fabulous holidays in exotic places, and a walk in wardrobe full of designer clothes is a crime, then arrest me 'cos I'm guilty as charged!"

Even in my withdrawn mental state I ached to intervene, resisting nevertheless.

And I soon became aware that we had become becalmed in a commercial break. Melissa was leaning forward to give me advance warning that she would shortly be calling upon me to voice my opinions once the show had resumed. I replayed Melissa's charming little anecdote about not being sure whether she would speak or hurl. Now I knew exactly how she felt.

"Are you OK?" Melissa enquired of me, I guess understandably perturbed by my faraway demeanour.

"I'm fine," I intoned flatly, presumably doing little to put her mind at rest.

"Time to welcome my new People Person," she declared, hoping to waken me from my self-induced trance, if only I hadn't been stuck on pause.

I could see Melissa staring at me, encouraging me, urging me on, begging me to say something, anything, which would justify her absurd idea that she could take a girl out of the bleachers and turn her into a TV star. And then I spoke.

"Things are not always what they seem," I began in unnaturally hushed tones, "nice, shiny surfaces can be deceptive, a façade designed to deceive and distract from something rotten festering underneath," I continued building inexorably to a crescendo, the guy now clearly in my sights. "You are guilty as charged, guilty of cruelty by neglect."

You can imagine, it was as if I had unleashed wild dogs in the studio. The husband was complaining, demanding an apology or he would walk out. The crowd was booing, threatening to revolt by storming the set. Even Melissa was losing her cool and signalling for me to pull back. But amid the mayhem I continued regardless.

"I'm not saying you're a bad man - quite the opposite, in fact. Your problem is that you measure your love for your wife by the amount of material possessions you lavish upon her, yet I suspect give her little of yourself. Am I right?"

His silence confirmed my point.

"Perhaps without realising it, you have drained your wife of her personality, and having done so, you are tired of this empty shell." Even Ellen was flinching at my unflattering description of her.

I uncomfortably realised I could have been talking as much about my old self as I was about Ellen. *Get a grip*, I cautioned myself. *It isn't all about me.*

"And it's not all about him, Ellen. You have to rediscover the woman you once used to be, the one he used to be in love with. And then he will come back to you. Trust me, in time, he will. But until he does, get out there and do stuff like learning to paint water colours, reading

Madame Bovary or enrolling for salsa lessons, where you can dance with hot young guys – and who knows where that might lead!"

The audience whooped suggestively.

"I deeply resent that. I didn't come here to be humiliated," railed Joe the husband.

"Don't let your anger towards me become the issue," I cautioned him. "Why not woo her like when you were young? Just maybe, she will fall for you all over again, and once more forsake all others."

"Let's take a break, I think we all need one," said Melissa, clearly troubled by the show so far.

"Easy, girl" she whispered into my ear. "What are you trying to do? Incite a riot?"

"No, just tell the truth," I replied.

"And perhaps stir things up a little too," she speculated, which I confirmed with a smile.

Back came the music – Let me at 'em, I whispered under my breath. I was really getting into the swing of this television thing, ready to take on Iran if it thought it was hard enough. Instead, a bigoted male boss was thrown to the wolves, accused by two of his female ex-employees of refusing to promote women to positions of real responsibility, always preferring to appoint a man to a senior position, even when a better, more highly qualified woman had applied for the post. He shamelessly defended himself by detailing what he considered to be women's inherent deficiencies by quoting such perceived flaws as being either over emotional or horribly bitchy, an inability to concentrate on one thing at a time, a tendency to abandon the office without warning to look after their sick children and above all, an unfortunate predisposition to pregnancy.

As I'm sure you can appreciate, these accusations only succeeded in unleashing uproar, further inflamed by one foolishly brave guy in the bleachers who testified that women in the workplace were more trouble than they were worth and that never in a million years would he agree to be subservient to a female employer.

With the studio ready to erupt, instead of further fanning the flames of debate I decided to build a bridge over troubled water by calmly citing other traditionally female character traits such as diligence, co-operation, multi-tasking, advanced social skills and high emotional intelligence.

"What boss in his right mind wouldn't want those attributes in the modern workplace?" I challenged the boss, to near universal acclaim.

"Well, when you put it like that," he said, slowly surrendering to my charm offensive. His repentance even engendered a trickle of sympathetic applause as the audience welcomed a perceived sinner back to the path of righteousness.

"So do the right thing," I urged him – could that become my new catchphrase as a presenter on TV? – "And if you faithfully promise that next time you advertise for a new employee you agree to give applicants a fair and equal chance, I hereby promise to give you a long and lingering hug."

"I don't mind if I do," he exclaimed.

I unfurled my arms invitingly, nowhere near able to encompass his considerable girth whereas he enveloped me with ease. If you'd ever had the misfortune to be embraced by a rather moth-eaten, sweaty old bear then you would have appreciated exactly what I was going through, self-inflicted though it may have been.

"Hey, he likes you," I heard Melissa exclaim from outside the bear hug.

"You'd never believe how much," I replied, rolling my eyes.

"Too much information. Let's take a break," Melissa announced, and as soon as the cameras stopped rolling the boss was prised from our embrace – what a relief. The things I do for television, I reflected.

Next on the agenda was a needlessly jealous guy who stridently objected to his sexy, vivacious girlfriend wearing clothes which in his opinion "left nothing to the imagination" and created what he claimed was excessive attention towards her eye-catching, hourglass figure.

I felt the wind in my sails. Or was I sailing too close to the wind? The production team and Melissa were on the edges of their seats in anticipation and dread of what I was going to say next.

"When you're in love with a beautiful woman, it's hard," I said reciting the words of an old Doctor Hook song, far too ancient, I guess, for a girl of my age to be quoting.

"So you secretly suspect she might actually enjoy turning a few heads as she goes about her daily life? Too right she does, cos she's a woman. It's in her job description, and there's one person above all she wants to impress, and that person is herself."

"Where the hell is this going?" Kyle grumbled into my earpiece.

"So what to do?" I continued unabashed. "Be proud that she's hot and don't hate but celebrate every guy who eyes her, who eyes her lovingly, because unlike any of those poor losers, she's going home with you. How great is that?"

"Awesome," said Melissa, a view later shared by Angelo, who had been watching on a special feed at Wolf Network HQ – I would have died had I known – recognising what he described as my raw talent and predicting success, provided I submitted to his expert guidance. In his dreams!

At the end of the show even Kyle was forced to concede that I hadn't been a total disaster – high praise indeed – although he still found cause to criticise numerous aspects of my performance at the post-show discussion, where Melissa and the team gathered around the imposing rectangular table to dissect the show into its constituent parts.

"I so wanted to hurl when you grabbed hold of that big, sweaty boss," he bleated. "And imagine suggesting infidelity as a solution to a failing marriage. How 1980s was that?"

I suppose he could have accused me of being sensational too, the very last thing I had wanted to be, apart from boring.

"It wasn't meant to be taken literally," I patiently explained. "I did it to shock the guy out of his complacency, a way of announcing that it was time for him to wake up and smell the coffee."

"That's smart, although you had me fooled for a moment," Melissa decreed. "So, let's talk turkey." She escorted me into her office with a maternal arm draped around my shoulder. It was there that America's Number One Talk Show Host informed me that she wanted me to become her People Person for at least another ten shows, on a weekly basis, and that "Your people should speak to my people without further delay."

"A star is born," said Posy as she popped her head around my dressing room door in the afterglow of the show. "Can I borrow two minutes of your precious time?"

"A minute and counting" I said, pretending to be grand. "And what the hell is that?" I enquired, the smile rapidly disappearing from my face as Posy placed a shiny black box reverently upon a table in front of her.

"Cartier," said Posy, as fondly as Homer Simpson pronounces the word 'doughnuts'.

"It's him, isn't it?" I speculated, correctly. "He really does thing he can buy me. I don't think so," I said turning my back on the offending object with a show of exaggerated distaste.

Posy shrugged her shoulders in dismay that I, Melissa's very own People Person, could dispense such terrible advice to myself.

"Go on. Open the box. You know you want to," Posy teased me mercilessly.

"Haven't you got some clothes to iron?" I taunted her back.

"It may not be my place to say…"

"Well, don't say it then!"

"But I think he's behaving impeccably."

"Is that so?"

"Having invited you to a movie premiere where you will be expected to dress, how shall I say, expensively, he is simply enabling you – thanks to his great wealth – to look like a million dollars."

"That's a very generous interpretation."

"So, if you hate him that much, then by all means, pass him on to me."

"Hands off," I said finally getting real.

Reluctantly, I admitted to myself that I yearned for Angelo unconditionally, and my guilt at receiving expensive, unsolicited gifts began to recede.

"Omigod! Omigod! Omigod!" I heard Posy exclaiming

upon opening the box, bedazzled by the beauty of the exquisite diamond pendant and the matching *caresse d'orchidées par Cartier* diamond stud earrings.

I tried so hard to be unimpressed, only to fail miserably again.

CHAPTER SEVENTEEN

"I slept with my daughter's boyfriend. How gross is that?" said Elaine recounting Kyle's most recent idea for Melissa's show. You can imagine how squeamish I felt at the mention of it.

"Can you hear that?" I said cupping my ear. " It's the sound of barrels being scraped."

Elaine didn't quite get it, like so much of our relationship these days, which had lost its easy-going natural flow. Our misunderstandings were creating undercurrents of mild irritation between us – and that was on a good day. It was as if I had become her 'frenemy'. I had been sensing unease between us ever since the honey trap hit on Brad, unsurprising when you also consider the way I had upstaged her television career, truly the last thing I had ever intended.

We met at our favourite Italian restaurant, Is The Pope Catholic?, in a last-gasp effort to breathe new life into our ailing relationship. Our first course consisted of forced compliments to one another which left a bitter taste of having bypassed the heart. And when I made a complimentary remark in passing about the desirability of the guy who waited on our table, Elaine reacted by condemning all Italian waiters outright, arguing that they were only ever after one thing, and were none too discriminatory about who they got it from.

"So unfair," I condemned her. "It's not just Italians, or waiters for that matter, who are slaves to their hormones. And there's plenty of women too."

"Some more than others."

Was that a veiled reference to my honey trap hit on Brad? She'd already implied I was a whore.

"So have you seen Jennifer Aniston's new hairstyle? If that isn't making a statement to Brad Pitt, then I don't know what is."

"He can't even look you in the eye," said Elaine.

"Pardon me?"

"I'm talking about Brad, my Brad. It's like he's got something to hide."

Things were being said that would have been best left unsaid, and an unexpected appearance by Hannah did little to help defuse the situation. If anything, her presence proved incendiary.

"So do I sense an atmosphere?" said Hannah unhelpfully, inadvertently launching the question, which should never have been asked.

"Did you or did you not sleep with Brad?" Elaine demanded of me.

How the Piers Morgan did I answer that? It was deeply disturbing for me while Hannah was shocked to her English core. I watched her painfully recall that distressing Sunday morning when she had walked in on Brad and me in bed together, vowing to reveal all.

I was trapped in a prison of my own making, having no means of escape and being painfully aware that should I deny Elaine's allegation, Hannah was conveniently on hand to re-arrest me with truth.

"Yes, I slept with him, but not in the way you might imagine," I confessed.

I would have explained further, but I was drowned out by an angry cacophony as Elaine stormed out in disgust.

"Slave to our hormones!" she yelled at me from across the restaurant, "and you lady, are the greatest slave of them all."

It was just like old times at home in Valley Stream – Elaine bawling at me, me wanting to cry, except this time it was so much more catastrophic with utterly insurmountable issues tearing us apart, and no family ties to bind us in pursuit of an eventual reconciliation. And if that wasn't emotionally disastrous enough, a traumatised Hannah, having surveyed our table, laid waste by Elaine's distressing departure, earnestly assured me that she hadn't disclosed anything whatsoever about that Sunday morning in the apartment. In the midst of so much mayhem, I was truly touched by her concern and willingly accepted her explanation, so much so that I felt compelled to help her in return.

How could I not? To let her carry on thinking that Marty had genuine feelings for her would have been as good as making me an accomplice to his twisted plan. With that in mind I concluded that I must furnish Hannah with the inconvenient truth about how Marty was using her, as a friend in possession of disagreeable information is bound to do.

"You see, he's got this warped idea that by dating you, he can somehow get back together with me," I helpfully informed Hannah. She reacted as if I had just thrown a pitcher of pee in her face.

"I would never have believed you could stoop so low, inventing such a wicked story just so you can get your hands back on Marty again. Slave to your hormones indeed!" Hannah too stepped stridently outside.

Two down, none to go. If the road to hell was paved with good intentions then I was that well-intentioned, hell-bound driver, left cruelly rejected and utterly alone.

"I should have stayed in and washed my hair," I wearily commented to Silvio, the handsome waiter fussing around me. Judging by his demeanour, he would have been only too happy to be a head and shoulder for me to cry on. I opted for my own company, taking refuge in a bottle of Frascati and demolishing it, like my friendships, in a matter of minutes.

"I'm moving out," I later slurred to Silvio when he presented me with the check.

"So perhaps you like to live with me?" he mischievously suggested.

"Truly, I don't think I'm a living with other people kind of girl. I vant to be alone," I said, imitating Garbo.

★★★

Somehow I still had to live with these people who now, without exception, resented the very air I breathed. The best we could manage was to tolerate one another, while all my attempts at reconciliation with Elaine were rejected out of hand. It had the atmosphere of an uneasy standoff between two warring parties, me on one side, confronted and outnumbered by Elaine, and Hannah and more often than not Brad, on the other.

For me, it had become an intolerable place to live. Escape became my overarching priority, my mission to guide Elaine now beyond repair. I was forever being blanked by my hostile roommates, who practised malign indifference against me. I would have preferred it had they simply told me to pack my bags and get the hell out of there instead of incessantly grinding me down, making me feel worse than worthless. And I could have soldiered on having lost the respect and affection of both Brad and Hannah, but to be cut off by Elaine after we had become closer than I would ever have believed possible hit me horrendously hard.

So much for my supposed reason for being there, to

protect and point Elaine in the right direction as she confronted life's problems. If that really was my purpose, then boy had I screwed up. Maybe mothers and daughters can't be friends after all, at least not in the way girls of the same age can share clothes, exchange intimacies and go out on the town together. It seems obvious now, but motherhood is so much more complicated than that. I had been deluding myself that I could be both mentor and friend to Elaine.

Boy, how I yearned for a friend to listen to my tale of woe. And just when I couldn't have felt more isolated or lonely, out of the blue an email arrived in my inbox from a total stranger called Bonnie Knox. And to think, I nearly deleted it without reading.

I've got my finger on the pulse, it read, *and I have it on good authority that you have what it takes to be the next big thing. Let me make it happen for you. Regards, Bonnie.*

How could I not like her style? Had she have been a Jehovah's Witness I would have signed up there and then. She offered me hope when all around me negatively reigned, and besides, she represented the esteemed and prestigious William Morris Agency, who even I knew were extremely picky about who they agreed to take on as clients.

Without even meeting her – although I did click on her website to view her beguiling picture – I replied, accepting her kind offer - actually more like snatching it in desperation. Who cared about percentages? I needed help.

I called her on my cellphone, and at the other end was none other than Bonnie Knox, like some 21st Century Fairy Godmother, her voice warm yet suffused with strength.

"Remember, I'm here for you. Whatever you want, I can fix it," Bonnie assured me, faithfully promising me that should any problems beset me, I could call her day or night.

"Get me out of here. I don't belong any more," I sobbed down the phone.

"I will initiate the necessary arrangements and get back to you without delay," Bonnie said, undeterred by my neediness. True to her word, within 48 hours Bonnie had secured a prestigious two-bedroom apartment on the Upper West Side, overlooking Central Park. Who needed a magic hobo when you'd got Bonnie?

Before departing I sat down to write Elaine a handwritten note. How to explain what had happened between us? Bordering on impossible, I guess – but I tried nevertheless.

I began: *I should have known better than to agree to the honey trap hit on Brad, however much I tried to persuade you against it, although that can never excuse me for my inappropriate behaviour.*

I paused a while, and then wrote:

I will never forget your awesome kindness, inviting me into your home when nobody else cared, and for reasons that are beyond explanation, however much you hate me, I will always love you more.

CHAPTER SEVENTEEN

I looked around the deserted apartment one last time before I walked out of the door, and with everybody away at work I took a few moments to reflect on my troubled stay there. I clearly hadn't fitted in as I'd longed to, and yet it had had all begun so unbelievably well, with me becoming closer to Elaine than I'd ever been – that was until Brad came between us. I shut the door behind me, trying to console myself with the thought that at least I'd been able to rescue Elaine from the twin evils of Alice and honey trap, and by freeing her I'd enabled her to pursue a proper, legitimate career in TV, even though I would have preferred it to have been medicine.

"Are you ready to leave, miss?" said the smart-suited driver of the pitch black Mercedes parked incongruously outside our bohemian apartment block.

"Get me out of here before I do any more harm," I replied as I handed him my suitcase.

We made our stately way through the congested Manhattan streets, although I was weighed down with guilt by just how close I had become to betraying Elaine with Brad. But I hadn't, and know I never could, I told myself a thousand times over.

Suddenly, appearing on national TV alongside Melissa didn't seem to matter any more. Only thoughts of Angelo lifted my spirits.

So we were heading towards the Apthorp, a luxury early twentieth-century apartment house in the heart of the Upper West Side, and as promised, Bonnie was there for me on the sidewalk, wearing a life-enhancing smile and radiating rather more warmth than simple professional duty required.

"Hi Jennifer, you're safe now," she said, greeting me with a warm hug. "Say hello to your new home, Apthorp," she added, waving towards the building up above.

"This is awesome" I said, using one of the most overused words in the American language. though for once it was well chosen. "I'll never be able to afford this."

"Oh yes you will" Bonnie replied.

She activated the iconic wrought-iron entry gate as we walked across mosaic floors into a large interior courtyard accented with magnolia trees, evergreens and subtle lighting, and then into one of four residential lobbies, where a concierge summoned an elevator on our behalf. While awaiting its descent I marvelled at the Italian Renaissance Revival architecture, redolent of a more sophisticated age when the likes of Cary Grant and Audrey Hepburn still walked the earth.

"I've already got three clients living in this building," said Bonnie with a conspiratorial air. "You'd die if I told you who they were."

We alighted at the third floor, where Bonnie escorted me towards my jaw-dropping 5,000 square foot apartment with its modern minimal style of white lacquered floors throughout. In the living room I sat down on a pale yellow mid-century chair opposite a clear Lucite desk, alongside a white rectangular Italian couch, the style of the furnishings in sharp contrast to Apthorp's exterior of limestone arches, plaster relief sculptures and wrought-iron railings.

"I really don't deserve this and I definitely don't belong here," I said to her.

"You so do, but you just don't know it yet," Bonnie replied, leaving me to become better acquainted with my breathtaking new home.

CHAPTER EIGHTEEN

"After today you cease to be a private person. You belong to America now," Melissa informed me as we prepared to watch the transmission of Men Who Put Women Down amid the luxury of the Groucho penthouse suite.

The opening titles cut to the familiar signature tune, evoking memories of my heart-stopping terror in the studio – I was getting déjà vu nervous all over again – and when Melissa finally introduced her new People Person to the world I shielded my eyes, finding it impossible to view my likeness on the screen. I just couldn't bear to watch, until curiosity eventually overwhelmed me, and I stole a glimpse of somebody who claimed to be me. This confident young woman was dispensing advice to anybody who would listen – and even more surprisingly, they all did.

"That isn't me," I protested.

"Time to introduce yourself to the person you've finally become," my mentor proclaimed. "And without doubt, it was one of the finest television debuts I have ever seen, so don't go getting any better or you might put me in the shade."

I heard her warning, and within minutes of the broadcast ending my agent Bonnie – would I ever get used to saying that – called to sing my praises. OK, it was her job, that's what I paid her for, but I sensed she really meant it too. In her excitement she outlined plans for what she predicted would be my burgeoning career, citing the immediate need for photo shoots, celebrity endorsements and the 'must have' requirements to be seen in all the right places. So when I casually let slip that I had already been invited to the premiere of *Ravishing* you might have assumed that I'd just announced I had an audience with the Almighty himself, such was the force of Bonnie's piercing scream.

"Wear something memorable," Bonnie instructed me.

"You can depend on it," I replied.

Having been given permission by Melissa to leave early – "have fun" she had said, if only she had known, still blissfully unaware that I would be walking out with Angelo at a high profile Premiere that evening - I felt dreadful for not having informed her, whereas Bonnie, Posy and my hair and make-up team were all in the loop, having been sworn to secrecy about my big night out.

I proceeded along the long corridor, weighed down with gifts from well-wishers, my heart aching upon seeing Elaine approaching from afar, who flamboyantly ignored my 'hey' by tossing her head away from me, producing her cellphone to make what was probably an imaginary call just to blank me out.

CHAPTER EIGHTEEN

Having forsaken all my relatives I had only one friend in the world, and I had to pay for the privilege of pouring my heart out to her, although Bonnie again managed to create the impression that she somehow really cared. Of course, I wasn't naïve enough not to appreciate that she had professional reasons too. I needed to know exactly who it was that she had just signed up if she was to provide me with a comprehensive service as her agent.

"I want you to take a deep breath and tell me everything – and when I say everything, I mean everything about your personal life past and present," she said, probing me. "And remember, I'm on your side."

I didn't know where to begin. Too much information and she would drop me quicker than Charlie Sheen from *Two and a Half Men*.

"Is there anybody out there who might hold a grudge against you?" Bonnie helpfully prompted me.

"Where shall I start?" I mused, eventually opting for "I used to seduce strangers in bars - as a honey trap," as if that was justification, of a kind.

"A girl's gotta earn a living," Bonnie replied. Where had I heard that before?

"And my boss, who hit on me, didn't want me to quit, and reckons she had the power to force me to return to her agency whenever she chooses. And my room-mate thinks I slept with her boyfriend, which I did, but only in a drunken kind of way, no sex".

"It's OK. Relax. Nobody ever said I'd signed Mother Teresa," said Bonnie.

It wasn't all interrogation under the lamplight from Bonnie – mostly she did nice things, using her influence to good effect; one call from her and I was rapidly enthroned in the chair of celebrity hairdresser Sam McKnight, whose clients included Cate Blanchett, Madonna and Lady Gaga. Impressed? Well I ought to have been. How lucky was I, unlike normal mortals without fairy godmothers who would have to wait six months for an appointment.

After our initial consultation we agreed upon the look he wanted to achieve, although he did let slip that he'd been in receipt of suggestions from Angelo when they'd recently met at a television event. Maybe it was Angelo who had dictated I wore my hair as a throwback to Hollywood's golden era, updated by Sam as he reinterpreted Veronica Lake's classic waves for a new century.

Building the Pyramids must have been a walk in the park when compared to Sam's ambitious construction. His tools, volumising spray and a space-age dryer combined to give plentiful shine and lustrous volume, further enhanced by the forceful application of a round Ibiza brush while drying, then followed by sectioning hair and rolling it back into hot rollers. Next he brushed out the curls, swept them to one side and finished by applying a small lake of hair spray. Voilà, there you have it, a wannabe small screen blonde goddess ready to go – if they could see me now in Valley Stream.

Sam gave me strict instructions not to expose my locks to the elements at any cost. "Otherwise I will have just wasted two hours of my valuable time," he warned me. I wonder if he spoke to Madonna like that?

Thankfully, I got back, courtesy of a chauffeur-driven BMW, hair unscathed, soon to be followed by a visit from our gorgeous make-up artiste Charmaine and her Groucho colleague Posy, who arrived at my fancy new apartment bearing weapons of mass beautification.

"Oh to be dating in a quiet restaurant, seated at a discreet table for two instead of having to face the world's media," I confessed.

I watched them exchanging knowing looks.

" So I guess I'm one of those annoying people who just can't do happiness."

"Fame and beauty are seriously wasted on the fabulously gorgeous," said Posy. "Why so much weary indifference to a shimmering night out with the stars?"

"I so get it. She simply wants to keep her hot date all to herself." At least Charmaine understood my mood as she prepared to get down to work.

She explained that she wanted to use make-up to create a look that was chic without giving the appearance of having tried too hard. Talking me through it as she worked, Charmaine applied Giorgio Armani Luminous

Foundation in Light Sand sparingly, then a light dusting of translucent loose powder. Next she swept a rosy blush onto my cheeks, using a light hand to emphasise what she described as my piercing blue eyes. Brushing eye shadow from my lash line to brow bone, she lined my upper lashes with a thin line of black eyeliner, then applying a generous coat of mascara in black. Finally, she filled in my eyebrows with a light brown pencil and then the finishing touch, a swipe of pink lip gloss to complete the effect. Ta da!

"If you get any more gorgeous they will have to declare you illegal," she said upon finishing, standing back to admire her latest and what she claimed was her greatest creation – I bet she said that to all the girls.

"Let me through, I'm a fashion doctor," Posy interrupted us, next in line to take to the floor in the transformation of me, Jennifer Gold.

"First, say goodbye to modesty. Bra off," she said, declaring that it would be surplus to requirements given the intricate architecture of the Armani Privé dress.

"Omigod," said Posy, resting her hands on my absurdly pert breasts for longer than might be thought seemly. "I can't wait to tell my boyfriend that I actually grabbed Jennifer Gold's boobs. It will be better than spiking his drink with Viagra."

"Hey. Give them back," I said pretending to be offended. "So glad that I can be of service in spicing up your sex life, although your boyfriend will have absolutely no idea who I am."

"But he will after tonight," Posy countered. "Once your picture has been splashed across every newspaper and magazine you will not only become intimately familiar to my boyfriend but to millions more people besides."

"Go tell that to the marines," I replied.

As Posy and Charmaine continued to fuss around me I became drawn to the mirror, shocked to see that from the side view the black dress, glamorously adorned with sparkling sequins, had all the coverage of a bikini top.

And should you have forgotten, my dress actually plunged to my navel and scooped controversially low at the back, my modesty only partially saved by a strategic intervention from Posy, who applied a piece of sheer mesh which kept the neckline from gaping wide open. And as if that area of my body needed any more attention drawing to it, I wore a massive Cartier diamond strategically placed on my chest, my other accessories including diamond stud earrings, a clutch by Roger Vivier and platform heels by Jimmy Choo. I was all dressed up and for once I did have somewhere to go.

"Ta-Da!" I twirled around before them.

"Supercalifreakinfragilistic," said Posy.

"Expialifuckingdocious," said Charmaine, similarly impressed.

"All this," I said gesturing to my over the shoulder blonde waves, the tastefully understated translucent make-up and that daring dress. "It's not me. It's you."

"We were just the midwives. You're the babe," said Posy while adjusting the million-dollar Cartier diamond necklace which hung from my neck.

I thanked them sincerely for their miraculous work as they departed to give me time and space to get my head around the night ahead, and most significantly, the impending arrival of Angelo. While I might have felt a little queasy about how I would deal with the media glare, afraid the world would be able to see right through me, finally exposed as the fraud I really was, it was only the prospect of Angelo being by my side which persuaded me I could handle the night ahead.

I suppose I just about looked like I belonged at a premiere – thanks to a designer dress and hours of preparation, not to mention a miraculous transformation. So when the buzzer sounded far too early for it to have been Angelo I assumed it must have been one of my hard-working backroom team returning to collect an abandoned hairbrush or a mislaid make-up bag they had left behind.

"Who is it?" I shouted nonchalantly through the intercom.

"Your escort awaits," replied the deliciously deep honey coated voice.

"You've come early."

"Not something I've often been accused of," he mischievously replied.

"Pleased to hear it," was the best I could manage and when he announced that he had just summoned the elevator to transport himself to my apartment I dissolved into a bottle of panic.

"Stay exactly where you are. I'm nowhere near ready yet," I snapped at him, addressing him no better than I would a dog. "Sorry that didn't come out right," I apologised.

"Just close your eyes and inhale deeply," he counselled me over the intercom. "Hold it! Now breathe out, and just feel that negative energy ebbing away."

How ridiculously new age was that, and yet incredibly, I did exactly as he instructed, as I breathed heavily down the intercom. Not a good sound for a first date.

"Now you're ready to go. I'll be waiting for you in the North Lobby," he concluded like a man who was familiar with achieving the required effect.

"What was I like? A volatile mix of anticipation and fear – anticipation that he would be as gorgeously all-consuming as I had always imagined him to be, and fear that reality would never live up to the impossibly high standards set by my incredible fantasy.

Whichever, his Zen-like instructions appeared to have alleviated my distress, emboldening me to descend four floors to where he was waiting for me, as promised, in the lobby.

"No words," he said upon seeing me, "except to say, your beauty honours me."

"You're too kind. And you're not so bad yourself."

I wished I hadn't replied. He placed his hand at the base of my spine and struck flesh, sending a shock wave of seismic proportions reverberating through me, and so early in the evening too. How was I going to survive a car journey, a movie and a reception without ripping off his jacket and shirt? I had to be single-mindedly pure. I conjured up childhood images of nuns singing *Edelweiss* from *The Sound of Music* to help get me through, as we surrendered to the warm embrace of a Manhattan summer evening.

With the extravagant sweep of an arm he ushered me towards the white Excalibur limousine parked outside my apartment block, the uniformed driver courteously closing the door behind me. I slid a decent distance away from Angelo on the back seat, but not so far as to signal indifference. I suppose you could describe him as the strong but silent type.

"What a beautiful evening," I commented.

"Silence is nothing to be afraid of," he replied.

"So you're not one for small talk then?" which he conclusively proved by ignoring my question.

"So please allow me to cut to the quick. Would it seem utterly and absurdly ridiculous if I told you that I have been imagining you all my life?" I asked him, recklessly going for broke.

Mercifully Angelo appeared unperturbed, emboldening me to go further.

"And not only have I imagined you, I have seen you in fleeting moments in times gone by, and when I walked into your office I had this insane feeling that we had actually met before – you know, the stranger at my wedding?"

He smiled imperceptibly, as if he was humouring a troublesome child.

"Déjà vu. An illusory feeling of having already experienced a present situation," he patiently explained.

"Just ignore me. Maybe you've just got one of those faces," I said, backtracking rapidly. "I'm the closest thing to crazy you'll ever meet."

"I like crazy. Sanity is so mortal," he replied in his pseudomystical manner. He lightly touched my arm, sending more shock waves of pleasure through my already sensually-charged body.

And yet he remained a mystery to me. I speculated whether he was raised in a happy home, if he always treated waiters with respect and most controversially of all, was he married? I guess I should have Googled him.

"You like silence too," he observed.

"Oh, just lost in thought, you know, wondering whether I should have really worn this dress."

"You were made for one another," he observed.

Well, he would say that, wouldn't he? He chose it, and just about every other accessory too.

I looked up and saw the searchlights Twentieth-Century Fox style illuminating the night sky above Radio

City, while underneath a pack of ravenous photographers devoured the celebrities as they emerged in all their transient glory from stretch limousines. He seemed to sense my apprehension upon seeing the scene which awaited us – so he was sensitive to other people's feelings after all – as he gently dispensed invaluable last-minute advice about how to handle the premiere.

"Just keep on smiling until your face hurts, even though it will seem like the most unnatural thing you've ever done in your entire life" he murmured. I followed his instructions implicitly as I emerged smiling resolutely to an audible and collective 'wow' from the crowd. I was confronted by a blinding array of flashlights.

It was surreal. The photographers only had lenses for me, even evicting the gorgeous ex-tennis player Anna Kournikova from centre stage. Only seconds earlier she had been occupying their undivided attention.

"Who's that girl?" I overheard a photographer enquire of one of the more seasoned autograph hunters propped up behind him, wedged against a barrier at the front of the crowd.

"It's that new girl from the Melissa Parker Show. She's one to watch," he explained, waving his autograph book manically in the air in a frantic effort to attract my attention. How could I decline? Although I had to remember to sign my name Gold, not Green.

I guess you never forget your first time signing an

autograph. Angelo looked on proudly, having discreetly stepped aside, diplomatically abandoning the limelight so that the paparazzi could devour me unhindered as I sashayed my way along a line of ravenous cameras, feeling so surprisingly accomplished, like I had been parading semi-naked in front of strange men all my life. I genuinely hadn't realised that only yards away from where I was flaunting myself officials were looking on anxiously, watching me use, and in their estimation, abuse, my moment in the spotlight. Unknown to me, Angelina Jolie, leading lady of *Ravishing*, and her partner, Brad Pitt, had been outrageously forced to wait in line, delayed by me, this presumptuous newcomer, spurred on by Angelo shouting "work it girl" from the wings.

Eventually an official stepped in to intervene – I thought for one dreadful moment Angelo was going to land a punch on him – and escorted me out of the spotlight to allow Miss Jolie to claim her rightful place centre stage.

"That was sensational. I couldn't have asked for more," Angelo whispered into my ear upon rejoining me, just as if he had planned it all himself, which on reflection, he probably had.

Having made maximum impact upon the assembled media – Angelo's work on my behalf now done – we were escorted to our seats by a genial guy who opportunistically patted Angelo on his bottom, supposedly to shepherd him and me to our seats.

"Hands off, he's mine" I whispered playfully into his ear.

"To die for," he mouthed back at me, as if I needed telling.

After a brief introduction by the film's director, Sofia Coppola, who expressed her hope that the film embodied the enduring spirit of New York, the lights faded, although my thoughts stayed resolutely focused on Angelo throughout, regardless of the fact that Brad Pitt was sitting directly in front of me. While the audience began imperceptibly to drop their guard and slowly surrender to the film's siren appeal I retreated into my own little bubble, too busy thinking about Angelo. I recalled the first time I ever saw his face on what should have been, and ultimately became, the greatest day of my life, which had been less about marrying Greg and more to do with laying eyes on this incredible, amazing man as he materialised while having our wedding photographs taken, seriously tempting me to break my vows within fifteen minutes of having made them. Perhaps that was why I had initially been able to forgive Greg for his affair, having already been unfaithful to my husband, in my mind at least, on the very day we married. Almost unforgiveable, I had reckoned, until I discovered that old letter from Greg's mistress, recounting her ecstatic response to his declaration of love for her.

When you said you loved me, my heart skipped a beat.

Surely, that put my inappropriate thoughts into

perspective. I was certain that he had committed the greater sin.

So I had sought out my incredible fantasy man again and again, having seen him on a bus, a railway station or passing through check-in at an airport, forlornly chasing after him, helplessly watching him board a Greyhound, a train or a plane. Like a ghost he had haunted me, yet now in the darkness of the cinema I actually squeezed that apparition's hand, prompting Angelo to reciprocate, my irrefutable proof that I no longer lived in the imagined world.

"I found you" I said to Angelo as the lights went up and the credits rolled, the audience applauding rapturously.

"What took you so long?" he enigmatically replied.

At the post premiere party, in spite of glamorous people in abundance, I had only Angelo on my mind. In fact, I couldn't take my eyes off him. I was like a stalker, watching his every move. A shot of jealousy surged through me upon seeing Angelina Jolie throwing Angelo a sideways glance graduating to a full-on stare, while only seconds later Brad Pitt had eyed me, igniting a look of rebuke from his film star partner. Now I suppose I ought to have been utterly delirious, knowing that I had made Angelina Jolie, arguably the world's most beautiful woman, jealous of me and that Brad Pitt had admired me across a crowded room. And do you know what? It just didn't impress me that much. I only had eyes for Angelo.

While he became embroiled in a series of serious conversations with other media movers and moguls a tide of eligible young men washed upon my shore, all trying to make a splash. I could have done without the pugnacious independent movie producer who pleaded with me to consider auditioning – auditioning indeed! – for his next project, The Attack Of The Cyber Sluts, which he reckoned would be the ideal vehicle for my particular talents.

"You must ring my agent," I said while surveying the horizon for Angelo.

And how could I possibly not be dismayed upon seeing him in an animated conversation with Anna Kournikova, who was eagerly encroaching upon his personal space.

"New balls please," I said intervening, adamant that he'd be in need of some should he not remove himself from her personal space pretty darn quickly.

"Thank you for rescuing me," said Angelo.

"And you me," I replied, my meaning heartfelt and profound.

We retreated to a secluded corner, away from the prying eyes of lustful celebrities and seedy producers, and sat together, holding hands like two love-struck teenagers.

"Happy now? Your wish is my command," he assured me.

"So you will do whatever I ask of you?" I provoked him teasingly.

"Nothing is out of bounds."

"Then fire Kyle," I commanded him.

"Kyle?"

"That conniving, devious, dishonest producer who contacted you about our plans to claim the higher ground by producing Men Who Put Women Down."

"He's already gone."

So it was him.

"You'd do that for me? I thought he was your new best friend."

"He means nothing to me."

"But Melissa rates him so highly. For some unfathomable reason she thinks the sun shines out of his derriere. Believe me, she will never, ever allow Kyle to be fired."

"If you want it, it will happen," he whispered.

Holy Capone! It was as if I had the ear of my very own friendly neighbourhood Mafia boss, menacingly ordering in softly spoken terms an execution at my request. He had seduced me into savouring the illicit pleasure of being able to influence and then harness the power of a dangerous, ruthless man, and do you know what? I loved it.

The night was young, and so were we. As we climbed back on board our ludicrous limo I prayed to the dating goddess in her pink paradise that she would use her powers to redirect our swanky, smart, over-the-top car anywhere but home, maybe to an all-night diner followed by a short drive to an isolated parking place from where we could enjoy a romantic view of Brooklyn Bridge together. Of course Angelo had other ideas. Maybe he was already tiring of my boring presence, as with a sinking heart I recognised that the driver was heading back towards my apartment. What else could I do but value the time we had left together anyway, nestling up to Angelo, who radiated immense strength. My head was resting on his muscular shoulder, his arm enveloping me. I never wanted the journey to end.

"Do you wish me to come inside?" he enquired of me.

Omigod! Don't panic – It must be just his unfortunate way of asking if he should accompany me to my apartment. I couldn't say I wasn't tempted, either way

"It's been such a wonderful evening…"

"So let's make it even more wonderful," he oh-so-persuasively argued.

"On our first date?"

"You said earlier that you'd known me all your life, so this hardly counts as a first date, does it? We're almost intimate"

"Nice try," I said alighting on the sidewalk.

Climbing Mount Everest wearing six-inch Christian Louboutin heels would have been easier than forcing myself to be anywhere else but near to him when every fibre of my being wanted to be in his presence, partaking of him.

"Until the next time," he said as he stepped out alongside me to kiss me on my cheek.

If only I could have paused the world on freeze frame, relishing every one of those microseconds while his lips rested on my face, trying so agonisingly hard not to kiss him back on his cheek, on his lips, on his belly button – why precisely that last one came into my mind, Sigmund Freud only knows.

Once upstairs I gently shut my apartment door, kicked off my Jimmy Choos and switched on my iPad. I selected Billy Joel's *Uptown Girl* and played it loud, really loud, dancing around my palatial new home like a demented love-struck teenager before collapsing on the sofa. I was yearning to call somebody – anybody who would listen – irrespective of it being three o'clock in the morning. And then I considered who I might call. I did not have the longest address book in history. With the exception of my agent Bonnie, who was paid to endure me yakking on after all, I couldn't think of a single person I hadn't already alienated, upset or offended. Sleep was my only friend.

So in dreams I returned to Angelo, images of him lying in bed next to me thrusting into my mind as I slept – the scent of him, the power of him, the sex of him, all of them fabulous to behold.

I had only been asleep for what seemed like a matter of minutes when the phone rang, although in reality it had been six and a half hours.

"Hey," I said sleepily.

"Hold the front page," a disappointingly female voice

announced. I'd hoped that it might have been Angelo, calling to reflect on our first night out together, or even better, arrange the next one.

Or maybe he didn't care for me at all.

"Oh Bonnie, hi," I said, barely able to disguise my disappointment as my mind finally caught up with my ears.

"Are you alone?" she tactfully enquired.

"Naturellement," I said, slightly resenting her insinuation.

"Remember, we mustn't have any secrets if I am to represent you effectively," she reminded me.

"I guess you're right," I said still in a haze.

"Anyway, read it and tweet," Bonnie continued.

I could detect the excitement in her voice as she gleefully informed me of the incredible amount of newspaper, television and internet coverage of the *Ravishing* premiere, with one person above all dominating the column inches and the screens.

"You're everywhere. Splashed all over the front pages, lead story on TV entertainment news shows, chat room sites multiplying in your honour. The nerds love you. How does that make you feel?"

"Alarmed?"

"You've even succeeded in relegating Brad and Angelina to page seven. They'll hate you forever."

"And that's good?"

"Good? It's gargantuan. And you should read the

headlines!" screamed Bonnie, the sound of rustling newspapers audible in the background. "How about, Angelina Outshone by Gold, TV's People Person KO's Brad's Babe, and Angelina Not So Jolly Now."

"How strange. And tell me, how are things in the Middle East?"

"Nobody cares, unless she's young and beautiful and wearing an Armani Privé dress."

I thanked Bonnie for her support and enthusiasm and as I turned off the lights to steal a few more minutes' sleep, never did the phrase 'the world's gone mad' seem more appropriate.

CHAPTER NINETEEN

If I'd been expecting to be welcomed with open arms by my colleagues at Groucho following my celebrity exploits at the premiere of *Ravishing*, I would have been more disappointed than if I'd been at a bachelorette party in Teheran. And it didn't exactly help that the first person I encountered on arrival at Groucho was Elaine, who appeared seriously engrossed by the front page of the *New York Daily Post*.

"Hey," I said, in the forlorn hope that she might at least come around to tolerating me again.

"I've nothing to say to you," said Elaine. "Why should I, when I can read all about you in this morning papers?"

While I might have expected to have encountered hostility from Elaine I didn't expect to get trashed by the Groucho high command too. You could have tasted the atmosphere with the tip of your tongue.

I wasn't so far down de Nile as Cairo that I didn't expect repercussions about failing to inform Melissa of my night out with Angelo, but I couldn't quite get my head round why everybody at Groucho seemed to regard Angelo as the nearest thing we had to a sworn enemy.

"Have I done something wrong? Is it because I'm late?" I naively required.

"That's forgivable," said Kate.

"So how am I unforgiven?"

"Could having just lost the best producer we've ever had, forced out by your new best friend, Angelo, have something to do with it?" said the Senior Producer, tapping her fingers on the desk in irritation.

Boy did Angelo move fast – your wish is my command he had said, so I nod my assent and abracadabra, he makes Kyle disappear.

"I'm sure if Kyle is as good as you all think he is he'll have no problem getting a job elsewhere."

"So it was you," Kate triumphantly confirmed.

"And there will be no shortage of talented applicants waiting to take his place and work on Melissa's show," I said, desperate to move the argument on.

"Is that supposed to make us feel better?"

"So what if I told Angelo the truth about this creep who betrayed us. Surely you must realise by now, he was nothing more than a liar and a cheat whose only interest was to sabotage our efforts to make a better kind of show."

"So who do you suggest we appoint to take his place?" Kate contemptuously enquired, pointing at the scheduled recording date emblazoned threateningly across her rota, due to take place the very next day.

"Elaine," I replied without a second's hesitation.

In my head I'd hit a home run. Elaine was the perfect choice. I reminded them who'd been responsible for supplying the ammunition for Men Who Put Women Down, courtesy of her excellent research notes and astute choice of contributors. How could Kate possibly disagree?

She began to waver, probably due to having no alternative to hand. Finally she announced that she would run the idea by Melissa.

I immediately went back to my office and penned a note to Melissa myself, apologising unreservedly for my oversight and assuring her that my relationship with Angelo, such as it was, could never compromise my relationship with her, and what happened in Groucho would stay in Groucho. I scribbled a note to Kate along similar lines, although a little less apologetic, as I considered Melissa to be both my mentor and friend.

I hadn't expected Elaine to shower me with kisses upon learning that I had recommended her for the job, and she didn't. "Don't even think this begins to make things right between us," she warned me, although I was consoled to detect her joy too. As her mother, I could see behind the hurt façade.

When Melissa eventually agreed to my plan, Elaine immediately took a firm grip of the next day's show, staying up to the early hours of the morning, I later learned, to type notes, check on research and ensure that all the show's contributors had already arrived at the their Midtown hotel. And it didn't take long to discover that we were both capable of putting our personal differences aside as we prepared to record a show which examined whether it was possible for couples to forgive one another for cheating.

Ouch!

As regards Melissa, she didn't hesitate to let it be known that I mustn't allow my personal life to intrude upon my role at Groucho, and then after a few hours of frostiness she appeared to forgive me anyway. So, how could I possibly object?

Being professional to her core, Melissa redirected her attention towards preparing that day's show, ably driven by Elaine, who didn't let any personal issues with me prevent her from producing a boisterous yet thoughtful debate. In truth, I felt far happier in her hands than Kyle's as she quietly directed me through my earpiece, to intervene or hold back as the moment required.

"Thank you for coming to our rescue," Melissa praised Elaine at the post-show conference.

And how I wanted to hug Elaine to celebrate her successful debut as a producer, but I guessed that a shake of the hand was about the most she would tolerate.

So a sort of uneasy truce broke out between us as we set about making challenging talk shows, cleverly constructed by my new producer, who confidently guided me – my star now very much in the ascendancy – to even greater heights.

I began to feel uncomfortable however at the way my success always had to be at the expense of somebody else.

"Jennifer's the best thing about the show. So much more entertaining than Melissa," I overheard two members of staff saying in the rest room while I remained unseen in a cubicle only a few feet away. It was only the opinion of two people, but then I began to notice how I received longer and louder rounds of applause when we made our respective entrances on to the studio set, and in no way encouraged by me, I might add. And as Melissa's doubts about the wisdom of hiring me must have multiplied in her head, so the show's ratings grew too, pressurised by the Network, I guessed, to promote me from one to three appearances per week.

As a production team Elaine and I formed a formidable professional partnership, although "let's keep this purely professional shall we," she once warned me when I innocently enquired about Brad.

While my professional life blossomed, Angelo proved to be a slow starter. I'd had visions of him banging on my door, forcing himself in, throwing his jacket to the floor, taking me in his arms as I feigned minimum resistance, eventually submitting to his iron will. Still in my dreams! OK, so he did send me a beautiful hand-,delivered card strewn with red rose petals expressing his gratitude for what he described as our enchanting night together. Omigod, he wasn't gay was he? After all, he didn't flinch when the gay guy in the cinema accidentally/deliberately touched his bottom. And how the Rock Hudson did the cinema attendant even know that Angelo wouldn't be offended by his inappropriate touch? Gaydar, I guess. But then I recalled his long lingering kiss on my cheek as we parted. That wasn't gay. So I was worrying unnecessarily, wasn't I?

So it must have been me then, although after what seemed like an eternity since our date – it was actually five days – he eventually turned up in person. I was less than delighted that he chose to show at Groucho, really wanting to keep professional and personal entirely separate. I had given my word to Melissa, yet there he was in the front lobby, a picnic basket under his arm, inviting me to a lunchtime assignation in Central Park. I was conscious of the other staff there all staring at me – they knew exactly who he was, and were fully aware of my reprimand from Melissa for accompanying him to the premiere – all of them wondering whether I would dare to accept his invitation.

"I'd better check with Melissa first," I properly informed him.

"So they don't allow you to take lunch breaks here?"

"Lunch is for pimps."

"I think you'll find it's wimps. Step this way," he said gesturing me towards the limo parked outside. I duly and willingly obeyed.

I wondered whereabouts exactly in the Park he was

taking me. Somewhere busy and flagrantly public? Or perhaps his favourite secret place where we wouldn't be disturbed; after all, he had 843 acres of Central Park to choose from.

We travelled in silence – I was getting used to it by now - alighting at Mid Park from 79th to 85th Street, Angelo instructing his driver to return 45 minutes later. It seemed disappointingly brief, if only I'd had the nerve to tell him.

We laid our picnic basket in a shady spot underneath the branches of a grove of canopy trees, the dappled Great Lawn on the south eastern edge of the Park, a perfect place for a romantic picnic. He presented me with roses – pink this time – then fed me the finest pâté from Normandy while plying me with Bollinger champagne. While I ardently hoped he would waste no time in carrying on where he left off at the premiere and graduate from kisses on the cheek to lips, he preferred to talk instead. I would have to wait. We discussed everything and anything, yet nothing which shone a light on our past lives, as if we were both devoid of history.

"Time begins now," Angelo said to me as a swallow swooped low over the ground only yards away from where we lay, the sun-drenched leaves on the trees rustling gently before they fell for the fall, encouraged on their way by a persuasive recurring breeze rising and falling in rhythmic motion, branches eagerly submitting to the will of the wind. If love had a sight and sound, this was surely it.

"Happy?" Angelo asked me.

"My heart is overwhelmed by bliss. There's no word invented to express how I feel."

"So let's invent one."

"My blissheart," I replied.

"Be still my beating blissheart," said Angelo paraphrasing a quote from Shakespeare. That inspired me to smile incandescently, indicative of my indescribable happiness, or blissheart, as it had become known.

***

Of course I had shows to present, and I didn't want to enrage Melissa any further, while Angelo had deals to close and important people to intimidate. The two of us were reluctantly dragged back to the demands of our respective brilliant careers. So we packed up our plates and silver service cutlery in the picnic basket and rolled up the blanket before walking arm in arm back towards Angelo's car.

Until I ran away from him. I grabbed a handful of fallen leaves and threw them into his lovely face. I just couldn't resist it. He dropped the basket and ran, chasing me to a standstill and showering me back with a forest full of leaves until somehow we became entwined and he kissed me vigorously on the lips.

Now that's what I called blissheart. I was hoping that he might now at least suggest we find a shady glade, or even better a room, where we could love one another to distraction.

"Time is on our side," he announced instead, reclaiming his basket and blanket as we walked hand-in-hand back towards the waiting car. How disappointing was that?

I was doing my best to compose myself when back on the sidewalk reality hit home. A forlorn figure in a ragged old field jacket was shuffling towards us through the piles of decaying leaves, his hand outstretched, mumbling incoherently, apparently begging for money, challenging us to empathise with his plight.

For one terrible second I thought he might have been the one who had sent me there, coming to reclaim me, just when at long last I was beginning to get real with Angelo. But as the strong breeze rendered the hobo's shock of greying hair ever more windswept, I concluded as he came into view that he was just another vagrant after all.

"Can you spare me a dollar?" he begged, addressing his request directly to Angelo.

Terror still held me in its grip – if he treated the hobo cruelly I would never want to kiss Angelo again.

"Take this, it's yours," said Angelo, handing the guy a 50-dollar bill, "and this too," he added, holding out a card bearing a telephone help line number for those in need of shelter. "It might help to turn your life around. What have you got to lose?"

I surveyed Angelo adoringly, knowing that our kissing days had only just begun. So underneath those stridently alpha male characteristics lay a social conscience after all.

I'm certain that it was then, and only then, that I gave myself unconditionally to Angelo.

He invited me on an upcoming business trip to Paris and did I decline, or even hesitate for a moment? – No I Cyndi Lauper well didn't, regardless of my commitments at Groucho. Of course, I later checked it out with Melissa, who reluctantly sanctioned the time away. And Kate clearly didn't approve either as she grudgingly agreed to re-schedule two shows to compensate for my absence.

Even my agent Bonnie gave me a stern talking to, counselling me to make my television career my top priority, although she did manage to wish me bon voyage.

CHAPTER TWENTY

If aeroplanes flew to heaven, then first class would be the only way to go. I considered it to be divine anyway, being more familiar with being cooped up in Economy with a plastic tray perched precariously in front of me than stretching out my legs preparing to be pampered, wined and dined on a luxurious Atlantic crossing. There were irritations though, none more so than the threateningly pretty Air France cabin crew who appeared excessively solicitous of Angelo's needs, puffing up his pillow at every opportunity. Upon returning from a visit to the bathroom I was tormented by the sight of him lapping up the undivided attention of a coterie of uniformed beauties, who quickly dispersed on seeing me return.

"Just in time," I said. "Looks like I've got in the way of your invitation into the Mile High Club."

"How do you know I'm not already a member?" he asked, provoking me further by suggesting that the Mile High Club would be a great subject for my show.

"One," I said pointing my finger in a pretence of threat at Angelo, "we don't do that kinda sub-Springer stuff any more – or didn't I make myself clear that time when I came to visit you in your office? And two, it's not my show. It belongs to Melissa."

"Not for much longer," he said. At first I failed to grasp the impact of the grenade he had just nonchalantly tossed into our conversation.

"What is it about female flight attendants that men seem unable to resist?" I said, oblivious to his plans.

"Gold," he said, handing me a glossy brochure with my name and photograph emblazoned on the front cover. It appeared to herald the title of a forthcoming television show.

"File this under garbage!" I said enraged, throwing the brochure back in his face. "And this is how you think I should repay Melissa for giving me my big break?"

"Who said anything about life being fair?" he said. "She wants you out anyway. It's inevitable. She regards you as a threat."

"That's ridiculous - isn't it?"

"Success breeds insecurity in others. It's only natural that Melissa should be suspicious of you, given your increasingly high profile. You'd be doing her a favour by quitting."

"Do you think I could possibly walk away from the show that made me without a backward glance to those who made it possible? What kind of person do you think I am?"

"The kind who wants to succeed."

"But not at the expense of others. Melissa always hosts

her prime time celebrity interview shows in the autumn season. Are you saying she would lose her slot to me?"

"Just call it progress. The chance for Melissa to spend more time at her mansion in Malibu with her money."

A long uncomfortable silence ensued, save for the whine of the 747 engines, and as the flight progressed, one cordon bleu meal following another, provocative thoughts burrowed deep into a place where my sense of right and wrong resided.

OK, so I'd committed to Angelo unconditionally, but did that mean I had to abandon any sense of morality if I was going to continue being close to him? Sure, he had showed great tenderness and concern when it came to dealing with the hobo outside Central Park, yet back in his natural habitat of television he transformed into this big beast, eat or be eaten, the King of the Media Jungle. No wonder Melissa mistrusted him, whereas I had foolishly thought he must be on Groucho's side. Just because I had become besotted with Angelo I didn't have to agree to his every idea and plan, did I? I would convince him of the error of his ways, by withholding favours if needs be, until he agreed to let me be and carry on working for Melissa.

I suppose there might have been a germ of truth in what Angelo had said about Melissa feeling threatened by me. As Posy had once said, it had been extremely brave of her to appoint a much younger and as she had described it, more gorgeous sidekick, going against all the known rules of television. And I couldn't help but notice the drop in temperature between us away from the studio, especially when compared with the early days. It was as if I had gone from being Melissa's favourite little girl to her annoying teenage daughter in a matter of months. Except I wasn't her relative, and with no family ties to bind us, maybe Angelo had called it correctly, and by resigning I would be doing Melissa a favour after all.

So nearly half an ocean later, curiosity finally got the better of me.

"What's in this show, then?"

"I wondered how long it would take," he teased me.

I listened intently, although pretending to be unimpressed, as he outlined the show's format. It was essentially a celebrity-based talk show in which I was supposed to flirt with the hottest and most bankable male stars in Hollywood, with Brad Pitt, Casey Affleck and George Clooney already expressing interest.

"Derivative," I commented dismissively.

Yet unbeknown to him, I do admit to having been just a little intrigued by the concept, although flirting would definitely be replaced by interrogating if I ever had anything to do with it - which was unlikely, as I was still firmly committed to seeing my contract through with Melissa.

Putting the future on hold, I turned my thoughts more presciently to this evening and the delicate little matter of our sleeping arrangements in Paris. You see Angelo hadn't betrayed anything so far about whether he would be inviting me to share a room with him, let alone a bed. Don't get me wrong - while I yearned to know him better, I couldn't help but interpret the idea of sleeping with him as sleeping with the enemy, a betrayal of Melissa and everything she had done for me. For me to have made love to him would have been as good as signing up to his plan to steal me from the Melissa Show and take over her prized prime-time celebrity talk show, replaced by me in the chair.

"The City of Love," he observed as we sped through the Parisian suburbs in our black chauffeur-driven Mercedes.

"The City of Light," I said, correcting him. We were soon arriving at our destination, which just happened to be one of the world's great hotels. How could I fail to be impressed stepping into the Art Deco grandeur of the lobby of the legendary Georges Cinq. I was endeavouring to remain laid back and sophisticated as I beheld the ornate chandeliers, seventeenth-century tapestries and sumptuous curtains, but I was not so distracted that I didn't overhear Angelo saying we were booked into separate but adjoining suites. I went from experiencing fantastic relief to abject disappointment in seconds, proving just how contrary my feelings were about Angelo.

Exhausted after our transatlantic flight, I could have tolerated going to bed alone, although I remained open to persuasion. Angelo however preferred to slip into work mode almost immediately, sending emails, making calls and fixing appointments for what I had naively imagined would be our romantic few days together. While he spent his waking hours hunkered down in meetings with executives from French television channels TFI, Canal Plus and M6 I was left to my own devices, forlornly sightseeing and disconsolately shopping, unaccompanied by day and alone at night.

I was forced to visit iconic landmarks on my own, staring at wherever I went with that strange mixture of contempt, curiosity and desire a young woman alone attracts, when not being propositioned by creeps and cool guys alike.

I sought consolation in the Louvre Museum, climbing the stairs and passing Winged Victory to the first floor, where I devoured one of the finest collections of Italian paintings in the world. Eventually I joined a slow-moving line to gaze on the Mona Lisa and her enigmatic smile, wondering how she would have played Angelo. Would she be smiling now had she been left to roam the city alone?

On day two I distracted myself further by viewing iconic impressionist paintings at the Musée D'Orsay, followed by the awe-inspiring majesty of the Cathedral of Notre Dame. I felt so lonely I would have eloped with the hunchback had he asked me.

At the end of every day on returning from his high-powered meetings Angelo, looking weary and dishevelled, would spring into life at the sight of me, asking me about my day, fixing me a drink, then draping his arms around me, kissing me on my ear, my neck, moving ever closer towards my lips. And then his wretched cellphone would ring, calling him away to another hastily-arranged meeting. He would promise to be back soon, although he never returned until the early hours, by which time I had already fallen asleep.

On the third day I paid homage to Coco Chanel by heading, on my own again, to the Rue Cambon to patronise the shop founded in 1915 by the revolutionary French designer, purchasing a classic little black dress as a souvenir of my visit there. Maybe my LBD would work its magic on Angelo as we sat in the splendour of our hotel's acclaimed Premier Restaurant that night. My spirits rose as I watched him slowly begin to unwind, talking animatedly about us, a promise of things to come maybe, or so I'd hoped, until he received another call on his cellphone – why couldn't he switch the darned thing off? – from an irate television executive threatening to undo their deal.

"Forgive me. Ten million dollars depends on it," he said, leaving me with nowhere to go but back to my room.

I confess to hitting the bottle – my disappointment would have driven a Mormon to drink – and downing dangerous quantities of chilled vodka to help deaden the pain of desertion. I guess I shouldn't have taken it so personally. How could I possibly compete with ten million dollars? Because you're worth it, I waited in vain for him to say.

I tottered around my room, slipping awkwardly into a selection of fabulous French lingerie I had purchased earlier that day to impress him later that night. In my dreams!

I moved unsteadily towards the balcony, stepping outside to drink in my intoxicating view of Paris by night, the Champs Elysées only a short distance from our hotel.

"Hello, bonsoir," a party of adolescent schoolboys on the sidewalk shouted while gesturing frantically up at me as I waved innocently back, smiling sweetly, wiggling my fingers at them, until I shockingly remembered I was wearing nothing but a bra and thong. I screamed, crashing inelegantly back into my room, and collapsed on the bed while giggling helplessly, a picture of corrupted innocence wearing a Lise Chanel Belle et Sauvage thong with matching plunge bra, decorated in a delicate and feminine floral print on an ivory base, embroidered with fine lace, there for nobody but schoolboys to see.

How sweet to fall asleep, to be reunited with Angelo in dreams where he'd been restored to the man I had always imagined him to be, attentive to my needs and decisive in their execution, the polar opposite of the career-obsessed character he had become in Paris.

I resisted the waking world for as long as I could sustain my dream, but agonisingly it soon ran out of gas, my fantasy man slipping away from my grasp as I tentatively opened my eyes.

To see Angelo, a white towel draped around his taut waist, standing manfully at the end of my bed. He was as awake as I was.

"You came for me!" I gasped, still uncertain if he was a phantom but wanting him nevertheless, whether he was of this world or the next.

"You complete me," he replied and held me aloft, carrying me through the connecting corridor into his bedroom where a king-size bed, strewn with rose petals and illuminated by a sea of scented candles, awaited me. He placed me as if I was a precious object upon the bed, stepping back in awe. "Your beauty is incandescent" he murmured. Men, eh? So how could this precious moment ever live up to expectations? After all, I'd been waiting for this to happen for most of my life.

And I wasn't about to be disappointed.

Without shame, his towel fell to the floor, and with all the confidence of a man who had obvious reason to be proud he moved purposefully towards the bed, a part of him growing in sympathy with every step he took.

Having descended upon me, he explored every part of me, a maestro of foreplay, conducting my body like an orchestra, a symphony in three movements. First he gently kissing my ear lobes, then sweetly stroked my neck and ran his fingers up and down my back, finally moving towards my breasts, where he began to tease my nipples to distraction, creating a connection with my sex so strong that I could have climaxed there and then, especially when he paused to whisper "Ti amo" in my ear.

In the silence that followed I encouraged him to lie back so I could explore his taut muscular chest by silkily sweeping my breasts rhythmically back and forth across him. He closed his eyes as I then ran my fingers along the outline of his six pack abs until I was inexorably drawn further south, where I held him intimately. Never had my hand felt so small, forming an O with my thumb and forefinger around it, then journeying outwards until I reached its majestic mushroom of a head.

Open wide...

"Oh so completely beautiful," I told him as I came up for air, when I really wanted to shout, wow, so incredibly big!

It's not the size of the boat but the motion of the ocean, I'd once heard it said, but Angelo was about to prove it didn't have to be an either/or situation.

I was still in disbelief that this most wondrous of men had actually chosen me, as he reclaimed control by creating erogenous zones on my body where they had no right to exist.

And at long last he partook of my sex like he loved it more than life itself, his ingenious tongue bestowing intense pleasure upon me. I came and came again, and when he finally entered me, so deep inside my breath took flight, I gripped his agonisingly provocative buttocks, inadvertently drawing blood. He appeared insatiable, rewriting the rules of the Kama Sutra by initiating a sequence of ever more ingenious unions. So when I went astride him I began to jump up and down for joy, riding a cock horse to Banbury Cross, shouting "fuck me! fuck me!" until he took me from behind, deriving pleasure only in giving until I became inundated with bliss.

And so it was that my ridiculous body finally belonged to me.

"I want you to come too," I begged of him, and ever mindful of my needs, he erupted inside me just as his lips met mine, our kiss igniting us both. In the afterglow we held one another tenderly, spent of passion but replete in love.

CHAPTER TWENTY ONE

I was sashaying on sunshine. Well can you blame me, with Angelo having come so spectacularly to life? Let me first list his qualities – caring towards those less fortunate than himself, a truly great listener, an excellent sense of humour - and what was that other great attribute of his? Oh yes, I remember now - being a sex god, if not a lip-smacking, long-lasting, totally brilliant lover. How could I possibly have forgotten that? He had taken me to places I didn't know existed this side of paradise. So I wasn't going to allow one little local difficulty – his ridiculous idea for me to host my own show at Melissa's expense – to rain on my parade.

I thought I could handle him, resolute in my belief that I would do the right thing by Melissa. Except could it be that I was weakening? I caught myself getting just a little bit too over impressed after casually enquiring of Angelo if there had been any more takers on this supposedly new show, which was never going to happen anyway…

"Hugh Jackman? The guy who plays Wolverine, and the star of Les Mis? But he's downright gorgeous, and extremely talented too," I replied.

"The selfsame one," Angelo confirmed, wearing this huge, great, silly grin, positively relishing my resolve dissolving under his duress.

"You've outgrown Melissa", he kept on repeating, and while I couldn't deny that my People Person role hadn't been a total disaster, there was no way I considered myself anywhere near ready to host my own show. Besides, I owed Melissa my loyalty, so I was more than happy to carry on learning from the best and continuing to work alongside a television icon. Yet when I should have been on top of the world at my small screen success I remained down in the doldrums as I struggled behind the scenes to reconnect with Melissa.

"Do you want me to take on the bossy sister or shall I leave her to you?" I had enquired of her in make-up before a show on sibling rivalry.

"I guess you will do what you want to do, as always," she disdainfully replied, "although I would prefer it if you would follow my lead."

I had dreaded the idea of going back to Groucho on my return from Paris. So I would demand a clearing-the-air meeting with Melissa to convince her that my relationship with Angelo posed no threat to her whatsoever, and that I would remain loyal to her come what may.

You have nothing to fear of me except fear itself, I wanted to tell her, except, sad to report, I never got the chance. She had already reached her own conclusions. She had barred me from entering the building as the same burly security man who had once treated me like the First Lady of Television, politely but firmly told me that I wasn't welcome there any more.

"Do you know who I am?" I was embarrassed to hear myself saying.

"I have instructions not to let you in," he officiously replied.

"Let me through. I absolutely demand to see Melissa," I begged of him.

"Unless you leave immediately I will be obliged to escort you from the building forthwith," he warned me.

"Elaine!" I shouted in desperation as she rudely brushed me aside on her way through the lobby waving a newspaper in her hand. "Can't you get this guy to see sense and let me through?" My pleading had no effect. Regardless of what had happened in the apartment, we were professional colleagues who enjoyed working together. Surely she would help me when I really needed her most?

"Gold Steals Melissa's Prime Time Celebrity Show," she said, reading a headline out loud from that morning's newspaper in what was becoming something of a habit.

"That's a lie. It was nothing more than a proposal which I've consistently rejected," I said, honestly protesting my innocence.

"I was almost beginning to believe in you again," said Elaine, clearly unmoved by my heartfelt plea. "I should have known better. After all, betrayal if what you do best."

In seconds, two more security guys had arrived to provide reinforcements. They manhandled me unceremoniously on to the street, all my professional possessions in a cardboard box not far behind. And just when it couldn't get much worse along came a press photographer, conveniently on hand to record my humiliation for all the world to enjoy – getting my just desserts, I guess Melissa would call it. He was soon to be supplemented by a bunch of opportunist kids who began filming me on their smart phones. YouTube here I come! Thankfully I resisted the temptation to give them all the finger – not a good image for a once aspiring star, I'm sure you'll agree – doing miserable and forlorn instead, much to my agent's relief when I recounted the story to her a few minutes later. Mind you, it wasn't Bonnie I had in my sights – I would have trusted her with my shoes – my target was Angelo. Hand on heart, he was to blame. I could picture the scenario unfolding in his mind. Having been unable to persuade me to leave Groucho of my own accord, he'd deliberately forced Melissa's hand by leaking the so-called story to the press. You see, I knew him so well.

I hightailed it down to Network HQ to confront Angelo, dragging him out of a senior management meeting so he could become properly acquainted with the depth of my disgust.

"Men Who Control Women!" I bawled at Angelo. "That should be the subject of my first show in this supposed new series, and you the principal guest!"

He adopted the expression of a little boy who had expected to be praised for having done something good and was being told off instead.

"I would never do anything to hurt you," he assured me. "I did what I did because I love you."

"You confuse love with control. Go consider" I said, departing his office, wanting so much to be angry and yet... he'd only gone and said he loved me. "I did what I did because I love you," he'd said, unless I was sorely mistaken – so let the bells ring out, may joy be unconfined and while I'm at it - given my re-discovered youth - OMG too. You see, however much I wanted to hate him, I just couldn't stop loving him back. It seemed he was my destiny, and you can't fight fate can you?

That didn't mean I'd forgiven him for what he'd done to Melissa, as I attempted to repair the damage. I made several attempts to call, email and approach her, even hanging about outside her Manhattan apartment until I was moved along by the police, who'd assumed I was a celebrity stalker.

In despair I sent an old-fashioned letter to Melissa, promising her that I'd never had any intention of deserting her show in favour of *Gold*, or stealing her celebrity slot either, yet I couldn't bring myself to blame Angelo, unable to bear the thought of her saying ‘I told you so’ when it came to her judging my relationship with him.

She didn’t reply anyway, which greatly disappointed me, although forcing me to look forwards and accept that I had been comprehensively cast adrift from Groucho Productions, washed up on the shore of my own show. I only feigned enthusiasm at first, still having great reservations about the format, focusing as it did on celebrities as opposed to real people, where my real strengths lay. I argued endlessly with Angelo about this obsession with celebrity culture, but he remained adamant that it was ‘stars or nothing,’ and I guess nobody would have really understood if I’d announced I was willing to sacrifice my career in television that early on over my refusal to hang out with Brad Pitt. In fact, it wasn’t long before Brad’s people signalled that he would be thrilled to be my first guest of the series and was ‘totally relaxed’ about revealing more of himself than he had ever done before, so I had little choice but to go where my career was taking me.

I guess it was more about control, keeping Angelo out of my professional picture, as I took up the challenge of multi-tasking as both producer and presenter. To be honest, it was beyond me, and I needed help.

“I will produce for you,” he volunteered.

“I’d rather you re-hire Kyle,” I replied, which obviously got him thinking.

So just twenty four hours later, lying in bed in the afterglow of our lovemaking – so it wasn't all bad - he inappropriately announced: "I've got your new producer."

"Won't you ever learn?" I said in exasperation, disentangling myself from his embrace before leaving the bed in an extravagant hurry. "Does the word 'consult' mean anything to you? Whoever it is, I'm not the slightest bit interested. I'll make my own decisions, if you please," I argued stomping my feet.

"So you're not at all curious?" Angelo temptingly enquired.

"Whoever, whatever. I couldn't be less interested," I assured him while emphatically covering my body with an abundance of clothes to deny him as much pleasure as was womanly possible.

"It's Elaine," he informed me regardless of my reservations, bringing my reverse striptease to a dramatic halt.

"No way! She'd never desert Melissa, let alone work with me."

"Everybody has their price, and hell, Elaine Green doesn't come cheap," he said, gloating all over me.

I called Elaine directly – surely she would have to speak to me now – if only to ask her, why?

"It was knowing that you had requested me personally. Otherwise, I would never have deserted Melissa," she explained.

"Welcome on board," I said congratulating her.

So Angelo had manipulated Elaine too. We were but Blu-Tac in his hands.

Looking back, I was beginning to become something of an expert in turning a blind eye to Angelo's excesses, although it hadn't yet dawned on me that however much I disapproved of his actions, their consequences were becoming increasingly beneficial to me. Without Angelo I wouldn't be preparing to present a high-profile prime time television show where I would be exclusively interviewing A-list celebrities, making must-see TV for an audience of millions, produced by my once estranged daughter.

The stakes were high. Elaine and I met up for our inaugural planning meeting, where we began to lay the foundations for our show.

"How to succeed?" I reflected, tapping my pen lightly on the desk. "And how to avoid churning out a bland, predictable rehash of everything everybody already knows about some of the most reported people on the planet?"

"By stripping away the façade of celebrity by lulling them into a false sense of security," Elaine proposed. "By asking them stuff they wouldn't expect, like is the human race getting taller, or can animals commit suicide?"

"Surreal."

"Impossible to answer maybe, more about giving the viewer an insight into how their minds work as they attempt to give an answer. And then we would throw them a curve ball kind of question, such as, if you could select a superpower, would you choose the ability to read minds, to be invisible, or to fly, and then to pursue, why?"

"More like psychoanalysis than an interview."

"You've got it. Stuff like what's your favourite word, would you rather be a flower than a tree, but never, ever, how did you get started in your career."

Although I approved of the direction she was going in I had to rein her in once or twice – just like I used to at home – to prevent this show from getting too far out.

Slowly my optimism began to grow. I could really see Gold being fresh, original and thought provoking, unlike any other talk show around, thanks to Elaine's ingenious pre-production – all of course subject to whether I could actually serve her ideas well when it came to my turn, to present and interrogate celebrities on screen.

I felt the weight of responsibility upon me and when my day in the studio finally arrived I couldn't quite believe it when I heard myself saying, "Ladies and gentlemen, would you welcome Brad Pitt". To make it even more unreal, he didn't show up at first. He kept me waiting nearly thirty whole seconds.

"What kept you?" I said as he took his seat.

"Well, the last time we met at the premiere of *Ravishing* you kept me waiting a helluva lot longer than that," he joked to wild applause.

"So you're like an elephant, Brad. You never, ever forget."

"I guess so. After all, it's your memories who define who you are. Isn't that true?"

And off we went; no plugging of his latest film, book, or CD, just personal insights, exactly as we had planned it.

And OK, maybe a little celebrity trivia too, getting him to admit that Angelina was sometimes forced to elbow him in the ribs when he talked in his sleep.

"I'm so glad you don't snore, otherwise a trillion women's dreams go up in smoke," I said flirting with him, just a little.

"And I don't scratch my butt either."

"Pleased to know it. And what do you talk about in your sleep?" Elaine asked me to ask him through my ear piece.

"Just this. How dare that broad from Melissa's show keep us waiting? Doesn't she know who we are?"

And then I tailed it all by enquiring, "And if heaven exists, what would you like to hear God saying when you arrive at the Pearly Gates?"

"Your room isn't ready yet. Can you check in later?"

The crowd cheered, inspiring him to get to his feet with him singing, as God to himself, "get back to where you once belong."

"So God's a Beatle?"

"Yeah! Yeah! Yeah! It could be worse. He could be Justin Bieber".

***

We had got away with it, and there were kisses all around, even from Elaine. Angelo also approved as the ratings grew dramatically with every show, while the press also had their say.

"As an interviewer, Jennifer Gold possesses that rare gift of being able to relax a normally defensive over rehearsed star into a sense of false security. She flirtatiously pandered to a sometimes giant ego until that moment when his defences slipped and surgically struck to explore either an intimate secret or an unexpected profound opinion. And it was fun too.'

I think the guy liked it.

CHAPTER TWENTY TWO

A telephone rang.

In spite of Angelo's unrelenting ambition to control me professionally, I guess by any standard I had a thrilling existence, hosting my own prime time talk show, mingling with the most glamorous and cleverest people on the planet, and having a boyfriend who turned heads wherever he went yet only seemed to have eyes for me.

I picked up the receiver.

"I'm calling you in," said Alice.

Decisions, more often than not, are made in a split second, transforming lives either for better or worse. I could have simply hung up or demanded that she should leave me alone, threatening her with dire consequences should she ever call again, but fatally I hesitated.

"I just knew you wouldn't have the balls to cut me off."

"How the hell did you get my number?"

"Oh purlease! Surely you can do better than that?" Alice taunted me.

"What is it that you want from me?" I said, my voice betraying desperation, although inexplicably, not yet daring to hang up.

"You gave me your word," Alice reminded me, "that you would return for one more hit, at a time and place of my choosing."

"That was then – this is now."

"And now you are famous, but don't be deluded into thinking that makes any difference at all to our little agreement. A deal is a deal, regardless of who you are and what you've become."

"But why me?" I challenged her. "There must be at least a thousand other girls who could do an equally, if not better job than me."

"Modesty doesn't become you," Alice berated me. "Only you can pursue this particular hit to a successful conclusion," she added, subtly enticing me to investigate the hit further.

"You can flatter me all you want, but you can't seriously think that I could get away with a hit unnoticed. I'm on TV, in case you've forgotten."

"It's not a problem – the only thing this guy would ever watch on TV is news, but mostly sport."

"Alice – please get real," I counselled her. "I'm now on prime time television. What reason could there possibly be for me to work as a honey trap ever again?"

"But you promised me" she said like she was the one in the right. "And girls who break promises suffer consequences."

"Like what?"

"Like being exposed in the press as a former honey trap."

"You don't really think Angelo would let that happen?"

"I'm on speed dial to the *National Enquirer*, so you can kiss your career, and more importantly, I suspect your Angelo, goodbye."

Alice had struck a raw nerve.

"So you expect me to do just one more hit then?" I quizzically observed.

"And then I will set you free."

"Forever?"

"For sure, and this way, nobody need ever know about your colourful past either," said Alice, a threat lurking underneath her every promise.

I had no reason to trust her, and she had me in a corner, and yet I felt excitement too. Could I have been exhilarated by the idea of acting without Angelo's knowledge, actually escaping his all-pervasive control? Was that somehow spurring me on to reconnect with Alice?

Having become recognisable since I last visited Truth, I endeavoured to keep a low profile, my head swathed in a Hermes scarf, my eyes shielded by Ray Bans. On reflection the look screamed 'famous person in disguise'. I slipped surreptitiously into Eve Couture, browsing through jackets and tops until what had always been that heart-stopping moment when I was summoned to go upstairs.

"I'm so loving the show," said one of the assistants as

I departed the store – so much for keeping a low profile. Alice was lurking at the entrance to her apartment. She offered me an air kiss which I declined in favour of a formal handshake.

"As irresistible as ever," said Alice, eyeing me lasciviously. Her look that could have tempted a novice nun.

No matter how hard I tried to keep the meeting businesslike Alice just couldn't resist goading me about my well-publicised relationship with "that control freak," Angelo.

"How could that man ever satisfy you?" she taunted me.

"Expertly," I replied. Alice was visibly disgusted.

It was a relief to get back to business. She handed me a folder, explaining this victim was an unusual target in that she considered him to be approaching incorruptible. That's where I came in, my alleged gorgeousness still the ultimate test, at least in the eyes of Alice.

"His wife is a strange woman, like a ghost, almost as if she wasn't there" she said. "She is convinced he's cheating on her. Apparently he's done it once before – an affair of sorts – although this time around I strongly suspect it's all in her head."

Hell, was Alice going soft in her old age?

She continued recounting the wife's tale of woe. "You see, since her recently diagnosed clinical depression, becoming what she described as a shadow of her former self, she believes her husband has been looking elsewhere again, possibly high class hookers or a full blown affair. So we need to find out whether he's susceptible."

In the days when I made my living entrapping men, that moment when I first caught sight of the victim's photograph never failed to elicit fear and fascination, usually observed by Alice with wry amusement. Often the victim would look strangely familiar at first sight, sometimes leading me to believe mistakenly that I might know him, thinking it could be that officious hotel manager, the caustic cable guy or the serial flatterer who issued tickets behind the glass at Penn Station. This familiarity was almost always a trick of the mind. Until today.

The picture was of Greg, my husband.

Was I the victim of a truly mean trick? I knew exactly how much Alice would enjoy teasing me like that, her warped revenge for me having had the impudence to have become famous since we worked together. She scrutinised me closely, as I did her, not a flicker of a sarcastic smile to be seen anywhere on her lips, leading me to conclude that she hadn't set me up after all. But she didn't miss a trick, old Alice. Something about my reaction to the photo clearly disturbed her.

"What does this guy mean to you?" she quizzed me.

"He's my victim."

"And is there any chance he might recognise you?"

"None whatsoever."

Never had two truer words been spoken, my transparent honesty allaying Alice's fears that the hit might be compromised, thereby ensuring that the honey trap against Greg, my ex-husband, would go ahead as planned.

And I celebrated it when I should surely have declared a connection between us, ending the hit there and then. Well, what could I have said, that he'd been my husband in a previous life? As excuses go, a touch unbelievable. And even after everything I'd been through with honey trapping, and television and Angelo, still I cared about Greg. Of course, I positively relished the opportunity of putting my cheating, lying husband to the test – honestly not as revenge – so why should I care that you don't believe me? It was my gift-wrapped opportunity to discover whether I could ever trust Greg again.

It was irresistible.

Alice furnished me with the necessary details – Greg was in town for a seminar entitled 'Accountancy – Challenges and Rewards In the Twenty First Century'. He was staying at the Hilton Hotel, Times Square, for one night only. He would be in seventh heaven, I imagined.

I knew exactly how to dress for Greg - he was my husband after all. Nothing too slutty that might frighten the poor man away. I would strive to be smart but sexy in my navy blue Chanel suit.

I slipped unobtrusively into the hotel lobby, once more hidden by my regulation celebrity headscarf and glasses, picked up an accountancy delegate's abandoned name tag and replaced his name with a made-up one of my own. And then Greg walked right by me. I instinctively shielded my face, even though he would never have recognised me, unless he had been watching early evenings on Wolf TV.

How strange to be standing so close to him. Hans Christian Andersen knows if that was allowed under the terms of my reincarnation and whether I would turn into a frog as a result. But as no green skin was forthcoming, I carried on observing Greg. He didn't look at all the way I had expected. My heart went out to him, noting how he radiated tiredness and disappointment, in contrast to the other conference delegates mingling in the lobby, where much good-natured back-slapping was going on. If defeat had a face it would be Greg's.

A wave of sympathy mixed with guilt temporarily engulfed me. How I pitied the man I had first deserted and then condemned to living with a pale shadow of the woman I had been, and I don't think I'd forgiven him for his infidelity either.

While most of the delegates headed straight towards the hotel bar, I watched Greg politely decline their invitations and walk purposefully into Times Square, a hundred animated, illuminated signs shining brightly above and beyond him in the fading early evening daylight. I tracked him as far as 42nd Street when I decided to pounce.

"Mr Green, I think you might have left this" I said, waving a Parker pen at him.

"Not mine I'm afraid," he said hardly breaking his stride.

"What a seminar," I said pointing to my delegate's badge.

"Roxanne. That's your name?" he said slowing down a little to read my name.

He used to love that song by the Police. I had now reduced him to a more moderate walk.

"I didn't notice you at the seminar," said Greg. "I'm sure I would have remembered you."

I bet you would, you cheating, lying husband. But I decided not to say that. In fact, I momentarily ran out of words, as we ambled along together in silence, our delegates' badges the only thing that bound us together.

"I just had to get some air," he eventually commented. "I mean what a ridiculous title for a seminar, Accountancy Can Be Fun. Accountancy can be many things – lucrative, demanding challenging even, but fun?"

I had to smile – such a typical Greg rant. We were passing the Ed Sullivan Theatre where Johnny Mailman's great rival, David Letterman, was performed on TV nightly.

"Now that's what I call fun. Letterman, he's fun, or funny. I'm not really sure what fun is" he said. Given the nature of my mission I suppose I should have said, I'll show you what fun is, big boy, but that only ever happened in porn movies, didn't it?

"Did you know," he said as we completed our circuit

of theatre land back into Times Square, "that all building owners in this area are by ordinance obliged to display illuminated signs, whereas about anywhere else in the US it would be against the law to pollute the night sky?"

"Is that so? Fascinating," I lied again.

"101 Fascinating Facts About New York. It's a great read. I could lend it to you... if you like that kind of thing?"

"Hey, I'm a trainee accountant. How could I not? Can I collect it now?" I begged of him. This boring book was the key to his room, the place where I would be able to execute my hit on him.

"I'll bring it down to the morning session," he politely volunteered.

"I can't wait that long," I said a little too stridently. "I mean, I would so love to read it right now."

"OK," he said, looking at me quizzically.

"Let me accompany you to your room. I can't wait another minute."

First base, I thought.

***

He fiddled with his key card, looking guiltily both ways down the corridor as if he was doing something profoundly wrong before letting me in to his suite. He quickly disappeared into his bedroom to collect the book, which I correctly guessed would be right next to his bed.

"Enjoy," he said. "Don't let it keep you up all night."

A telephone was ringing in his room next door. "Must go," he said and ushered me out of the door, although I prevented it from shutting properly behind me. I waited a few seconds for him to pick up his call before going back in and draping myself across the sofa. I could overhear his conversation with his wife in Valley Stream.

"No, I'm having an early night," I heard him say, "I'm settling down with my Fascinating Facts Book for the evening." I already knew this was a lie. I heard him replace the receiver, then came the sound of splashing water, signifying a shower. I untied my headscarf and removed my sun glasses.

He didn't linger there long. He soon came back, a white towel wrapped around his waist.

"Hell, I thought you'd gone," he said as he feverishly adjusted his towel.

"Have you been working out?" I couldn't stop myself from saying it. I was genuinely taken aback by his newly-toned physique.

"As it happens, I have," he replied curtly.

"You'll have to forgive me' I replied. 'I guess I better leave right now. It's just that I didn't really feel I'd thanked you properly for the book, or wished you goodbye, what with the phone ringing," I lied through my lip gloss.

He wasn't going to throw me out now. Greg would never punish anybody for being polite.

"Can I get you a coffee?" he then enquired.

"I'd prefer a vodka and tonic," I replied.

"No problem, I suppose, especially after the day we've had," said Greg, stiffening defensively. "Please excuse me while I get dressed."

"Not on my account. I like you just the way you are," I teasingly said.

A short silence fell upon us while he fixed my drink. He was clearly uncomfortable in his semi-nakedness. I was relishing his unease.

"So when you're not cooking the books, what is it that you do for pleasure?" I probed him while sipping my drink.

"Pleasure? I'm married," he said, as if the two things were totally incompatible.

"Married? For real or in name only?"

He paused longer than was appropriate.

"Marriage is a serious business," he pronounced after what must have been an intense internal debate. "We've been together nearly 25 years. That cannot be dismissed lightly."

"An anniversary eh? Cause for celebration?" I probed him further.

"Of course," he replied with undue haste, "but we've had our ups and downs too."

"And are we presently up, or are we down?"

He hardly needed to reply.

"I can't claim to have been the perfect husband. Far

from it. I once had an affair with a girl years younger than me and I only owned up to it recently to ease my guilty conscience."

Aha! I so knew it.

"So why did you cheat on your wife?" I challenged him. The truth at last, or so I hoped.

"If I knew the answer to that I might know how to save my marriage," he replied enigmatically.

"Did it flatter your ego? Did you feel neglected by her? Was your wife rubbish in the sack? Did you fall out of love with her? Did you love Britney?"

"So many questions," he said. Then he froze. "I don't remember mentioning her name."

Whoops. "I think you've just had a senior moment. You so did! Just give me one answer, please!"

"I never ever loved that girl. I guess she must have appealed to the pathetic vanity of a middle-aged man, the type of guy who likes to read 101 Interesting Facts books."

"Are you sure?" I said pushing him further.

"I did once tell her I loved her, but I was infatuated and never, ever in love, only with the idea of love. I was simply telling her what she wanted to hear."

"And that's what you tell yourself, is it?"

"OK, so I'd been flattered. I even kept this juvenile letter from her until I realised just how meaningless it really was. The only woman I have ever truly loved is my wife."

"You should have destroyed it."

"I did" he said, looking at me strangely.

"Because if she ever found that letter it would break her heart."

"I'll check just as soon as I get home, and shred it if needs be." I could see he was panicking a little, wondering if he really had destroyed it.

Too late, the damage is already done, just look at your wife, I wanted to shout. Instead I just nodded sympathetically.

"I can't believe I'm opening up like this," said Greg. "Ever since our daughter left home, my wife has become increasingly distant."

I watched the weight lift from his shoulders at being able to unburden himself to another human being without danger or recrimination.

"She used to spend hours organising aid for the homeless. A waste of time, if you ask me. What's the point of helping people who don't want to help themselves? There again, even that would have been preferable to what has happened since – becoming a virtual prisoner in her home, having turned her back on the outside world."

"Like a recluse?" I asked seeking clarification.

"As good as," he concurred with a heavy sigh. "She gradually became addicted to trash TV and one evening when I came home from another day at the practice I discovered her slumped on the sofa watching some celebrity junk called 'Gold'."

Instinctively I bowed my head.

"She said 'That could have been me'. She was looking at this girl interviewing Brad Pitt. 'And I could have been the President of the United States', I replied, and she just broke down. She didn't stop sobbing for three hours."

"And how did that make you feel?"

"Angry at first, then irritated, concerned, disturbed and finally heartbroken," he replied, his voice drenched with emotion, an unfamiliar sound to my ears.

"And this wife of yours, do you love her?"

Greg paused to formulate his thoughts.

"I love her, but I don't love what she's become. It's as if she's gone missing, like her soul's been stolen overnight. It's like she's a wife in name only."

I don't think I knew the meaning of the word 'guilt' until I heard Greg say that.

"I want my wife back," he said pleadingly, eyes moistening, emotion threatening to unman him, "but I don't know how to find her, or even where to begin."

"Kiss her and she'll come," I whispered into his ear, and then I kissed him on the lips. Just for a moment.

"I think you ought to leave" he said, recoiling as if from something terrible. "I was unfaithful to my wife once, but I never will be again."

I was now more certain of my husband's future fidelity than any woman alive could be.

"But she'll never know", I said breathily.

"She'll know", said Greg, more poignantly than he had reason to realise.

Yet still I wanted to torment him and put him to the ultimate test. He looked into my eyes longingly. And just when I became convinced he was about to take me he moved, reluctantly, away.

For a moment I was unsure whether to celebrate or mourn his fidelity to me. After all, I was the only woman on earth he could make love to without being unfaithful, yet he remained incorruptible.

While I yearned to talk to him further I made my excuses instead, disappearing into the night, the hit accomplished to my own satisfaction, if not to Alice's. So many questions were producing just one answer.

He loved me still.

CHAPTER TWENTY THREE

I returned to the lobby wrapped up in a head scarf and dark glasses again – Audrey Hepburn, eat your heart out – so I was thankfully unrecognisable as Elaine appeared heading towards an upward bound elevator, en route, I supposed, to visit her father. In fear I hid behind a copy of *American Vogue* to avoid having to invent reasons for my presence in the hotel – it looked like I was finally running low on lies. That near miss, not to mention the emotional fallout of my hit, on Greg encouraged me to face up to Alice without delay.

"I tried, boy how I tried," I explained to her, happy to own up to my failure to seduce Greg. "Tell his wife he's not a bad man."

"Either he's a closet gay, or you are definitely losing your touch."

"He's as straight as they come," I said miming his arousal. Forgive me, but I just couldn't resist offending Alice.

"Too much information" she said. "You are so free to go." She was addressing me as if she owned me. "What use could I possibly have for a girl who's lost her power to infatuate?"

While I felt liberated by finally escaping from Truth, reconnecting with Greg had disorientated me. He couldn't have been more faithful – I'd seen it with my own eyes – and I had also been reminded of that lovely sense of security he used to give me with his old-world courtesy and politeness, and his generosity of spirit, lending me his *Book of 101 Fascinating Facts*, God bless him, whereas Angelo was a roller coaster of emotions, thrilling and dangerous and exciting in turn, a scream-out-loud ride in every sense.

Which way to turn? So I did what rich people without close friends to confide in usually do – I got Bonnie to book me a therapist.

"I saw this girl on the Melissa Show when I was just a viewer, long before I worked there," I explained to the distinguished female psychiatrist, who was more a follower of Jung and Freud than Oprah and Melissa.

"She was torn between two lovers, one safe and reliable, the other wild and dangerous, and from the safety of my armchair at home I had said, dump them both. Fast forward, and I now have two such men in my own life, yet suddenly I need them both."

"I see" she observed. My 2,000 dollars had clearly been well spent.

I told her about the other men who had recently been in my life too, knowing that she wouldn't judge.

"Maybe a man for every mood," she proposed. "Greg, when you're feeling insecure, Angelo when you're wild, Brad when you're adventurous and Marty when you're mellow."

"I suppose that's secretly what every woman wants."

"But practically, if you can only have one of them, then it's just a question of which of them ticks most, if not all of the boxes."

"Angelo" I said. "I've had a lifetime of safe and secure, although I do sometimes miss that feeling of security. Oh I don't know", I said in despair. That was assuming I even had a choice. And I hadn't even bothered her with Alice. I just hadn't got that much time or money to spend.

While I had been deceiving Angelo he had been plotting behind my back too, planning what he thought would be a momentous surprise for me at the forthcoming People's Television Awards. He had unilaterally decided I should be surrounded by my closest friends on what he argued would be my night of nights when he strongly suspected that I would blow away the competition to win a prestigious prize, if he hadn't already fixed it.

He had become full of good intentions. He was aware of an almighty falling out between me and my former friends in New York shortly before he met me, his inspiration for organising what he considered to be an overdue reconciliation between us all. And what better place than the scene of my inevitable triumph at a glittering awards ceremony in the heart of New York City?

In pursuit of his mischievous plan he had managed to lay his hands on my address book while I was sleeping, scribbling down the names and numbers of, among others, Alice Brewer, Marty Prime, Hannah Johnson and Elaine's boyfriend, Brad Tripp.

It was truly thoughtful of him, if totally misguided. Had I got wind of Angelo's plan I would have torn up my request to attend and stayed in to paint my toenails instead, while many of the names on that list would have been equally hostile or indifferent to me, and certainly astonished to have received an invitation from Angelo and Jennifer, especially Jennifer, of all people.

I saw first-hand how the People's Television Awards continued to occupy Angelo's waking hours, some said at the expense of his Network commitments, creating rumblings of dissatisfaction at Wolf TV. I had become his pet project, and he was obsessively devoted to making me more marketable than the iPad, lobbying the movers and shakers on the committee to give Jennifer Gold their vote. Should they need a gentle reminder he commissioned a giant billboard of me standing fifty feet tall in Times Square.

I didn't want to appear ungrateful, except that I began to suspect this wasn't about me, or even us, but him. I could feel myself becoming just an extension of his giant, all-consuming ego. Take the way he wanted me to look at the ceremony, dismissively ignoring my heartfelt plea to allow me to dress more conservatively than for my debut at *Ravishing*. "Your body is a weapon of mass seduction. We must use it," he decreed.

I was determined to put a stop to Angelo's nonsense and saw no reason why being madly, absurdly, blissheartedly in love meant I should have to abandon my own principles, beliefs and opinions in favour of those of a man who continued to confuse support with control. Yet however hard I battled to challenge him and assert myself in the face of his downright intransigence, still I doubted my own worth, suspecting that only Angelo knew what was best for me, given his immense status as a towering figure in the world of television. My resistance was low. Time and time again I surrendered to his supposed superiority, as if I had become his creation. Even my esteemed agent was eclipsed by the Svengali in an Armani suit.

While loving him might have been easy, liking him was harder to do. Even when he miraculously agreed to my demand to be allowed to wear a neck-high front at the People's Awards Ceremony, the back of my curve-clinging navy blue Guy Laroche dress just had to be spectacularly bare, didn't it?

Angelo triumphs again, yet however much I may have felt manipulated by him I couldn't truthfully deny that the dress felt heart-racingly gorgeous to wear, now that I had overcome my fear of being on display.

The paparazzi loved it too, not I suspect because of its striking haute couture or chic, elegant style but the way it exposed almost the entire surface of my toned, nude back. Those guys with the cameras were quickly becoming my new best friends. Why? Because I gave them what they wanted. Keep the boys happy, my new show business mantra, was enthusiastically encouraged by Angelo. I feared would have hung me naked from the top of the Empire State Building, had he thought it would produce results.

Having set the flash guns ablaze, I looked back to witness a commotion caused by an unfortunate coincidence. Melissa was tottering unsteadily down the red carpet, arm in arm with her new beau Kyle, as they arrived at the Art Deco magnificence of the Waldorf Astoria only a few feet behind us. Sensing an opportunity, the paparazzi hollered at me to return – and as I always gave those boys what they wanted, I duly obliged them. But I was horrified to discover that they wanted the two of us, Melissa and me, to pose together for the shot neither of us wanted but were both obliged to deliver.

"Judas!" Melissa mouthed at me through her Rouge Coco lip colour as I caught the acrid scent of alcohol on my erstwhile mentor's breath.

"That should never have happened. Heads will roll," Angelo pronounced once we were safely inside, and how could I disagree?

So the night had started badly. It was about to get worse.

"Wow, you look so delicious I could eat you," said

Alice, emerging unexpectedly from the crowd with a blonde starlet hanging decoratively from her arm. What the Ellen De Generes was she doing there?

I smiled artificially while acknowledging her compliment, then dragged Angelo away, pushing him through the door of the ladies' toilets before locking him inside a cubicle and refusing to let him out until he explained how come this disreputable woman had been invited to the People's Television Awards.

"It's my surprise gift to you," he protested full of hurt innocence, enough to make me throw a fit hissier than a bag of snakes.

"Simply why?" I railed.

"Because I adore you," he began, explaining how he thought I would enjoy being seated at a table surrounded by those I had loved, as he unfortunately expressed it.

"And how is that you know Alice? Have you been the victim of one of her honey trap hits?" I quizzed him frivolously.

"Don't be ridiculous. She was unknown to me until I read your address book," he replied, and I knew, I just knew, he was lying. In that brief moment I even considered the notion that he had been the one to commission my honey trap hit on Greg, not that pale shadow of a woman in Valley Stream, such was his all-consuming control over me.

I left him with a flourish. He looked surprisingly unperturbed when he later emerged from the ladies' rest room, unlike me when I saw Marty striding towards me, his once crooked smile now transformed to a lopsided grin.

"Over here!" I screamed frantically towards Angelo. Anything was preferable to being left alone with a seemingly deranged Marty, but my darling boyfriend had been intercepted by an obsequious independent TV producer.

"I'm here for you," Marty creepily informed me.

"And how's Hannah?"

"I was never good enough for you, was I? Always out of your league. Well after tonight, you will only have eyes for me." His forehead was visibly throbbing. He looked deranged.

Hannah's arrival signalled a sudden key change in Marty as he performed a less-than-convincing rendition of his sweet old self, whereas she greeted me coldly – gross bad manners I would have thought for a specially invited guest to my table – and then, oh joy of joys, along came Brad clinging on to Elaine for dear life, as if I was about to molest him.

Any normal person would have appeared appropriately mortified, their tail between their legs, after what I had done to Angelo, but when he rejoined us he stood totally unrepentant, confidently welcoming the assembled group with warmth and good humour. Although I couldn't help but notice that Marty regarded him warily.

A stilted conversation ensued as we all attempted to

cover up the cracks of our various dysfunctional relationships with comments about the beautiful table settings, the Hotel's Art Deco splendour and whether Brad should have one or two buttons done up on his tuxedo. All failed to recreate connections between us, until we were blown away by a passing superstar of such global immensity that she took our breath away.

"I'm loving your work," said Oprah to me with an air kiss.

I stared back vacantly at her smiling face. The magnitude of her intergalactic celebrity had sucked all sense from me. I was incapable of formulating anything resembling a coherent response, apart from a totally embarrassing nervous giggle.

"Miss Gold holds you in the highest esteem," said Angelo, intervening on my behalf. Now he was putting words into my mouth, such was his hold over me.

"Isn't this fun?" said Hannah as she took her seat alongside Alice and her decorative plus-one, the sensational Suzi, who was blissfully oblivious to the fault lines which were opening up, cracking under the weight of our collective history.

Alongside Melissa on an adjacent table sat toxic Kyle, another character in the catastrophic cast list of people I had either hurt or who had blighted my new life. All of them seemed to have come back to haunt me on what should have been my greatest night of the year.

The three-course dinner which preceded the ceremony would certainly rank as one of the most awful I had ever endured, more as a result of the company than the food. In between courses, while making small talk with Alice, I could feel Marty's laser beam stare scorching through me, in complete contrast to Brad, who averted his eyes from meeting mine at every opportunity.

Conversation continued to be achingly artificial until, having had his fill of booze, Marty began spoiling for a fight.

"Take a bow, Angelo. You've reinvented her. She's your finest creation yet" said Marty.

"You're too kind," Angelo replied, so far from being offended his heart actually swelled with pride.

I couldn't help but be amused by his reaction. Until he coughed, a sound redolent of strong tobacco and cheap spirits. That made me scrutinise Angelo ever more closely. I sensed something had changed, but I was unsure whether it was in him, or whether I was seeing him anew, as if through different eyes. I knew I had encountered him before at my wedding, but more often in the half light, in dreams or in fleeting moments, subliminally seen in passing cars or disappearing into a crowd on the sidewalk, always just out of reach. This time it was different. A cold chill permeated my being as an image formed in my mind of a dishevelled, failed man I had once met when my life had hung seemingly by a thread in a time gone by.

I began to study him, this time with the love light

switched off. His handsome features were morphing into the face of that chaotic, down at heel hobo I had dramatically encountered on Main Street, Valley Stream, in what had been my darkest hour. That had been Angelo too.

The lights dimmed as host Mike Postman's entrance was greeted with rapturous applause. His remarks about Oprah failing to return his calls were going over my head. My thoughts were racing irrevocably towards a shocking conclusion.

Recipients of awards came and went, presenting themselves to me as nothing more than a blur on the landscape, my focus decidedly elsewhere.

"Are you OK?" Angelo enquired, his voice lacking its usual authority. He was visibly disorientated by my faraway air.

I didn't reply.

"And the winner of the Outstanding Contribution to People's Television," Mike Postman announced, "is..." - he paused to open the envelope - "Melissa Parker."

A collective gasp emanated from the room, amplified by the pre-show speculation that Oprah had been an odds-on certainty to retain her crown, especially in light of her recent retirement from her iconic daily show.

Instinctively I leapt from my seat, back on Planet Showbusiness once more, to cheer and shout as Melissa made her way unsteadily to the podium to receive her trophy, bumping into scenery and then stumbling.

Postman reacted quickly, catching her before she fell drunkenly to the ground.

"Go girl!" I shouted. My words and my whooping and hollering were obviously discernible to Melissa and they had the healing effect of temporarily restoring her composure and inspiring her to a rousing declaration of how television can not only entertain viewers but encourage them to lead better and more fulfilling lives. Melissa and I were still singing from the same hymn sheet – God bless her – even after all we'd been through.

"And yet, I am not a role model, but a survivor, although by surviving I give others hope," she proclaimed. "For sooner or later we all take a fall. So what do I do when I come crashing down?" she enquired of an open-mouthed audience. Nobody dared to respond.

"I get back up again. It's what I do," she declared to thunderous applause, regally gliding back to her table in triumph and into the arms of Kyle.

As the applause subsided, I stared Angelo between the eyes, now in no doubt whatsoever about exactly who this man really was.

"And now, Best Newcomer," said Postman, heralding the award I was most likely to win. "Let's hope they've shut the bar," he quipped.

"And the winner is…" he announced, pausing both to read the name and predictably to prolong the moment for dramatic effect. The result was no longer of any importance to me.

"You're him, aren't you?" I said confronting Angelo, "the hobo I kissed at the diner. You made me who I am."

"Jennifer Gold," Postman declared, but I continued to remain resolutely seated.

"Go on!" said Elaine, tugging my arm. "It's the moment you've been waiting for."

"You go," I spat at Angelo. "You might as well. It belongs to you."

"Are you out of your mind? Don't let this control freak take all the credit!" Alice urged me. I should have said, it takes one to know one, but I was touched by her concern. Maybe we could have been good together.

"Jennifer Gold!" Postman repeated for the third time. "Has anyone checked the bar?" he joked, a small eruption of nervous laughter slightly relieving the excruciating tension created by my failure to show.

At last, like a ghost, I made my way to the podium.

"You've always scared me," said Postman as he handed me the shiny silver trophy. Then he slipped back into the shadows, leaving me alone, in a spotlight, on a stage.

"What to say?" I said almost inaudibly. "Thank you, but I don't deserve this. Yes, I know award winners always say that, but in my case, it couldn't be more true. I stand before you a complete and utter fraud."

The room was that quiet you could have heard a false eyelash drop, both the brave and the beautiful seemingly in awe at the intensity of my extraordinary confession.

"I've heard it said that inside every careworn middle-aged woman is a beautiful young girl trying to get out. Well it might surprise you, the reverse is also true."

I watched celebrities at tables exchanging bewildered looks, suspecting many of them must have been speculating as to which fashionable drug I had been inhaling prior to the show.

"I've done some terrible, wicked things. Melissa, you plucked me from obscurity, believing in me when nobody else would have either dared or cared, and having groomed me for stardom, how did I repay you? With disloyalty. Forgive me.

Elaine, you took me into your home and entrusted me with what was most precious to you, and I abused that trust. Forgive me.

Marty. By my thoughtlessness, I transformed a young idealistic boy into a bitter twisted man. Forgive me.

Greg, my husband – yes, I have one - unbeknown to you, I deserted you without so much as a simple goodbye, condemning you to co-exist with a ghostly stranger. Forgive me."

I paused to take a long lingering look at the trophy, resting like an abandoned baby, unwanted in my arms.

"I've stolen this award from its rightful owner, so I wish to return it to.... Angelo Ramirez, the man who made me!

The room turned as one to witness Angelo's reaction. There was collective surprise as they saw his composure still intact.

"Bring it on," I yelled, as if impersonating that mad woman who stands shouting at the end of every Main Street. "Come on! Get up here! Take it! It's yours!"

Apparently unperturbed, Angelo rose elegantly from his chair, silence greeting his inappropriately assured walk to the podium. I just knew what he was thinking – if there's one thing the public adores more than a goddess, it's a flawed goddess. I was being elevated to the ranks of Marilyn Monroe and Princess Diana, but unlike them, I was blissfully and indisputable alive. Kerching!

I watched Angelo as he walked towards me. He stepped onto the stage, momentarily distracted by the glare of lights.

That gave Marty an extra couple of seconds to produce a gun and take aim at the man he despised enough to kill.

But Brad saw what was happening. He lunged towards the would-be assassin, unbalancing him. A shot rang out and Angelo's face was bathed in blood and confusion. Screams erupted from the crowd. I saw Marty looking aghast at what he had done. The bullet had hit me. The girl he had loved beyond reason had been gunned down by a bullet meant for another.

In one swift move Marty elbowed Brad in the face, allowing time and space to fire again. This time the shot ripped into Angelo and felled him like a tree.

It was the disbelief, not the pain, which I remember

about being shot, lying there, next to Angelo, who appeared unsurprised as he watched me age before his eyes, years passing in seconds, my face barely recognisable, Gold turning to Green.

"In God's name, this can't be happening," a breathless paramedic, who had sprinted from the back of the hall, observed, as he watched me close up, flagrantly defying the laws of nature by degenerating into an old woman in front of him.

"Kiss me," Angelo begged of me. Hardly the time or the place, I thought, gasping in shock.

"But with a kiss I can save you," he pleaded with me, as both our lives ebbed relentlessly away. "Let me take you back to where you once belonged. Otherwise, you will surely die."

I grimaced. The pain, which had previously been confined to my chest, was spreading to my abdomen. I was losing consciousness.

"Tell me your name?" I heard the paramedic ask.

"Jennifer… Green," I replied.

"She's losing it. It's Gold," I heard Postman say.

"Kiss me," Angelo begged of me again, rolling painfully over to get closer to me.

"Like when you were a down and out," I managed to say.

"But you did it. Do it again, to save your skin."

Maybe I had outstayed my welcome in this life.

Through a haze I could see Marty, the guy who had shot me, looking down in desperation as two burly cops pinned him roughly against the wall.

"I didn't mean to kill her!" he screamed. "I only had bullets for Angelo!"

"Bring him to me," I begged of the bigger, burlier cop who, surprisingly, obeyed, probably believing he was granting me my dying wish.

"Why?" I asked of Marty.

"Because I love you."

"That's not love," I said, kissing Angelo fervently on his lips, "this is love". He kissed me back harder and longer, rendering me breathless. I felt transported to a place of safety, far away on high, morphing into mist.

I suppose scientists would call it an out-of-body experience. I travelled formless in clouds. I journeyed ever onwards towards a laser-bright light until a careworn middle-aged woman – the one who'd been living with Greg in my absence, that pale shadow of the person I once used to be – walked towards me.

"I couldn't make him happy, only you can do that, and maybe he can make you happy too" she said before disappearing into fog.

"Come back!" I shouted after her. Then I became distracted by the appearance of Angelo, looking gorgeous and in his prime.

"Submit to the kiss," he advised me as I began to take shape, once more unable to resist his limitless appeal.

"Why is it that I can't tell the difference between right and wrong whenever I'm with you?"

"Morals are for mortals. Let's kiss some more", he replied, though even as he spoke the sonorous, seductive voice of Angelo was deteriorating into that of a croaking old man.

"Oh, gross!" I overheard somebody else say as I recoiled from the disgusting, dishevelled hobo. I was back home, exactly at the point where I had left it, kissing a hygienically-challenged vagrant in front of a group of horrified customers.

"Gross and grosser!" I heard the traumatised youth on an adjacent table groan again, just one of many diners who had suddenly lost their appetite upon seeing us kiss.

I rinsed around a gulp of water in my mouth and then spat it out. Now once again I was middle-aged Jennifer Green, and once again the hobo sitting opposite me was licking his lips in the aftermath of our kiss.

"The show's over!" I bawled at the rubberneckers. "OK, so he might not be your idea of eye candy but in his day he was to die for." Then I stormed out into the street, the hobo limping furiously after me. "Let me be!" I bawled at him.

"Tell me, what am I supposed to have done wrong?" he demanded of me. His question acted as a brake, bringing me to a furious, foot-stamping halt.

"Where to begin? You deceived me. You were pretending to be somebody you were not."

"You and me both," he said coming right back at me.

"But you had the advantage of me, posing as this Angelo, knowing exactly who I was. I had no idea who you were whatsoever."

"I wanted to make your dreams come true."

"Nightmares, more like."

"Everything I did was with the best intentions."

"Ain't it always?"

"And I might have saved your life, after you attempted suicide."

"So did you?"

"Ah", he grunted apologetically. "You were going to live anyway, if only in a half dead kind of way. You drank the good glass."

I exhaled extravagantly.

"So tell me, what kind of insane arrogance could have driven you to believe that your life was nothing more than a disposable commodity?" he accusingly asked, taking his turn to go on the attack.

"I was desperate."

"And that's sufficient reason to kill yourself? Not when you had a family, and your health, and your wealth, and so many other reasons to carry on. However bleak you think your life might have been, it would have passed. And solutions follow problems, as sure as night follows day, if you let them".

"I'm not proud of what I half intended to do. In fact, I'm deeply ashamed."

"Find no place in your heart for regret when time is so limited. And don't waste it living someone else's life, either."

"So now I suppose you're going to tell me to be myself?"

"Be whoever you want to be, and if you choose yourself, that's bliss."

"And what about us?" I eventually asked.

"I have lived many lives. Time for me to move on."

"How convenient. Typical man, totally unable to commit."

"I don't think we would be a great match, do you?" he said gesturing to his scruffy beard and down-at-heel clothes, in striking contrast to fragrant, respectable me.

"I could get used to it", I contradicted him. "Nothing that a good shower and a spot of shopping couldn't solve – after all, appearances can be deceptive".

He smiled at me. What joy, I had made him laugh, although I doubted if I'd done enough to persuade him to stay.

"OK. So what of this Angelo, did he ever love me, or was it all just one big fat cosmic joke?"

"His love for you will live on for as long as he is alive, which for Angelo is forever."

I'd almost departed hating him, yet when he said he loved me my heart skipped a beat.

★★★

"Is this guy upsetting you?" the handsome, thirty-something young artist who had previously barely given me a second look, enquired of me, having watched these strange events unfold.

I was taken aback by him, glad of his concern, unnecessary though it might have been.

"Don't worry. He's harmless, but thank you for caring anyway" I replied.

The artist had been standing behind his easel, painting a view of the 100-year-old courthouse, I assumed, just as he had been when I had walked that way before.

"At the risk of you thinking that I'm some kinda stalker, I've been watching you for a while," he politely informed me.

"Is that so?"

"I was truly impressed with the way you sorted that guy out, showing strength, yet kindness too."

Was he being polite, or heavens above, could he be hitting on me? Surely not. No big deal for Jennifer Gold I suppose, but totally amazing for polite, respectable, middle-aged Jennifer Green. So how unusual and slightly lovely would that have been, to be admired, not as an artificially created being but for who I truly was. Just plain, boring old me!

"How kind. I should introduce you to my daughter," I said, as much a reality check to myself as a realistic proposal about Elaine.

"High school kids are of no interest to me whatsoever."

As if I would fall for such a cheesy line.

"I have to come clean, it wasn't only your safety that concerned me," the artist confessed. "I was beguiled by your enigmatic smile."

I laughed out loud. "Like the Mona Lisa. I don't think so! I saw that up close and personal in the Louvre quite recently."

"So you've been away on holiday?" he enquired.

"In a manner of speaking."

"And did she live up to expectations?"

"Do things ever?"

He sympathised, and then expressed his frustration at not being able to 'capture' the courthouse, having vowed not to let this challenge defeat him.

"I much prefer painting portraits though. In fact, I would love to paint you," he further confessed, handing me his card and then producing a portfolio of work from his case to rest decorously on his long, sensitive fingers.

"I'm sure you'll find somebody more worthy of your brush." My eyes were drawn inexorably south as I said it. And I thought I'd left this kind of lascivious behaviour behind me.

"I'm serious. I would so love to capture you on canvas. My speciality is life class. Think about it", he said.

"Believe me. I will," I replied, trying to refocus all my senses back towards my life as a responsible middle-aged woman living respectably with her husband in Valley Stream. I would consign all this erotic nonsense to a drawer marked 'history'. Instead I became Jennifer the homemaker. I visualised a place where the painting might hang, assuming the artist would agree to sell it to me, once the portrait had been completed

It was then that I remembered the hobo – I'd been seriously distracted after all. I looked round to see that he had vanished.

"I need to find this guy at all costs" I said, striding off the way I thought he might have gone, looking to left and right. I didn't explain why I had to find him.

"Why is he so important?" the young artist enquired, trotting along beside me.

"He used to mean everything to me."

"That guy?" the young artist asked in surprise.

"Yes, that guy. He's not what he seems."

"Then maybe you should let him go." He stopped, and so did I. I hadn't a clue how a limping hobo could have disappeared so fast.

"I think I should try to give him up, although I don't know if that's possible." I was already mourning his loss – so many questions left unanswered – and wondering if I would ever see his beautiful face again.

"Sorry, I've got to go" I said, now firmly resolved to get back to where I had once belonged with Greg. It was time to face home.

My car was still parked where I had left it nigh on a lifetime ago outside Forever Young, Valley Stream's beauty parlour of choice, a penalty ticket affixed to the windscreen. I shook the artist's hand as politely as a woman of my age ought to. And if I did detect a certain something between us, I quickly dismissed it as inappropriate and wrong. I took one last glimpse of him in the rear-view mirror as I drove off.

Life class? That's naked, isn't it? I remembered those words. I almost stalled my car at the realisation of his artistic intent.

I could just imagine the horrible outcome, with him interpreting my body as a sad symbol of the passing of time, all drooping flesh and tired limbs, and attempting to employ his charm to persuade me to fall for his plan. I was wiser than that. He was never going to paint me, clothed or unclothed, because I was now utterly devoted to Greg.

There would be changes, though.

With a heavy heart I entered the home I'd deserted such a long time – and such a short time - before. Where to start?

I opened a kitchen cupboard, and was profoundly disturbed to be greeted by the dispiriting sight of two drinking glasses, one blue, one green, one half empty, one half full, both staring at me malevolently. Reliving the despair which had earlier driven me to contemplate ending my life, I chose to rise above it by pouring the noxious cocktail which had been mixed in the blue glass down the drain. As I watched my death ebb miraculously away, I became momentously uplifted by the prospect of a second chance. I was reinvigorated, restored and alive.

On departing the kitchen I found each room more cold and empty than the last, Time to make some changes. A painting of a bleak winter landscape hung forlornly on the living room wall. That would have to go.

In the distance I heard unfamiliar voices. It was the soundtrack of an old black and white British movie, being watched by Greg in his study upstairs.

"You've been a long way away, thank you for coming back to me," a man was saying in the clipped tones of a bewildered 1930s husband. He was addressing his remorseful wife as she returned home after forsaking the man of her dreams for him.

"Hi, I'm back," I said, announcing my return with a kiss on the lips. He seemed happy, but bemused.

"Wow! What have I done to deserve this?"

"I think you know. You remained true to me," I said mysteriously, although lost on him.

He regarded me sceptically, as if he had become aware that something had changed in me, restoring me to somebody approaching my old self, yet better, shinier and sunnier than before.

"Forgive me for neglecting you. I've been away on a far distant planet," I said.

I showered kisses upon him, dispelling his confusion, then led him to our bedroom, where we made love as if for the first time.

Later that evening we made talk too, both of us being heavily pregnant with plans for the future. I was going to give it my best shot to try to save our marriage. I'd concluded that this really must be my second chance - and everybody deserves a second time around, don't they? I'd said that much on the Melissa Parker Show, and if it had been said on TV then it must be true, mustn't it? And why should love always have to come naturally anyway? However much *True Romance* magazine, the Greek God of Love, or writers from Mills and Boon tell you otherwise, you have to work at it.

And we would both have to be true to our real selves as well. That's why I talked animatedly about a fundraising scheme which I wished to pursue, whereby a magazine would be published to be sold on the streets by homeless people themselves, who would benefit from the profits to assist them in getting housed. I'd been told by an English girl of a similar system already operating in London. I explained it to Greg, who gave my idea an uncharacteristically warm response. He was just happy I guess to have his wife back and being positive and making plans again.

He responded by proposing that we should finally take the vacation to Europe we had long promised ourselves, remembering my long-held ambition to be serenaded by a gondolier on the Grand Canal in Venice, cheesy though that might be. After all, marriage isn't about being cool – it's far too real for that.

And then Greg adopted a serious tone, proposing that as a matter of urgency we should invite Elaine and her boyfriend Brad for the weekend to give them comfort and support as they attempted to recover from the effect of the appalling scenes they had witnessed close up at the recent People's TV Awards.

"Let's do it," I agreed.

"The girl who was shot used to share an apartment with Elaine. I think I might have met her once, or maybe I spoke to her on the phone," said Greg.

★★★

"Whatever happened to the winter landscape?" Greg asked the next day as he surveyed the empty space where the painting had once hung on the living room wall.

"Honey, I've disposed of it. It's time for something more affirmative".

★★★

I suggested we held a barbecue to entertain Elaine and Brad, to help give them an old-fashioned sense of normality after everything they'd been through. So we invited familiar friends and neighbours to join us. More than one of them commented on the difference in me when compared with the pale shadow who used to hang out in our house.

"You seem so happy and relaxed," said my neighbour, Betty.

"You're not kidding. I'll have what she's having," said my friend Annie from the Homeless Centre where I worked.

"Honestly, I haven't been placed on any new medication, this is the real me," I protested, without success.

And then the moment I had been waiting for, becoming teary eyed upon seeing Elaine standing on the doorstep, looking more vulnerable than when she had fallen over in the front drive, aged six. We hugged until our tears, inexplicably, turned to laughter.

Of course I welcomed Brad more cautiously at first, by conservatively shaking his hand.

"You look nice, Mrs Green," he said.

Suddenly, I wanted to hug and kiss him, which I did, his reward for remembering how I'd once advised him in a life gone-by how he shouldn't be afraid to compliment his girlfriend's mother.

"Call me Jennifer," I said.

"You're blushing," said Elaine, addressing Brad in tones of mock shock. "I've never ever seen you do that before. Reckon I'm going to have to keep an eye on you two."

I nearly blushed too, hardly appropriate for a woman of my age.

Eventually we all gathered amid the African daisies and butterfly weed which populated my garden, the women seated on uncomfortable garden furniture while the guys were strangely drawn to stand by the flaming barbecue with its primeval appeal. OK, so the jollity was a little forced – hardly surprising considering what everybody had recently been through – as we worked at it, laying the foundation for future happiness, truly learning how to enjoy ourselves again. I did notice, however, that Elaine twice refused her father's offer of an alcoholic drink. Kids and their health kicks, eh.

Just when I thought I'd been safely restored back into the comforting security of my family life, Greg clapped his hands and made an announcement.

"Ladies and gentlemen, boys and girls," he said, wiping the barbecue sweat from his brow. "As many of you might know, Jennifer and I will soon be celebrating an anniversary. Our twenty-fifth, in fact." Wild applause ensued. "You can't stop time, so I've decided to do the next best thing, to immortalise my wife of soon to be twenty-five years as she is now. And to make that possible, I've hired the services of Valley Stream's most acclaimed artist, Mr Will Ladislaw, who I have commissioned to paint Jennifer's portrait."

I could have died. Up stepped the handsome, thirty-something, genuinely agreeable, utterly unsuitable artist. He regarded me with as nearly as much surprise and shock as I greeted him, but he exploded into a big wide smile, whereas I must have worn a look of panic and horror.

"Oh Greg – that's so sweet, but I really don't think so. It's just not my kind of thing," I pleaded with him.

"But I know exactly where it will hang – a replacement for the country scene in winter – something more positive," he explained, eager to convince me. The rest of the party urged me on until I was forced to agree, the cue for an almighty cheer from people who should have known better.

"Life is full of strange coincidences," Will the artist greeted me.

"You better believe it. And don't go getting any ideas about inviting me into your life class."

"Don't worry. We'll do the portrait first, and then as I begin to gain your confidence I will ask you once again whether I can paint you naked."

"And which one of us is naked? You or me?"

"Both of us, if that helps. Perhaps it's only fair that the artist should experience what the subject is going through too."

Why couldn't Greg have just bought me a new washing machine instead? Something practical like he normally does; not a dashing artist promising a gallery full of artistic delights and Jackson Pollock knows what else.

"How exciting about the portrait," said Elaine, approaching arm in arm with Brad. "I suspect there's quite a few ladies round here would like to be painted by him."

"Shush, behave yourself," I warned her as Greg came to join us.

"It's lovely to see you looking so well," said Greg to Elaine.

"Radiant" I added.

"And there's a reason for that," said Brad.

"We're expecting a baby," Elaine quietly announced.

I screamed louder than a jumbo jet on take-off.

"Keep eating your burgers," I threatened the expectant guests, and then held Elaine close, as did Greg, as did Brad, as did we all.

And to think the journey which had started with me becoming a hot young babe ended with me playing the grandma in waiting.

Sure, I was thrilled - with reservations. What's not to like about creating new life? Except that Brad was the father, and whether he was anywhere near responsible enough I was as far from sure as Gene Pitney was from Tulsa. And whatever happened to that proposal of marriage that was so imminent I had to seduce him under instruction from my daughter?

Nothing was ever going to be perfect, I supposed. Take my determination to be true to Greg. As soon as I decide on it, along comes this drop-dead gorgeous artist who ridiculously desires me – the real me - to test my resolve, all part of the great stew of human existence, thrown into a pot and stirred up for our delectation, all mixed up yet delicious nevertheless.

The next day I purchased a posy of spring flowers and made my way to the Catholic churchyard to visit the grave of Javier, the young man who'd threatened us with a knife at the Homeless Centre on the same day I'd learned of

Greg's affair. We can be so careless with our lives, I reflected, as I placed the posy upon his grave, yet unlike Javier I had been given that precious gift of a second chance. I must not abuse it.

When making decisions I like to make lists, drawing a line down the middle of a piece of paper, one side for, and one against. To risk, or not to risk, having an affair by visiting Will's studio; that was today's topic.

At the risk of being accused of having hidden shallows, just to know I could still lead a desirable younger man a merry dance was about as unfaithful as I wanted to get. The love of my husband had become more joyous and precious to me by far.

So I chose to resist Will, and I would visit his studios as if to prove it. Well, what's the worst that could happen? It wasn't like anyone was going to die, was it? And me? I'd chosen life.

EPILOGUE

So what am I? The name's Angelo – I guess the clue's in the name. I was there for Jennifer. I had a hundred mortals on my watch, and I know you're not meant to have favourites, but what was I supposed to do?

I'd been trained to keep my distance and care for her from afar, but when I saw her on her wedding day looking heavenly in white, I knew I was falling in love with her. Even so, I would have continued to remain out of reach, had not her crazy uncle got involved and asked me to kiss her. And when I realised what I had done by directly intervening in her life – strictly against the Rules, incidentally – I was inevitably hauled before the Boss to answer for my actions.

I begged him not to take Jennifer from my watch, in spite of my gross breach of conduct – and he's a forgiving kind of guy. He put me on probation, decreeing that I could only observe her from a distance or materialise within her dreams.

So I religiously observed the terms of my probation, as you might say, for nigh on 25 years, keeping a watch over her from the sidelines. But when I saw that she was about to take her precious life – and unlike me, she's only got one – I just had to intervene. How could I not? Although I was almost too late. I willed her to drink the good glass and then appeared as a hobo to appeal to that caring nature of hers.

Having already flirted with death, she had more wisely decided to leave home instead, so as my reward to her I decided to send her on the journey of a lifetime, to be given a second chance by being young again, while retaining her 48-year-old mind. I knew it would be irresistible to her, and would be allowed under the Rules, as long as the purpose was to teach her a profound lesson or two.

"If only I knew then what I know now" I had more than once heard her say – and I could make that dream come true for her. And yes, you can mostly blame me for the way I recreated her, inspired by a magazine I had once picked up while waiting in a barber's shop in the 1950s called *Playboy*. I thought that's what she would have wanted – and she did have some input into her look anyway. Although what did I care? I was more in love with her soul than her body.

So even when I saw her screwing up in the apartment I didn't intervene, and wouldn't have if she hadn't stormed into my office where I hung out in the guise of a television executive, an ideal place. I could observe at least four of my watches from there, including Jennifer. I never expected her to crash in on me like that – you see, even angels don't know everything – but once I saw her up close and personal I knew I couldn't resist her a second time around. So I pursued her until she succumbed, loving every part of her, until inevitably I was summoned back by the Boss.

"You have broken the rules of your probation. I will condemn you to the other place unless you restore Jennifer to her rightful life" he commanded.

So I enlisted the help of Alice, a fallen angel from days gone by, to create a scenario where she could fall in love with her husband again. And please don't imagine I wasn't jealous, knowing that Greg loved Jennifer nearly as deeply as me. Of course I hadn't planned for Marty to shoot her, nor me neither, although it had provided us with a convenient, if somewhat bloody way to get back to Valley Stream.

And then she meets that wretched artist, who desires her because she's now in control and wonderful to behold for who she really is, although maybe she would get back together with Greg and live happily ever after anyway. Either way, I was screwed. I had set her free from her dependency on me, and she had become wondrous in her own right. What I hadn't accounted for was my dependency on her. How could I possible live without her?

As for my prospects of returning to active service as an angel, I've been placed on extended leave until my case is reviewed by two archangels and a former Bishop of Baltimore. I'm confident I'll get my licence restored – I've done what the Boss has asked of me and delivered her back to Greg, although the Rules would prohibit me from ever encountering Jennifer again… unless I was willing to put my immortality at risk. Who wants to live forever anyway?

So I vow, here and now, in contravention of those wretched Rules, that I will seek her out again, regardless of the consequences. Because I love her still.